EUNUCHS AND NYMPHOMANIACS

ANONYMOUS

EUNUCHS AND NYMPHOMANIACS
ANONYMOUS

G

GALLERY BOOKS

New York London Toronto Sydney New Delhi

G

Gallery Books
An Imprint of Simon & Schuster, Inc.
1230 Avenue of the Americas
New York, NY 10020

First Gallery Books trade paperback edition October 2019

GALLERY BOOKS and colophon are registered trademarks of
Simon & Schuster, Inc.

For information about special discounts for bulk purchases,
please contact Simon & Schuster Special Sales at 1-866-506-1949
or business@simonandschuster.com.

The Simon & Schuster Speakers Bureau can bring authors
to your live event. For more information or to book an event,
contact the Simon & Schuster Speakers Bureau at 1-866-248-3049
or visit our website at www.simonspeakers.com.

Manufactured in the United States of America

10   9   8   7

Library of Congress Cataloging-in-Publication Data has been applied for.

ISBN 978-1-9821-2897-5
ISBN 978-1-9821-2898-2 (ebook)

EUNUCHS AND NYMPHOMANIACS

ANONYMOUS

1

My legs are mostly for decoration.

I spent the day flirting online with a girl who looked very much like a guy, in a wheelchair.

After much to-ing and fro-ing she sent me an unasked-for, very frightening close-up of her bush.

I jumped when I saw it.

The surrounding body was tasty enough but her head looked suspiciously male. She said she had already met six men, one of whom "ran out the door when he saw me."

The only one I did fuck . . . (her phrasing not mine) turned out to be a homeless man who stayed the night.

He fucked me twice that night and once the next morning.

Like it was an accomplishment.

Her mind was refreshingly depraved and certain sex seemed imminent but I wanted to speak to her on the phone first to satisfy myself that the big unkempt bush wasn't concealing a dick. Her legs were now *completely fucked*, she said.

So much so, that even kneeling was no longer an option. She had actually tried to kneel after I alluded to spanking her on all fours. *Not possible. Not anymore.*

This implied that it had been possible at one point but perhaps since her condition was progressive the option had expired. She sent a picture of said legs in thigh-high stockings, and to be fair they looked pretty fucking good.

I can wrap them behind my head.

This put me in mind of a yoga teacher I had once had the pleasure of fucking who was lithe enough to fold her legs so far behind her head she looked, as I lunged into her, like she was listening to exquisite music emanating from her knees. Balled up like that I was able to rock her back and forth on my impaler. Dead legs might be even more flexible.

Oh and by the way, I know you're slumming.

Somehow this observation forgave me in advance for any future misdeeds. Meanwhile I scrutinized her photo for an Adam's apple. Her face was more masculine than I would have liked but her skin was pale and clean and she was very shapely and obviously up for an adventure. And it didn't look like any children had emerged from that hedge. I had already decided I wasn't going down on *that*. Not without a compass . . . or a Sherpa. I decided to refrain from masturbating.

I'd save it all up for the disabled girl's tits.

After all, the fuller my balls the less chance there was of a soggy erection when faced with the combined unknowns of atrophied legs, jungle-bush, and man-face. But then as soon as I generously agreed to travel all the way out to her place in Astoria, she canceled in favor of the homeless man. This was galling of course because I had wanted to believe I was doing her a favor but now I was being told I'd have to wait my turn? I began to get seriously turned on by the sheer twisted logic of it all. She was going to make me beg for permission to charity-fuck her. A text woke me the next morning.

I just sucked him off and swallowed his cum before he went to work.

The dirty cunt.

That should have been me.

Mind you, I wouldn't have stayed the night. But he was homeless so he had no choice. He was obviously using her. He had to be. Hang on, he had a job? Surely that was a lie so he could get away quickly after spending a free night in a real bed. Or did he exist at all? Either way I decided I would now have to come on her face *and* her tits.

When we finally met in a café near PS1, the sheer mechanical effort involved in wheeling herself over the threshold in what seemed to me to be a very cumbersome-looking wheelchair punctured any fantasies I might have been nursing. It didn't help that she was wearing a bulky coat that hid her shape and lent her the appearance of a very thin, deeply unhappy young man, complete with light mustache.

He ran out the door when he saw me.

I too could have left there and then but I didn't. I consciously decided to go through with it. I even turned on the charm because now that she was seeing me for the first time in the flesh, there was a chance she might, through some self-destructive subtext of her own, reject me.

The possibility of being refused sex by an androgynous paraplegic after spending two hours subjected to the indignities of the New York subway system was not something I wanted to encourage. This resulted in me being actually relieved when she said: "You'll see what I mean," referring to the layout of her apartment.

I was in.

But her apartment presented another challenge in that it was disgustingly disheveled. There were cobwebs everywhere. How long did it take for cobwebs as large as these to form? Years? Decades? And how difficult would it be to clear them? Housework had to be difficult in a wheelchair but one swipe of a cloth and they were gone. I chose to believe they served some sort of gothic aesthetic. That the reason they blossomed all over the apartment and clung to every corner and ledge like Halloween was because they were intentional and not the result of years of apathy.

While I was still inspecting the living room she had already wheeled herself into the bedroom. Mercifully her attitude was that of an able-bodied beauty. Her self-assurance in this regard was impressive. Either that or she chose to plug the gaping fissures of self-doubt with false confidence. I did not get the sense that there were drugs involved.

It was necessary to lift each leg separately out of the wheelchair and position them on the stale-looking bed strewn as it was with all manner of domestic detritus: Q-tips, clothespins, two spoons, and a shoe. Had I seen pictures of this I probably wouldn't have agreed to meet. And even now it should have been enough to send me scrambling for the elevator but no, I had decided to go through with it. Once we extricated her legs from her jeans I saw she was wearing the same style of woolen thigh-highs that had once looked so stunning on Marian.

They mocked me now from these lifeless legs. Closing my eyes I tried to kiss her with only my tongue in the hope that if my lips were peeled back I wouldn't be able to sense the peach fuzz of her mustache.

Luckily I was able to hoist an erection and more importantly maintain it. Responding enthusiastically to my manual ministrations she came easily and frequently and loudly. I began to feel as flattered as I should have been from the start. I read once that Norman Mailer would sleep with women uglier than himself because it was nice to feel like the pretty one for a change. I had hoped I'd feel like a pale beauty being molested by a beastly ogre but since I was using both hands to get her off it was hard to convince myself of this. I was, however, feeling confident enough to tell her exactly what I wanted her to do with my dick.

It was obvious she wasn't as worldly as she claimed.

To my delight she orgasmed repeatedly when I squeezed her nipples very very hard. At first I hadn't wanted to go so hard on them but she squeezed my finger and thumb with her own to indicate that she liked it much much harder. Reacting to her moans and breathlessness I was virtually jerking her nipples off like stiff little dicks.

She also came very loudly when I spanked her pussy.

I couldn't tell if she enjoyed this more aggressive treatment because she was losing sensitivity to her encroaching disease or whether she just liked it rough. Maybe she needed the extra velocity to feel anything through all that vegetation. She told me proudly that she hadn't trimmed it in fifteen years. Maybe she felt she was a more successful seductress for not having to try.

He ran out the door when he saw me.

When I first saw her I forced myself to stay seated. I joked that she should laminate a menu of potential excuses from her dates to choose from. And it should look like it belonged to the café. The fact that she found this funny endeared her to me. It was humble and charming. The waitresses were ridiculously beautiful. Traditionally beautiful like eighties models. And they were so attentive to me when I first arrived I blushed in advance knowing that I would soon be seen with a girl in a wheelchair.

Looking back at her on the bed after I'd already come explosively (I felt a hot spurt hit the underside of my own chin), she was now sitting up and pontificating about how the female orgasm had been co-opted by the patriarchy. This was prompted by a sticker on her bedroom door that I'd read aloud in an attempt at making conversation as a prelude to leaving:

CHRIST OUT OF MY CROTCH. It wasn't the sticker I was drawn to so much as the door.

Now that she was sitting up the inert legs sunk under her into the mattress, and I was reminded of something I couldn't quite place. I had the sense of not being able to tell if it was a prediction or a memory, but as I feigned interest in what she was saying it came back to me.

A film called *Freaks* from 1932. There were moments in it when I was concentrating on the plot only to be rudely reminded by a wide shot that the story was being narrated by a torso. ". . . and just because I came doesn't mean we're done . . ." she was saying.

This was happening for real, right there on the bed in front of me in an apartment in Astoria. She was leaning so far forward her lame legs were concealed; the effect was that only her stockinged feet were visible. It was now imperative that I get out before I said something regrettable. After all, I'd done it. It was over. I had successfully researched my sexual equivalent of *Down and Out in Paris and London*. All I had to do now was nod as convincingly as possible and edge toward the door. I imagined the neighbors unable to eat their evening meal so disgusted were they at the sounds emanating from their handicapped neighbor's apartment.

She was loud but I was even louder.

I hoped I wouldn't have to meet anyone in the elevator and be forced to imagine their thoughts: *So that's what a guy who has sex with a girl in a wheelchair looks like.*

I couldn't pretend she'd been servicing me and that I had just been passive because she had been the more vociferous of the two of us for at least the first hour. In other words I was the type of guy who made a paraplegic come. But standing there nodding at her as she slowly disappeared into her mattress I began to get that old familiar sensation that the girl I'd just had sex with was feeling underserved.

That she wanted to go again.

But we would not be repeating the experience. As promised, I left her a signed copy of my book and after consuming it in a day she texted her review.

> ### IT WAS SO HONEST, I FOUND IT UNBELIEVABLE
> —Girl in wheelchair

Behold my doorway.

The portal though which so many of you would be unsouled.

When I first broke up with Marian I had a dream where thousands of girls thronged the streets around my building and jostled up the stairs to my door. In the same way the million-strong Persian army was lured into the Thermopylae Pass, I would bottleneck and bang New York's female elite.

My website received a steady flow of messages from women interested in finding out more about the mysterious underground author. It was like a customized dating site where I was the only guy listed. And since they'd read my book and hadn't objected to the content I was forgiven in advance for behaving like a cunt.

In fact, it was expected of me.

I began insisting we meet in my apartment, ostensibly to preserve my anonymity but in reality because it brought them that much closer to my bed, itself a literary phenomenon consisting as it did of eighty cartons of my self-published book with a mattress on top. I sent them photos of my shabby chic apartment along with one rather flattering (read "youthful") selfie wearing a raffish bowler hat and a fake Victorian villain mustache. Also attached was a confidentiality agreement I found online. If they were considered worthy of an audience with Anonymous they were expected to bring it with them already signed.

Among the many hopefuls was a professor of poetry studies at Columbia who was keen to pick my brains about my adventures in self-publishing. Having already stalked her Instagram and deemed her worthy of fucking I wondered if I might solicit her opinion on, and maybe even an endorsement of, an idea I had for a book.

No one was more astonished than I to learn that the majority of my readers were girls under twenty who regarded the murk in which I slithered to be the stuff of romantic fiction. Often recommended on Amazon under the heading "if you liked that you might like these" were books of romantic poetry with pastel covers and one particular novel about a man who, on learning his wife has Alzheimer's, takes it upon himself to reignite their relationship daily by wooing her anew. And because everything he achieves one day evaporates the next he has to continuously work his ass off to win her affections.

How romantic.

For her.

Tellingly, the most popular male equivalent featured a girl whose clitoris is located in her throat. I thought about mashing up the two stories: a woman with Alzheimer's wakes up each day complaining of strep? Anyway, it was while exploring the intersection of *The Notebook* and *Deep Throat* that I stumbled on what I thought might be the title of my next book.

Beowatch.

Relocating the Old English epic poem on the beaches of California, I'd introduce hentai-style, orifice-raping sea monsters to tentatively clad swimsuit models in a genre-breaking, post-apocalyptic romantic comedy with a message: the message being, *Anonymous is a fucking genius.* My name would be even more widely unknown than before.

Drinnggggg

Her ass was so big it was visible from the front.

Okay so sex was off the table but a quote from the professor who'd written her thesis on Seamus Heaney's revered translation of *Beowulf* would still make all the difference on the dust jacket of my reboot. She had just settled into my couch when another worrying issue arose. She was only an adjunct professor. Even I knew *adjunct* was just another word for *pretend*.

I needed the real thing if I was going to get a quote.

A huge ass attached to an imposter.

Never mind, maybe I could still get into her students'

pants if she let me in front of them. I thought of all those young, bookish, bespectacled, upturned faces awaiting the arc of my ejaculate. But then she did something that made even that prospect unattractive. She began to pitch me *her* book.

"In the same way photography captures images, I want to harness the humble paragraph to do the same thing.

"I call it *Paragraphy*. It's pronounced *Par-ug-ruff-fee*. Here, you see?" She showed me an example on her phone.

> **TIED TIGHTLY AT THE TOP, THREE TINY ORANGE CERAMIC DEER STRAIN AGAINST THE RESTRICTING SIDES OF A CLEAR PLASTIC BAG. THIS OMINOUS INCARCERATION COULD HAVE BEEN FOISTED ON THEM BY SOME ANTI-SANTA OR THEY MIGHT BE ORNAMENTS FOR SALE. ONE DEER IN PARTICULAR HAS BEEN CAUGHT MAGICALLY IN MID-PUNCH LEAR-LIKE IN HIS FUTILE ATTEMPT AT PUSHING BACK THE INEVITABLE**

"Paragraphy," she read, "is more personal than photography. In the same way we all have our own idea of what a character in a book looks like, Paragraphy invites the viewer to create their own visual understanding of the content."

She described a world where large-format books containing limited edition prints of typographically crafted *Para-*

graphs adorned the living rooms and gallery walls of the culturally informed.

I felt conned. I'd been maneuvered into a very uncomfortable position on my own couch. As she paused to let me absorb the brilliance of her idea, I was able to confirm she was not worth the effort so I pounced on her.

It was easier to pretend to want her and be rejected than to find a way to get rid of her. Apart from some adolescent kissing and hugging I was enthusiastically rebuffed.

She was more embarrassed than angry, flattered on some level maybe. Or she didn't want to be seen as easy. But most likely she didn't want the subject changed.

"We should take things slow," she said.

The more gallant I appeared now the greater the insult when she never heard from me again. I was about go beyond the call of duty and pretend I gave a flying fuck about her *Par-ugh-agghhh-raphy* when my phone shuddered on the table.

It was Alice.

I'm heading out now . . . be there in 40 minutes.

It was almost midnight. We had arranged to meet the following day at noon but she was coming over now? Could she have misunderstood? I received another message; a mental text sent from somewhere inside me: *Lose this cunt and replace her with Alice.*

"I'm so sorry. That was one of my sponsees. He's only got five days sober and it looks like I'm going to have to . . ." I paused here to look deeply concerned into my phone before continuing. "I'm really sorry but as you say maybe we can pick this up the next time?"

When she finally understood that she was being asked to leave she reluctantly put her phone away. You could say she was *Lear-like in her futile attempts at pushing back the inevitable.*

"I'll send you the link," she said, laboriously hoisting herself off the couch.

"You're not afraid I'll steal your idea?"

She glowed.

Apparently I was impressed by her idea *and* I wanted to fuck her.

"I trust you," she said.

How malleable I was going to be.

When she finally figured out how to open the door I had to resist pushing her through it.

Meanwhile more texts arrived.

I'm half way over the Williamsburg bridge.

Alice had indeed mistaken noon for midnight but I laughed it off like it was something I did all the time.

Hahahahahaha

I might have asked if she thought it a little too dark to be midday but the JPEG she'd sent earlier in the week wearing a garter belt and thigh-high stockings muffled any misgivings I might have had about her sanity. Or mine.

Drinngggggg

Twenty minutes later she was standing in my doorway looking gorgeous and sounding crazy. Absolutely gorgeous. Absolutely crazy. It was crucial to her that I be made immediately aware of what drugs she was on. Presumably this was so I could brief the emergency staff if she passed out. Like it had happened before. And though I marveled at her ability to pronounce the names of the drugs without slurring or missing a syllable I mentally pressed *mute* so I could focus on her undulating lips as they made all manner of cock-friendly shapes. After a dazzling camera-flash of a smile the tongue-twisting polysyllabic nomenclatures of pharmaceuticals subsided in favor of what began to at least *look* like normal speech.

"I fucked a guy this morning."

Or evening, depending on whose time zone you subscribed to. Could this be some sort of joke she played on fawning idiots like me? Was that a brooch-shaped camera on her lapel? Was this going out live on RealDatesRealLife.com? Maybe one of the many young men I'd duped into buying my book had hired her to enact this sting. Right now he was ensconced in an armchair somewhere watching us on a widescreen. I thought about waving just to let him know that I knew, but such an act would make Alice the sanest person in the room, and that was unthinkable after seventeen years in AA.

She handed me a brown paper bag with a broken bagel inside it because in her poor befuddled mind: "Breakfast."

Paradoxes crackled in the air around her.

She was a devout Christian and relied on Jesus even though she had just told me she had committed adultery that morning (which in reality must have meant the previous night). Her husband had served her with the divorce papers so she didn't feel like she was responsible for the failure of the marriage. She did, however, confess to an ongoing campaign to emasculate him. So much so, she felt like she was now married to a woman and she told him so. In fact she kept returning to this: her husband's lack of manhood. It made me want to assert mine.

"So do you think, do I have any chance of . . . you know . . ."

I nodded at the general area of her groin. She seemed amused by this and immediately shook her head.

"Oh no, doubtful, I don't think so, shall we go to bed?"

All in the one sentence.

"Are you sure you want to stay? I mean if you want to go I won't be hurt or angry."

She was standing up now looking around her, unsure, her nipples visible under the expensive lamb's wool sweater.

"Awww?" she said as if these were the exact words she had been waiting for me to say.

And just like that we were kissing.

She was like a thin, young, underfed man in my arms. I fretted for a second that she might be transgender and that I was about to feel the hot bulge of an erection against my own. But no, she was just another ex-model who had confused day for night and her husband for a wife. Shaking her pajamas from the tote bag she began to prepare for bed right there, right in front of me. She was topless now as one arm searched for a sleeve.

She had woken up at eleven PM thinking it was eleven AM and rushed out to meet me for what she believed was a midday coffee date. It worked out pretty well though because once we got under the covers she turned out to be very loving and sensual. She was unusually slim but chubby in exactly the right places. I motioned her bony fingers to my cock and she fell easily into sexual step.

The drugs prevented her from having an orgasm, she said, but she was looking forward to mine. Her son had been a caesarean birth because she wanted to preserve her pussy. I slipped my thumb into it from underneath and with my other hand tapped her clit from the front. A deep moan escaped from her as she pushed my hand away and plunged in there with her own. I thought she was going to finger herself but she was checking to see if she was as wet as she thought she was. She stared first at her glistening fingers and then at me as if maybe her trip hadn't been a waste of time after all.

"Oh my gosh, you have skills. I'm surprised, I mean, I wasn't expecting . . ."

I kept at it because basically I didn't have anything else to do. I hadn't been sleeping since I broke up with Marian so I might as well finger-fuck a drug-addled gash as binge-watch four more episodes of Renaissance TV.

"I don't feel like I'm doing enough for you."

She insisted on sucking my cock and although it was nice (she looked up to ask if she was doing it right) the best thing about it was the sight of her slim body and those pointy tits going in and out of silhouette. Like a seventies actress lit by an

16

Italian cinematographer, or, and I tried not to acknowledge this but I couldn't help it, like Marian was back.

"If I wasn't on all these drugs I'd have come four times by now."

She was worried that divorcing her husband was a mistake. The guy she'd fucked earlier wanted her to watch porn with him.

"Men who watch porn are disgusting."

When I told her most men were like that she began to talk about how good a catch her husband was in comparison. She married him because he was the opposite of her womanizing manipulative father but now he bored her. She went on about her reliance on Jesus, which was laughable because her reliance on drugs was so much more obvious. And her beauty. She said she used men instead of mirrors. If she wanted to know whether she looked good on a particular day she gauged the level of her attraction from the looks she received from men in the street. Women hated her, and having to be so overly pleasant to them was exhausting. She said the love she felt for her young son was reminiscent of an adolescent romance. Her second chance at first love. Having made life hell for her husband for so long, she knew he would eventually have to divorce her. He was now using the fact that she was on drugs to prove she was an unfit mother.

This was how it worked. They decided it was all over when they were still with you. They starved you of sex and affection. Watched you dry up. Burgled your balls and then delighted in your attempts at retrieving them.

Trazpene was one of the more pronounceable drugs she mentioned and after looking it up I learned that it was an extremely strong antidepressant and that one of its many side effects was a sense of confusion about the time of day and location.

Drinnggggg

Kennedy eventually arrived at 10:10 the following night after originally agreeing to eight PM, but I didn't mind at all because of her pleasantly ditzy demeanor and all that unexpectedly exposed pale luminous skin. What a rollicking fuck she'd be. Mischief didn't quite describe what she had in her eyes. Self-destruction maybe. A spirited innocence. As if life itself was crammed into that tiny frame.

At twenty-one all things were still possible. Maybe even sex with the likes of me. She wanted to develop a VR helmet that stimulated the part of the brain governing the orgasm. Not as outlandish as it sounded when you learned that she had spent a year assisting one of London's top brain surgeons and had already clocked up many hours of valuable experience in the operating theater. She'd resigned though, after some upperclass twats, as she called them, performed a totally unnecessary procedure that went horribly wrong and as a result the patient was fucked-up for life. It was all covered up of course but she couldn't bear the idea that she was working for such assholes. It didn't help that they'd mocked her accent. I was left to wonder what offended her more—the malpractice or the accent shaming. But then as if to erase any good impression she might have made she announced she was desperately looking for tickets to Burning Man. One glimpse of her blinding white cleavage and I was tolerant even of this.

The sparkle of a lit fuse.

That's what I saw in her eyes. She looked out from within herself in the knowledge that time was limited and the game was excellent. The latest contestant in this wobbly-wheeled trolley-dash through the cosmic supermarket. I must have seemed jaded to her. A spent force. Someone who'd had his shot and missed. She excused herself as she thumbed a lengthy text into her phone.

"Sorry, I know this is rude."

She had already decided I was a nonstarter so there was no need to stand on ceremony. Suddenly her face froze. Reaching for my teacup, my hand had caught her eye like something that had crept onto the table from the floor. Following her gaze I saw why. There, to my horror, and obviously hers, was the indented impression of the side seam of my jeans. Yes, I was old enough to have skin where marks such as these lingered.

She all but shivered with disgust.

Did it now become the subject of her text?

Please call me . . . I'm sitting here with a dirty old nasty-assed man who has obviously lied about his age (and his height) but I'm too nice to tell him and anyway why should I be the one to set him straight . . . please call me so I have an excuse to escape!!

Or maybe she had seen all this as soon as she walked in two hours late and there I was licking my lips far too happy to be allowed near anything as luscious as her. I had actually taken the entire day to wash my jeans and shirt and socks and generally prepare for my big date.

Mercifully Alice called as I watched Kennedy texting. I let my phone hum and revolve on the table long enough for her name to be visible for anyone who wanted to know.

Kennedy might not want me but there were those who did.

But then a text: *WHO ARE YOU??? PLEASE STOP CALLING ME*

She didn't remember who I was.

I darted a look at Kennedy just as her eyes returned to her own phone. She was going to pretend she hadn't seen it but I could already see the blush on her cheeks as the interior entertainment looked for an outlet. Then her phone began to vibrate right there between her texting fingers. She answered it.

"Okay great I'll be right over."

A friend had just been offered two free tickets but she'd have to leave immediately to pick them up. Did I mind? We could pick this up *next time*. I was now on the receiving end of the same technique I used only now I had to pretend I didn't know. My audition was over. Any optimism she'd had about meeting me had been very efficiently snuffed out by meeting me. The Extinguished Man.

• • • •

She was capable of looking so much better.

And though it was a huge relief not to want to fuck her I couldn't help feeling cheated that she hadn't made more of an effort. Even if it was just to show me what I could no longer have. The fact that she hadn't given any thought to her appearance was a clear statement of disinterest. I shouldn't mistake this meeting for anything more than a platonic lunch.

Marian was dropping off a fold-up table she'd lugged all the way from Park Slope. This was where she now lived. *The place where dreams go to die* was how I had once described it when we were together. But I wasn't about to remind her of that now as I helped her wedge the thing between the diner booth and the wall. It must have been quite an undertaking to get it onto the subway and up the escalator. Such Herculean effort seemed to indicate that she approved of my latest idea to sell books. I had been reluctant to shut down the fake dating profile that harnessed some of the more intimate photos I'd taken of her. Setting up that profile had been an undeniably scummy thing to do and I would have understood if she never spoke to me again.

But the fact that she was sitting there across from me now seemed to me to imply there might be an outside chance for us. At least she was willing to meet me. Or maybe she was just enjoying the prospect of seeing me on the street trying to sell books to uncaring New Yorkers.

It wasn't going to be easy.

This approach would need to be more successful than a beautiful, seminaked, supposedly French photographer/model who promised sex in exchange for buying a book. How could a guy standing behind a table compete with that?

She picked up the salt shaker.

"You want me to balance it?"

This referred to the time, three years earlier, when she had caused an identical shaker to stand at an impossible angle, propped invisibly on a couple of grains of salt. I was transfixed at the time not so much by the trick itself but by the flush of triumph in her face as she pulled it off. I had taken a photo, ostensibly of the leaning salt cellar, but I made sure she was very much in focus. It turned out to be one of those heartbreaking photos I could now hardly bear to look at.

She looked ravaged.

By the city? By me? Did she sense this had been a beautiful moment in the early flush of our romance? How skillful of her to revisit it now juxtaposed as it was with the stalemate that represented our present feelings for each other. It was the same technique a film director used to make his audience cry. First make them fall in love with the characters. Invite them to share in the laughter and charm. Seduce them, stir their souls, open their hearts, wait until they're enthralled. Then start the arguments and show the disagreements. Begin breaking the spell so that by the time the on-screen couple are sulking and separated the viewer is also hardened and resigned. That's the moment to remind them of the halcyon days with a surgically placed flashback.

The specific brand of folding table in question was no longer being manufactured and was actually quite sought-after. She knew this because her roommate had at one point used it to sell jewelry on Brooklyn sidewalks. Basically Marian was calling my bluff. To be fair, I had lied to her (and by association, her roommate) so many times already they couldn't really be sure what to believe.

If I was ever going to fondle that lovely pale ass again I would have to go through with it, but I couldn't shake the feeling that having announced my intention to self-flagellate she had just made me the gift of a beautifully crafted whip.

Drinnggggg

She had to be at least seventy years old.

Maybe more. Everything seemed to hang from her: clothes, hair, skin.

"Bridgit left you a message?"

The head of a little dog poked out of her tote bag.

I had of course seen her in the corridor many times and nodded or exchanged banalities about the weather or the corresponding holiday depending on the time of year.

I was indefinitely indebted to Bridgit for getting me into a two-bedroom rent-controlled apartment in the East Village. If I had a first-born she would have been well within her rights to it. She was welcome to whatever favors I could muster.

Mrs. Sejenko, my downstairs neighbor, was leaving for a week to visit a relative in Kansas and she couldn't take her Chihuahua with her. Would I mind keeping an eye on him for a few days? Keeping an eye on him sounded like something I could do from a distance. It sounded like the equivalent of watering a few plants. So I agreed. But apparently a dog needed to be taken out at least twice a day and fed too. And Chihuahuas were particularly needy little fuckers.

A plant would have been preferable.

Anyway, I was introduced to a beige rat called Barney and handed a leash and some blue plastic bags (for picking up his shit) and a bag of edible pellets with which to manufacture the shit. Pre-shit. Shit-in-waiting.

"Thank you so much for doing this," she said, handing me a piece of paper with some handwritten instructions and a phone number on it. She seemed overly grateful. I found out later that real dog-sitters charge as much as $300 a day.

But Barney seemed cool.

Until she left.

As soon as the door closed, there escaped from his little throat a kind of unremitting shriek that seemed to enter my skull under my eyelids and stab at the interior with aural knives. I was virtually a hermit apart from the occasional female so this was definitely going to be an imposition. But a hermit needed a cave and I was eternally grateful to Bridgit for providing me with one.

I would do her this favor or any other she asked of me. In her email she had tried to sweeten the deal by reminding me that girls love to see a guy walking a dog and though it seemed like salesmanship I was eager to test out the theory. I didn't tell her that I already knew the reason women were attracted to men with dogs was because they imagined they'd make great fathers.

Or more accurately that in owning a dog he demonstrated a willingness to deal with all manner of excretion. Not something I wanted a girl thinking I was good at. Anyway, as it turned out I didn't attract even one girl. But Barney did. They began smiling fifty paces away. As Barney's butler I would receive no more than a salutatory nod. And yet I could see how such encounters could be intensely erotic. When two dogs met they made straight for the other's genitals. Or tried to. In fact the dogs behaved in a way that all New Yorkers would if it weren't for the cultural constraints that bound us. But these women ignored the conversational potential of two animals basically eating other out until the unfettered carnality taking place at our feet was reduced to a cutesy interchange. *Oh he's so cute!! How old? I love his collar!!*

I had been looking forward to sharing a bench with the models I'd seen in the Tompkins Square dog run, but line three on my sheet of paper forbade me from bringing him there since Chihuahuas were known to be "antisocial." Basically I should walk him twice a day, pick up his shit, and feed him.

After one of our walks on a ridiculously humid day we got back to my apartment, I kicked off my sneakers, and Barney pounced thirstily on my feet. His long pink tongue protruded and retreated in and out of the nasty sweat-filled crevices between my toes. The nastier the toe-jam the more frenzied his slurping. He looked like he'd lost all reason. Whatever dog-logic had governed him up to that point dissolved. If I moved my foot to get more comfortable he whined in panic, pawing at my toes. The frantic scratching and screaming only stopped when I spread my toes again, giving that darting tongue access to the most unmentionable nooks. Here it seemed was where the gold resided. The unexpected effect was a cooling down of my fevered frontal lobe as if my brain was being magically air-conditioned. Barney got busy. Whenever I tired slightly of holding my toes wide he helpfully slid a paw sideways between them, ensuring continued access. Of the week he spent with me it was obvious that he was happiest at moments like these and so, I have to admit, was I. He had no interest in me after I showered. None whatsoever. So much so I felt rejected.

He literally turned up his nose.

An unbidden thought arrived in me: *If it feels that good on your feet . . .* One day after a grueling trudge around the block in ninety-degree heat we arrived back up the stairs and as was customary for me in such conditions I shrugged off my sweaty shorts, sneakers, and T-shirt and made straight for the air conditioner. But on this day I decided to try something new. I stripped off as usual but this time I lay on the couch. I didn't need to invite Barney to join me since he was already licking my feet before they were even out of their socks.

The scent drove him crazy.

I would tease him by drawing the sock back and forth over the dizzying fumes. He'd scrape at the sock hoping it would just fall away but he had to learn that carnal desire is all the more satisfying when it is denied. Barney would know the anguish I had had to endure in my pursuit of human honey. But who among us can refuse the repeated attempts of such persistent passion? To be the custodian of so much joy was in itself intoxicating. In the end I acquiesced and yes, he would have his wicked, stinky-tongued way with me. After a mind-cooling minute of this sort of wanton bacchanalia (Barney never quite stopped, he just slowed down) the frenzy gave way to a more methodical, less intense tongue and slurp. He had already consumed the cream and was now merely mopping up. Soon he would lose interest and begin licking what there was left on his lips. Reason would restore itself and he'd resume his hunt for a perfect nesting place around my apartment, scraping crazily at cushions as if they were mounds of earth. This was when I opened my thighs. He actually looked at me. I blushed. Would he growl? I had obviously crossed a yet-to-be-drawn line between the animal and human kingdoms. Surely something instinctive would intervene, some genealogical cock-block that prevented the birth of unspeakable creatures. Barney didn't have a word for what was happening and neither did I.

But it was happening.

• • • •

People strode past with such regularity their passing vertical forms created a strobing effect. It caused an illusion where my table appeared to be moving. It made me queasy. Or maybe I was just sick with myself for being out on the street trying to sell books to cliff-faced New Yorkers. Eye contact was tantamount to physical assault so apart from the occasional sad sympathetic smile, I was completely ignored. How embarrassing for them to have to acknowledge the vagrant behind his table. Why should they be subjected to this? The sidewalk would be that much wider without me. I repositioned my sign.

> **NOT SO MUCH A MEMOIR AS A LITERARY SELFIE**
> #TheOxygenThiefDiaries

They could have given a fuck. Just as well I'd brought along some alternatives.

> **HAVING TROUBLE GIVING A FUCK?**
> #TheOxygenThiefDiaries

This got some wry smiles and one girl even crouched and took a photo but still nobody stopped. Someone shouted behind me and the queasiness blossomed into paranoia. I'd be stabbed in the spleen by the street vendor whose spot I had surely stolen. Looking nervously around while at the same time trying to induce passersby to stop was dizzying. *Man Stabbed on Prince Street*. I'd be on the evening news. Would Marian see it? At least she'd realize I was serious about getting her back. What photo would they use? Would they show the book? I'd be okay with losing a kidney if the book got a mention on national TV. But I could be lying dead in a pool of blood and these fuckers still wouldn't stop. They'd probably quicken their pace. This was now my life? I selected my most philosophical sign. I'd been of two minds about using it since it wasn't exactly the most cheery of my quotes but they were leaving me no choice. I placed it in front of the others.

> **SPOILER ALERT, WE ALL DIE AT THE END**
> #TheOxygenThiefDiaries

If nothing else, I had plenty of time to think.

How lucky I'd been to have Marian. How stupid I was to lose her. How tolerant she'd been of me when in fact I'd thought I was the one tolerating her.

A graphic example came to mind.

The day she gave me the table, she escorted me to Prince Street, partly, I thought, to see if I really was going to go through with it. Unloading my repurposed laundry cart, I became aware, as she read my signs for the first time, that she had noticed something on one of them. Half-raising her arm she looked like she was about to point it out but then seemed to think better of it.

I wanted her to believe that the only reason I was out there was to demonstrate my willingness to generate sales *without* using photos of her ass. That shutting down the fake profile was the only option open to me because doing right by her was more important than booksales. This was bookselling at its most self-flagellatory. I wanted her to watch as I humiliated myself trying to get New Yorkers to give a shit about my brutally honest memoir. Surely any man willing to prostrate himself thusly was worthy of a second chance.

But the truth was datemedotcom had shut me down.

Someone complained.

Actually a lot of people complained. And the yacht-owning entrepreneur who had initially acknowledged my brilliance as a marketer disappeared when he realized he wasn't going to meet the beautiful Françoise. That, in fact, she didn't exist.

Marian retrieved her hand and instead made a comment about it looking like rain. This was an explosive enough subject to distract a fledgling street vendor like myself from remembering to ask what she was going to say. Rain had taken on new significance, representing, as it now did, the urgent need to pack up my wares and seek shelter. But as her hand returned to her side and I sacrificed what little dignity I had left to the frenzy of packing up, I forgot all about it until some months later when a would-be wag in a tweed suit and a flat cap took enormous pleasure in pointing out a typo located in exactly the same spot Marian had decided not to draw attention to.

F. SCOTT FITZGERALD FOR THE IPAD GERNERATION
—Richard Nash, Soft Skull Publishing

Tipping his pretentious thirties-style James Joyce cap, he bade me adieu and strode away, shaking his head at the good of it. I was humiliated of course. Especially since I had just spent ten minutes trying to convince him that Lars von Trier's production company was looking at a treatment of the book. But even more humbling was the realization that Marian had considered our relationship so irreparable there was no point in bringing the error to my attention. I'd only accuse her of enjoying my misfortune or of kicking me when I was down. Or had she decided it was more satisfying to let me stand out there represented by typos?

She'd already told me that when we'd split the bill in restaurants she secretly accepted less than half the full amount since I objected when the total came to even a penny more than the menu price. Being European I conveniently ignored the need to factor in tax and tips. To keep the peace she paid the extra dollars without telling me. Really? Charming wonderful me? The advertising hotshot who once thought nothing of buying hundred-dollar dinners for his dates.

FROM MIDAS TO TIGHT-ASS
#TheOxygenThiefDiaries

I would soon learn there was only one trustworthy indicator of rain on Prince Street and that his name was Stone Cold Joe. A Korean jewelry vendor who read the surrounding environs like an Aborigine. Three droplets of moisture on the surface of his table was tantamount to exfiltration. And he wasn't fooled by artificial rain from air conditioners or the jettisoned contents of airline toilets. He'd been doing this for twenty-five years. In fact if you googled *Prince Street* you'd see him and his table from three different angles on *Street View*. He was as much a part of the street as the hydrants. No surprise then that the moment he began to disassemble his table the rest of the vendors followed. Within seconds, two, three, sometimes more Asian men appeared out of nowhere pushing shopping trolleys stuffed with every imaginable sort of umbrella, racing for the best spots on Broadway. They were already giddy with excitement since the sight of Stone Cold Joe packing up meant they were about to make a killing.

"You wan a yellow?"

This was what he called a banana. Presumably if the concept worked for an orange then it was worth extending. I must have looked downhearted because he offered me one now.

He had inherited the wife of a friend, another Korean vendor, who had died some years earlier. The street vending license passed to her. Every day at noon he helped Mrs. Lee set up shop next to me. They were the closest thing to a couple we had out there. They'd argue pleasantly over who should pay for the disgusting trays of slop silently delivered to them by a fallow Asian on an electric bicycle. He waited patiently while Mrs. Lee, who was regularly mistaken for Yoko Ono, and Stone Cold Joe went through the charade of trying to secure from the other the privilege of paying.

Stone Cold usually won. But not without a fight.

The real Yoko Ono lived around the corner in a loft on Greene Street and when, on the rare occasions, she walked among mortals our resident vendor of hats (in summer) and socks (in winter) filmed her on his phone and posted the results on @HatsAndSocksTom.

Mrs. Lee sold onesies with the legend PARTY IN MY ROOM 4AM BRING A BOTTLE emblazoned across the front. People, women mostly, stopped, pointed, and went limp with laughter before taking a picture and making a purchase. The onesies sold steadily at $15 each but on more than one occasion I noticed an artsy type, usually a man, considering not just the onesies but Mrs. Lee herself. Before long, others stopped to stare at what he was staring at. This happened so often Mrs. Lee recognized the signs and in a bid to deflect the unwanted attention covered her table and sauntered off up the street in the hope that they'd lose interest and be gone by the time she returned. But the more she avoided them the more likely it seemed to the culturally astute that Yoko Ono was curating a sort of postmodern consumer-centric comment on the nature of capitalism.

After all, such occurrences were not without precedent.

Only a few blocks away the elusive and anonymous graffiti artist Banksy had hired an elderly actor to sit with his paintings and pose as an artist/vendor, and no one realized it until the story broke the next day and the man who paid $20 for a painting learned he was a millionaire. New York's intellectual elite would not be caught out twice.

Beginning with tentative nods of the head it evolved to finger-pointing and escalated to the taking of pictures. Before long, a crowd gathered around her table. The attention might have been welcome had they bought onesies but they were too busy trying to keep Mrs. Lee in focus. Having learned that the best thing to do was just walk away, thereby removing the temptation, she'd sometimes arrive at my table with her entourage in tow. I took photos of her holding my book and Tweeted it under the caption *Cultural Icons*. It was retweeted so much and attracted so many comments and likes I would have clarified that we shouldn't confuse a widowed Korean vendor of onesies with the woman who broke up the Beatles, but such a complex idea was impossible to convey in less than two hundred and forty charac

Drinnggggg and *Ping*
I'm outside
Marian was about to take me on a road trip to New Paltz.

She insisted I bring some laundry because she knew a cool fifties-style laundromat there. The trip had all the makings of a memorable outing. I knew I couldn't overtly point to anything romantic but all the ingredients were in place should the opportunity arise.

Fearful that she'd get honked at for holding up traffic I pummeled down the stairs and burst out the door to find her already out of the car and sauntering toward me. This was so unexpected I stopped in my tracks. She wore a tiny black cardigan buttoned over a black T-shirt and skintight black leggings that stopped just short of a pair of matte black ankle-high cowboy boots.

It certainly didn't help that she looked better than I'd ever seen her. Had she selected this outfit especially for me? It had to be for me because we were about to spend the day together.

"Fucking hell!" I said.

It was so uncharacteristic.

She had never gotten out of her car like this in all the time we'd been together. She hated idling in the street because Manhattan's drivers only allowed a few seconds' grace before the honking began. I hoped it was because she wanted me to absorb the full, unfiltered force of her attraction before we set off. She met my hug halfway but stiffened on my approach like she was bracing herself against a chest-high wave. The result was an extremely awkward misdirected kiss to her neck.

And as if to confirm my sense of alarm a car honked behind us. Having done such horrible things to her I was surprised she'd want to be with me under any heading and yet here she was. There was a luminous flash of calf above the short black cowboy boot as she turned to get back in the car, and her logic-melting ass made a momentary appearance before concealing itself in the driver's seat. I stood in the street transfixed as she slammed her door and adjusted what looked like a new pair of Jackie O sunglasses helmeted by the oh-so-French-looking bangs.

Another honk and then two more in quick succession.

And she was being so chatty. Again this was unusual for her. Since we were en route to the town where she'd gone to college, every hydrant, road sign, and storefront evoked memories and stories only half-related before the next prompt arrived around a bend. It was as if her better self waited for us in the town ahead and she couldn't wait to introduce me. She looked like a pale East European art student, amazed at everything. I felt fortunate to be in the car with her, to be allowed to look at her. This was not the girl I had so cynically gotten rid of. This was the beauty I'd felt unworthy of when we first met.

She wanted to revisit a forest trail that led to the ruins of an old mill she'd explored years before. The denuded forest stood ankle-deep in brown and yellow leaves and blushed in the deepening orange of the setting sun. I couldn't decide how to behave. Weren't we supposed to be just friends now? Was she showing me this secret place so I could get to know her better?

To see new sides of her? Or was I just castrated company on a trip down memory lane?

Astonishingly, she posed for pictures.

She wasn't afraid I'd use them for another fake profile? This was a good sign. She even tolerated a minor adjustment to one of her poses. Surely there had to be some feeling left over from our three years together. I decided to behave like we were still together. It was all I knew how to do. If nothing else it'd remind her of what she was missing: the lighthearted, witty, confident, easygoing, self-effacing Irishman.

She smiled, acknowledging the effort from the perspective of a detached observer. It was as if she could see how well it would work on someone else. This went on for longer than I would have thought bearable. For the most part she said nothing, only breaking her silence to correct me. I had just referred to the sunset as being *azure* and pronounced the word with as much of a French accent as I could muster. There was a time when she would have loved this.

"Yeah, azure is blue," she said matter-of-factly.

No apology, no concern for my feelings. She might as well have been out for a walk with someone with Alzheimer's. As if she knew the correction wouldn't register but she was duty-bound to make it. The sky was so orange now it tinted us. I tried to alleviate the tension by offering to take her picture in this light and she immediately folded her arms in a playful *gangsta* pose. She looked incredibly beautiful in that instant but she was gone again as soon as the picture was taken. I had until that moment always imagined that *azure* meant *orange*. It was shameful for an award-winning art director to be humbled by this glowingly lit girl.

"Will you send me those pictures?" she said, regretting the need to have to ask me for something.

We managed to get our laundry loaded into the washers and with an hour to kill as the machines churned we decided to get something to eat. But as soon as we sat down in the cute little blue-and-white café serving Greek gyros I gave in to an urge to blurt. She was keeping me at a distance and it wasn't fair. Surely we needed to clarify what was going on.

She looked embarrassed. For me, not for herself.

"I'm in the same place," she said, which I immediately mistook to mean we were on the same page—that she agreed with me. But hang on. *In the same place?* Meaning the same place she was when she said *no* the last time. And yet she didn't seem at all sure of what she was saying.

I began to cry.

It wasn't something I had planned.

She looked so good and loving through my tears. She even kissed one or two away, which only encouraged me to emote all the more. If tears got me kissed then tears it would be. She held my hand over the table and smiled kindly, more comfortable now in the role of nurse.

But she was nurse and malady in one.

She seemed more relieved than I was. Did she need to see me in tears before she could believe anything I said? Maybe she was just enjoying the sight of me suffering. I had been a complete cunt to her while we were together, but I felt justified since I was sure she just wanted to trap me into cohabitation, marriage, and baby-rearing. She was extra sweet to me now almost as if she approved of the crying. I would have been mortified if she had been the one crying in a café with other people around but she actually seemed proud of me. It was the first time since I'd known her that she wanted to show me off.

But since I now had her full attention I ventured further out onto the ice. I told her that I now found myself in the position where I was yearning for a text or an email from her and that when we met I was all trembly about what she was going to say next and that when I was away from her again I was obsessively checking my email.

"That's how I was when I was with you."

I'd lost her again. In the car on the way back to New York she held my hand tightly like she was afraid I'd drift out the window into the passing trees. She pretty much drove with one hand all the way back to New York and I pretty much cried all the way, partly from necessity and partly because I knew she liked it.

When we arrived back in New York she turned to me.

"How are you doing?"

I had recovered and was enjoying myself far too much. I was giddy in fact.

"How am *I* doing?" I was so happy, I thought I might start crying again. "How are *we* doing?"

She looked disappointed, I had ruined not just the moment but the entire trip. I got out and found the trunk already popped. She was now in a hurry to get away. A car honked behind me. Retrieving my laundry bag, I hugged it without meaning to. It would absorb the force of the recoil as she accelerated away from me.

I began to compose an email.

Thank you for the clarity today . . . as I think you could see it's just too difficult for me to be around you when there's no chance of us getting back together . . . maybe we should take a break from seeing each other and see how that goes?

• • • •

Isabel was a spherical Haitian woman who wore the most amount of color I'd ever seen on one person. The effect was that she seemed already audible before she spoke. Her table was the next one down from Stone Cold Joe and Mrs. Lee. Not that you could see it buried under the proliferation of scarves, sunglasses, bracelets, and beads. Sitting on a fold-up chair, she looked like her wares had spilled off the table into a human-shaped heap at one end.

I marveled as she repeatedly employed her fail-safe sales technique on the countless customers who tried to bargain her down.

"That's racist," she announced in a voice loud enough for everyone to hear.

They immediately bought hats, scarves, and sometimes sunglasses, the better to hide their shame. It was an interesting strategy. Draw on the bottomless well of Caucasian guilt and slake your thirst for revenge and recompense. Inspired, I harnessed a less intense but equally entrenched source of prejudice.

NO, I DON'T HAVE FUCKING TOURETTE'S, I'M IRISH
#TheOxygenThiefDiaries

A tall angular young man stopped abruptly. I waited for him to congratulate me on my new sign but it was the book that caught his eye. He sent worried looks up and down the street and I got the impression he would have liked to check under my table but he was exercising restraint. His eyes continued to dart left and right before returning to me, obviously disappointed.

"I read this book . . ." he said at last and then stopped himself, as if regretting having told me. As if he was being forced to reveal information he'd rather hold on to.

"A friend recommended it."

"Really?" I said. "Who was that?"

"This really hot chick said I should read it if I wanted to meet her."

I was careful not to overreact.

"And . . . you read it."

"Yah."

"Did you like it?

"It was all right."

"Did you meet her?"

His eyes searched mine. I thought for a second he was going to lunge at me but instead he looked around again hoping the object of his desire would return from her coffee break. Maybe I could provide a clue to her whereabouts. He was reluctant to leave. I tried to imagine some further use I could make of him but as far as I was concerned he was a spent force. A wandering soul. He'd obviously bought the book on Françoise's recommendation, but selling him the sequel, in which he was listed among the gullible fools stiffed by my marketing prowess, would expose me as the Oxygen Thief and put my precious spot at risk when he returned with his friends looking for satisfaction.

"No. She just disappeared."

He stood there hoping I'd contradict him.

Ping

Tilden Beach? Saturday?

It was the owner of the very ass that bewitched this poor guy. Far from addressing my email suggesting we take a break, she was just going to ignore it. I obviously hadn't meant it so she was saving me the embarrassment of having to acknowledge I'd ever sent it. Where did she get the confidence to know I was so besotted with her? That Saturday I answered my own question.

"You look like a fifties film star."

I didn't care how she took the information, I just wanted her to know it. Why keep it from her? That was what I'd always done, withheld compliments so she wouldn't have power over me. I didn't dare look at her directly in case she thought I was waiting for a reward but I imagined her resisting a natural urge to smile. Why would she resist smiling? Because she knew its dizzying effect was like drugs to me and she would want to deny me that. It was gut-wrenching not being able to touch her or be in any way romantic and yet I was grateful to be beside her in the passenger seat. It was as if we were learning about each other for the first time. Or maybe I was now willing to open myself up to her since I had concealed so much the first time around. *The first time around?* My emotions were like the children of divorced parents desperately trying to dress up a platonic trip to the beach as a romantic reunion.

Three years earlier, if I noticed something distasteful

about her I'd ignore it because well, what was the point? She'd soon be dumped and there was no sense in wasting time nurturing something that would soon be discarded. But now that I wanted her back this could never be said out loud: *Marian, for the three years we were together I didn't care what you said or did because I knew I was going to dump you, but now that I might want to keep you around I'm willing to at least entertain the idea of understanding you . . . can we have sex now?*

I had no way of knowing she had put on a bikini under her clothes so when she began to undress right there in front of me any hopes I had of seeing her naked plummeted like shot-down doves. Stepping out of her shorts, she spun round and basically slapped me in the face with the sight of a bush so unkempt it had outgrown the confines of her navy bikini bottom. So unchecked was its proliferation it had begun to encroach on the beautiful pale skin of her inner thighs and the world in general.

I was instinctively insulted.

Its progress said more about her feelings for me than anything she could ever have articulated. And she was so proud of it, brandishing it around in front of my meticulously shaved head and face. I felt hot. Panicky even. The ocean began to look inviting not just because I could soothe my fevered thoughts but because it would conceal the tears I felt welling up inside me.

The term *bushwhacked* presented itself.

I sensed her disgust at my subjugation. I needed to get away from this. I needed to take what I'd learned, if anything, away with me. We couldn't ever get back to where we once were. This girl didn't even like me now, let alone love me. None of this was acknowledged of course, and I tried to behave as if I was squinting philosophically out to sea.

I tried not to ogle a very shapely girl who got up from a blue towel beside us and sauntered toward the ocean. She looked like a model in a commercial. She was probably in her late thirties but she had a quiet contented smile that made her seem much younger. I would have loved to spend the day with her instead but I felt I owed Marian more opportunities to torture me. To avenge herself. I had no say in how she took this revenge; all I could do was turn up and stand still while she obtained satisfaction. It seemed fair. Hopefully she'd get it out of her system and we could move on.

"Nice butt," she remarked as the girl sashayed past.

Now we were buddies checking out chicks?

"I prefer yours," I said, and she immediately made a face.

It was time to jump in the ocean.

At one point a huge wave knocked her over and when it subsided she sat in the surf dazed with her bikini top knocked sideways and her gorgeous tits in plain view. Smiling in the way people do when they're not sure what has just happened, she looked around trying to catch her breath. Still blinking the water away she looked over at me. I said nothing. I was far enough away that she couldn't make out how longingly I looked at those perfect breasts or how satisfied I was to see her knocked on her ass. I had been knocked a couple of times too and I wondered if she had enjoyed that sight as much as I was enjoying this one. She had certainly laughed hard enough.

A mean, impractical laugh. She must have wondered why I was still standing there up to my waist in water looking at her because suddenly her head dipped and she realized she'd been virtually topless for the preceding forty seconds. Without looking at me she quickly adjusted herself and those lovely tits disappeared forever.

Drinnggggg

I'd try to plug the Marian-shaped hole with Courtney.

In her email she referred to herself as an aspiring psychologist. She marveled at how well I had managed to so realistically convey the behavior of a sociopath in my writing. But she was careful not to infer I was one. In fact, the accusation was conspicuous by its absence.

But I made it very clear to her that the Oxygen Thief and I were very much the same person and to prove it I slid up beside her on my couch and kissed her on the neck. Halfheartedly pushing me away she embarked on an unconvincing visit to the restroom that seemed to me to be just an excuse to break off so she didn't explode with lust all over me.

I was grateful she did because it gave me a decent look at her ass, which, though it was depressing compared to Marian's, wasn't half as bad as I'd feared. Having read about my penchant for thigh-high stockings, she hinted that she might be wearing a pair if I visited her in her office all the way up in Washington Heights. She needed clients to practice on and hosting as I did a veritable smorgasbord of neuroses and mental tics, I was the perfect test dummy. I received all sorts of offers from therapists. I think they saw me as a challenge. And having me as a client might even be good for business.

But a therapist in thigh-highs?

Suddenly the trip to Upstate Manhattan didn't seem so bad. Her "office" turned out to be her apartment and her therapeutic technique turned out to be . . . well . . . confrontational.

"Didn't you say only sluts swallow?"

I had to concede that I did at one point express that view in one of my books, yes. "So you've changed your mind since?"

I replied that I hadn't yet gathered enough evidence to make a decision. "I think we need to explore this idea."

While we talked she pecked politely at a glass of whiskey, so I couldn't help thinking she'd probably had more than that before I arrived. She referred to me as a therapist's starter kit, a beautifully disturbed, human simulator on whom to rehearse.

"The proof being that you're flattered by the description." She adjusted her thigh-highs, obviously enjoying herself. *Prnggggggg*

I had no intention of answering my phone but I couldn't resist a peek.

MARIAN

A little red blister indicated she'd left a voice message, and I immediately began to agonize over its contents. I tried to look unconvinced as Courtney continued to expand on how useful we'd be to each other. The depth of her psychological insight was astonishing.

"I'm going to give you two blowjobs in a row." The idea was that I would indicate a preference. Swallow vs. Facial.

The *Sophie's Choice* of blowjobs.

On the way home with my balls basically glowing in the dark, I heard Marian's voice say she missed me and that she was driving to Maryland and . . . the next few words were frustratingly muffled as the receiver moved away from her mouth but then clarity returned and one isolated phrase broke through the murk: ". . . some surgery might be required."

There she was, the girl I was supposedly in love with, en route to having some worrying condition dealt with, and I was too busy having my dick sucked and my cum swallowed to answer. How could I ever be a decent boyfriend if I couldn't be there for her in situations like this? But had she made other calls before me? And were there other calls made after? She had just wanted to kill time while she drove. Guilt gave way to resentment as I began to wonder if she had only been looking for sympathy.

I decided to show I wasn't ignoring her but at the same time clarify that I wasn't available for counseling. Courtney had strongly suggested I cut off all contact with her since it was too confusing for me. But hearing her voice was like sunshine in my veins.

I needed to wean myself off her.

"You can't cross an ocean if you don't have the courage to lose sight of the shore." So said my trainee therapist, between mouthfuls of molten me.

I sent her a text.

I honestly appreciate that you're concerned over a health issue but on a social level I'm just not ready to hang out or chat. I hope everything goes perfectly though.

Pressing send was like detonating my life.

A hurricane was forecast that weekend and it seemed apt that I should batten down the hatches and steel myself for an onslaught of Marian while gales raged symbolically without.

But in the end all it did was rain a little.

HURRICANE CANCELED DUE TO RAIN
#TheOxygenThiefDiaries

Minutes into our second session Courtney got straight to the core of the problem.

"How would you like to come?"

While I tried to think of a witty riposte she set about effortlessly inhaling the contents of my balls. And then making a point of licking her lips she walked her newly medicated patient to the bedroom. I felt myself being helped out of my clothes and placed between the cool, clean, crisp, sheets of her bed.

We talked.

Or rather I talked while she listened like a proper little psychologist-in-waiting.

It was such an effective form of therapy.

A mouthful followed by an earful.

A voice inside me cautioned: *This is how they get you.*

But I loved talking to her. After all I was allowed to talk about my favorite subject (I might not think much of myself but I did it all day). And in the few rare moments where she was allowed to get a word in edgewise she actually managed to make some very astute observations.

For instance, my technique of gaining people's trust by appearing to be overly honest allowed me to secretly hate them for their gullibility. This in turn cemented my reluctance to show them my real self. Her analysis was unnervingly accurate but she preempted any potentially prickly pronouncements with a gentle cupping of my still-tingling balls. Her hand was already in place so it was just a matter of a slight *recup* at the appropriate moment. She was definitely onto something here. How easy it was to divulge oneself psychologically having already been unpacked sexually.

But there was something sad about her.

Surely all the attention I received was an attempt to hide from her own feelings. Was this why she wanted to be a therapist? Much more fun probing around in other people's heads than her own. When I mentioned this I felt my balls being fondled.

"It's probably because I'm about to turn forty."

She broke the silence by making some reference to what we'd have for breakfast.

In other words she invited me to stay the night. But I preferred the idea of finite sessions and I told her so as I began to get dressed. She sent an email on ahead to greet me when I got home.

Is it too maternal to ask if you made it home okay?

It was, but I said nothing because I wanted more of that mouth.

And yet the sensation of having my sludge siphoned for the second time already seemed less heavenly than the first. I couldn't help thinking that her sexual subservience was just a ploy to trap me into being her live-in pet in her pristine apartment. Ideally before she turned forty. She could never compare with the depth of feeling I had for Marian. The very thought of whom made me want to cry. But that would have to stop. Wouldn't it? I felt desperately that I should be with her and yet I could clearly remember hating her when we were together. *Hating* her. Was it really all just a trick? If so, why? For whose benefit? Did we fall for this sleight of hand over and over again just to keep the planet populated?

Courtney said I shouldn't be afraid to approach the cage where I said I'd locked up *The Thug*. I should hear what he had to say. If I did, I'd realize he was gone. That what I was feeling was only the memory of the fear of him. She was just about good-looking enough to inspire a hard-on but not so beautiful that I was in danger of falling in love. At one point as we lay in her bed, she told me to take my arm out from under her because I was obviously trapping myself. I was impressed with this until I realized that it was just more strategy.

Lock him to you by setting him free.

"Imagine I'm you and you're *The Thug*. What would you want to say to me?"

She was enjoying her faux session but this was starting to unsettle me. I imagined all the horrible things *he* would want to say to me. She'd never be able to understand how much I wanted to eviscerate that stupid, short, fat, bald, ugly, small-dicked fool she now represented. I didn't want to risk exposing her to such vitriol in case it interfered with my supply of blowjobs, but I knew I had to give her something.

"I will cause you to underlive," I said at last. "I won't let you live to your fullest capacity. I will limit you. I will ensure you are with a girl who does *not* make you happy. *Not* in an atmosphere where you'll thrive. *Not* make enough money to live comfortably."

I stopped myself.

I had given her too much. A girl who doesn't make me happy? What? She nodded to herself. Thinking. Cogitating.

Her conclusion was that I saw myself as some awful force that people needed to be protected from, but that in her opinion I was wonderful and smart and unbelievably kind. She said I could figure things out in an instant and though this was an admirable trait it also told her how often I'd had to do it in my life and that this was sad. She also said she thought Marian was systematically punishing me for what I'd done to her. She then took my soft, frightened penis in her mouth and made it hard again without using her hands.

• • • •

I climbed the three flights of stairs to the sex addicts meeting. The sign hanging on the door said SLAA. What did the *L* stand for? Love. Their full name was *Sex and Love Addicts Anonymous*. This was stunning to me.

Yes I was prone to sex: the endorphins released before, during, and after the act, but addicted to love? To the machinations and sleight of hand, to the seduction and manipulation, to the power of having someone on a string. This had never occurred to me before. It explained a lot. In fact it explained everything. There were SLAA guidelines for dating; no French kissing for the first three dates, no long lingering phone calls, no *rain-checking* (postponing dates in order to continue the illusion of a relationship), no pressure dates (fancy dinners or opera tickets).

But if love was an addictive substance then women were the dealers. A bottle of booze or a drug had the decency to sit on a shelf and wait for you to use it. Not so with a woman. She got up and walked around, made decisions, went on vacation, interacted with other potential suitors. If a woman held the key to your stash then you were in deep shit. When your drug of choice can refuse to be imbibed that is a problem. Women, it seemed, had what I sought. They carried it around with them. I had thought it was their pussies but now I could see it was much more serious than that. It wasn't sex I had been chasing all those years, it was approval.

There was a lot of talk about fantasy.

Not the sort of fantasy involving a convent full of lesbian nuns, but the romantic daydreaming that took place between dates. The cottage-building, rose-tinted, soft-focus longing that reality will always fall short of.

I sat in a circle and listened as a reasonable-looking man shared that after having an affair with his best friend's wife he had now become an outcast. He was blocked, unfriended, and very much unfollowed. The wife had been forgiven but he hadn't. He was deeply annoyed by the sheer inconvenience of it all. Like he'd lost his wallet. He resented his best friend for not forgiving him. After all he *had* apologized. And to be fair he wasn't the only man she'd had an affair with. There had been others. She was the one who had broken her marriage vows, not him.

I could see his point.

An older man shared that he fantasized about having sex with miners and while I imagined him being sodomized by soot-covered Welshmen, he spoke falteringly about how it was their innocence and lack of criticism that turned him on, and I suddenly realized why he looked like a child molester. *Minors.* And even more worrying was the fact that I had identified with his attraction to innocence and lack of criticism. I looked around the room searching for support. This guy was disgusting, right? I was impressed that no one took me up on it. This really was a safe place. There was no judgment. But didn't they hear what he was saying? Shouldn't someone be calling the police?

This was when she walked in.

She was twenty minutes late but her body language, or more accurately, her body, apologized for it. We shuffled sideways to make room and when her turn came she shared how she used to *act out* with complete strangers. Sexually explicit terms and phrases were discouraged since they could trigger *bottom line behavior.* In other words, someone might start wanking. One of her favorite places to *engage her addiction* was in elevators. She'd simply press the stop button and that was that. She loved the finality of it. That it all took place in a mirrored container and that when it was over she left the guy there.

She had all the power.

She was never refused and she never saw any of them again. It turned her on to do it.

To think about it beforehand and replay the memory afterward. She'd keep a memento. A tie. A cufflink. A lighter. A glove. Like a serial killer. She was absolutely gorgeous. Upperclass and very well made. I would never have expected to find a girl of such quality in a place like this, saying things like that. I looked around the circle again. This time for sympathy. I couldn't take this. I was so jealous of the guys (were there girls too?) fortunate enough to have been *engaged with* by her. I felt like she had to be prick-teasing us with the concept. Surely she was still active. Her face flushed at the memory. So did mine. I was shocked. I couldn't explain it. I was jealous of her too. Her power. Her beauty. It was like meeting a real-life billionaire.

I never went back because all I felt was rage that I had never had an encounter like that with a girl as beautiful as that and I suspected I never would. Far from discouraging me I simply got new ideas. Hearing that a girl like that was capable of such escapades only encouraged me to return to the fray. I was like the mild-mannered traffic offender mentored by murderers. I wanted to cry when I heard her say she hoped she'd never debase herself in that way again. When the meeting ended, all the men, myself included, waited for the elevator.

She took the stairs.

I DON'T GET LAID ENOUGH TO BE CALLED A SEX ADDICT
#TheOxygenThiefDiaries

I took Courtney's suggestion to attend these meetings not because I thought they'd work but because they'd prove useful in my ongoing campaign to show Marian I was working on myself. And if attending them meant there was a good chance Courtney would continue sucking me off well then, all the better. But on exiting the elevator I got a text from her saying she'd met a Wall Street trader who seemed to be interested in a relationship. It had the potential to turn into something permanent so she was going to give it a try. Apparently he was more fucked-up than I was and consequently needed more help than I did. He had massive trust issues and she wanted to be able to assure him that he was the only one in her life.

She was dumping me for not being fucked-up enough.

By text.

I walked straight into a Codependents Anonymous meeting that was just starting in a depressingly hot room on the ground floor of the same building as the SLAA meeting. The chairman was obsessed with allotting equal segments of time to each person to share. Dividing the overall amount of time (an hour) by the number of people in the room (nine) ended up being an exercise in futility because he had to start all over again when someone walked in late.

It was Beckettian.

The best part was at the end not just because it was the end but because he went around the room asking people what they were feeling at that precise moment. It was humbling to realize that what they announced was not at all what I thought I saw on their faces.

"I'm tired and sad," said one girl who looked anything but.

"I'm confused," said another who looked like she had her shit together.

"Overwhelmed," said the next guy who admittedly did look a little flustered but it was quite a revelation to understand the chasm between inner thought and outward appearance.

Don't compare your insides to someone else's outsides.

Apart from that it was the same stuff I heard in AA.

"Don't give away your power." One guy was going through a separation and he said he was fine during the week but when he had his kid for the weekend he wanted his wife back. But overall, looking at it coldly he realized the cons significantly outweighed the pros.

"Basically she was hot and the sex was great but apart from that she wasn't a nice person. She wasn't a companion. She didn't treat me well."

There was a lot of talk of "having your needs met" and references to putting your life on hold to benefit someone else. Disappearing into another person's personality so as to avoid having to develop your own. A joke was told.

What does a codependent see when he's drowning?
Someone else's life flash before his eyes.

There were knowing nods and grunts of recognition but it was new to me. I saw a lot of Marian's behavior in there. She liked to find out what was going on with me so she could get into the mix of it and hide from her own issues. And I welcomed it as long as I got what I wanted. Namely sex. And I began to see how controlling I could be. I'd be more than happy do something for her but I'd seethe if I didn't receive payment.

Sexual payment.

I'd take long walks with her, visit museums, have lunch with her parents, whatever she wanted as long as she fucked me afterward. And when the sex eased off I'd suppress my rage since I was so ashamed of its origin. Getting angry about it would expose the fact that I only wanted her for sex. And then behind that there was a certain relief involved because I could harness the sexual rejection as a reason for not staying with her. *See? She's just a frigid cunt. I'll have to dump her soon.* Which meant there was no point in making any plans for our future. It was a stalemate.

I was a stale mate.

They talked about boundaries and trust issues and taking on other people's feelings. I was thinking about inviting Marian to attend a meeting until I heard one of them say that fixing people was in itself a symptom of codependence. *We fix others to make ourselves more comfortable.* Like families where one person took on all the work to keep the peace. They put their needs aside for the good of the whole. This was what I had done in advertising. Obsession, compulsion, and insecurity were great traits to have in the workplace because you're always over-prepared and at your desk early but those same characteristics were disastrous in a relationship. And yes workaholism might get you promoted but hiding in a job wasn't living.

They called it *miming in the choir.*

I'd never been married or allowed myself to be in a real relationship because I was never going to trust anyone enough to let them in. My behavior with Marian was classic. Push her away. Hurt her. Whatever it took not to let her in, or better yet make her not *want* to get in.

"I liked hurting girls . . ."

Later, on the phone, I told her I had identified with some of the things I'd heard in the meeting and instead of saying *Yes, me too,* she said, "Well yeah, I've been trying to tell you that for ages."

At least we could agree on one thing.

I was an asshole.

• • • •

"You're a misogynist."

The girl held my eyes making sure I understood it was an insult. At first I thought this might be the feminist who had emailed to say she might stop by my table at some point that afternoon, but leading with an attack didn't seem like her style since her email had been quite flattering. She stood there waiting for me to leap to my own defense but I ignored her in favor of a homeless man who loomed up from behind.

"Ahh, yessir, good afternoon, thank you for stopping."

She walked away shaking her head.

The homeless *loved* to be sold to.

So accustomed were they to being shooed away they only met your eyes to decide if you were mocking them. After exhausting my spiel I'd get thanked for going to the trouble of pretending to sell to them. They were like fat girls grateful for the attention. But they were less likely to be a nuisance if they were treated as potential customers. Otherwise, knowing they were a deterrent, they'd hang around waiting to be bribed. The truth is I had no way of ensuring they would stay away other than to give them no reason to come back. After more than one failed attempt at banning a multi-coated individual I realized I couldn't dictate to a street dweller where in the street he could dwell.

If anything I was the trespasser.

This particularly grimy example of the genre declined to hold my book when I handed it to him. Not because he was demonstrating his taste in literature but because he didn't want to soil it. The poor bastard stepped back to save me the horror of contact with him. He (I think it was a "he") smelled so bad the dominant fumes of piss and feet brought tears to my eyes.

"Thank yooooooo," said a voice from somewhere inside the clump of matted hair and coats as it shuffled away.

Minutes later a sixty-three-year-old, impeccably groomed, self-confessed feminist called Delaney presented herself at my table and appeared to be far too impressed. I was suspicious. Since she had referred to herself as a "hard-core feminist" in her initial email I was braced for some sort of intellectual assault, but as she spoke I felt my shoulders relax as I realized she was hinting at the possibility of having me as a guest on a podcast she hosted called *The Seethesayer*.

Surely it was a trap.

I'd be publicly roasted by bull dykes with overgrown vaginas and end up taxidermed in reception. But I couldn't refuse the exposure. Or the potential for pussy. All those college students producing soup to the sound of my lilting Irish accent. And a radio interview was perfect because I'd still be anonymous. There was no harm in hearing her out.

So later that night in Cafe Ost we had an excellent chat about media and gender and all things patriarchal. The usual stuff. Stuff I had became accustomed to speaking about in a convincing manner.

"I'm surprised there aren't cars on fire in the street," I volunteered.

"What do you mean?"

"Well, where's the rage? Men have been treating women like retarded rabbits for centuries. Why are you not angry? Because the patriarchy is so effective, it's trained you to police yourselves."

She was definitely well connected and not unintelligent, but she seemed to be just now discovering things that should have been old news to her. If anything she seemed *too* impressed by my observations. I wondered if she might be about to offer me a slot with my own show. Or at least confirm the time and date of my interview on hers. So when she stopped me outside the café just before parting, I was expectant.

"Can I ask you something?"

"Please do."

"Was this a date?"

I wanted to laugh. She was over sixty years old. I wouldn't have fucked her if she paid me; well, maybe if she paid me a lot. She had just spent three hours sitting there under the impression there was an outside chance of us having sex. She saw my eagerness to philosophize as a measure of how strongly I was attracted to her. In other words, I and everything I had talked about was reduced to a cosmetic she applied to her aging cheeks. And this from a radical feminist. It made me revise everything I'd said. One statement in particular.

"I'm not a misogynist, I'm a misanthrope with a hard-on."

Now I could see why she'd beamed at this.

I was thinking I had at last found someone capable of navigating the vertiginous canyons of my brilliance but in her mind this was the moment she became convinced she would get some dick.

She sent an email the next morning.

As I walked away last night I got the feeling that "he's just not that into you."

If she walked past my table again she could read my response.

HORMONES NOT SO MUCH RAGING NOW AS COMPLAINING
#TheOxygenThiefDiaries

Marian invited me to her workshop in Bushwick. It was thrilling to be shown around her inner sanctum and I was determined not to fuck up. She showed me how to make some simple metal designs from a sketch I drew of a skull. She was so sweet and caring as she explained the various techniques. Her hands touched mine as she positioned my fingers on the cutting tools. A tingle ran up my arm and splashed in my chest.

"You should always make sure you cut away from the body."

How thoughtful.

She obviously wanted me to see her in action.

To show me a side of her I hadn't seen before. She'd made it clear that she'd have to leave by six PM to be on time for a dinner party, and I nursed a barely acknowledged hope that, depending on how the afternoon went, I might be asked to join her. After making much of my skull-shaped aluminum key ring I felt I had passed whatever test she had set for me, because at 5:50 PM she announced she wouldn't be going to the dinner party at all.

Glee ran around inside me looking for an outlet.

I could have gone home there and then and it would have been a momentous day but there was more to come. Without warning she held my shoulders, drugged me with her famous smile, leaned forward, and kissed me on the lips.

I couldn't believe it.

Was she mocking me? I felt so undeserving it was almost painful to receive it.

Did she know this?

"Oh," I said, stupefied. "That seems . . . that was . . ."

"Do you need more reassurance?" The smile was actually still there.

"Hourly," I said, beaming.

I felt such a surge of joy it verged on religious. I didn't dare jinx it with speech. It was too delicate a moment to support the weight of spoken words. When I first sat down in her workshop I was determined not to let her know how fucking gorgeous she looked. My idea was to reemploy the technique that won her three years earlier. Back then I made a point of being nice and witty and respectful and resisted any temptation to make a move. This eventually proved to be a successful strategy. Apparently it was going to work again.

We crossed the street from her studio into a café.

A rich French art dealer had hired her to install a collection of rare figurines in one of his coastal homes near San Francisco. She'd be flown out there in a private jet and met by personal assistants. I was jealous that she'd be brushing shoulders, and perhaps other parts of her lovely pale sleek body, with wealthy young men who were going to appear very attractive compared to me. She showed me pictures of the guesthouse and the taste level was worryingly astute. Expensive but not tacky; simple, laid-back, bohemian.

And I couldn't help but notice the double bed.

She asked me to help her pronounce some artistic phrases like trompe l'oeil (*trohm loo-aye*), penchant (*pong-shong*), and fleur-de-lis (*flure duh lee*) so that she didn't make a faux pas (*foe-paw*) at dinner. Ordinarily she'd dismiss such niceties as unworthy of discussion but now she blushed as she rehearsed them with me. Either she was out to impress her employers or she was chumming for ceauk (*cock*).

To change the subject I produced some DVDs that we might watch that weekend. Inexplicably her arms began to flap like a flightless bird. I thought at first that she was excited by the titles until I saw the tear roll down her cheek. Leaning across the table she tilted her face up at me and kissed me first on the cheek and then after a moment's consideration, micro-pecked my lips as if she was worried she might burn me. As if she understood the intensity of what she had dammed up inside her and didn't want to hurt me with it. The lovely smile was just a memory now as she began to cry in earnest. I felt my stomach twist with self-disgust and suppressed rage. It was a reminder of why we were no longer together.

What the fuck was I doing with this myopic girl?

"They remind me of all those nice nights we spent watch-ing movies," she said.

Something broke open inside me.

My latest fear had been that she'd turn out to be a lesbian (that unruly bush had rocked me to the core) or that maybe we would get back together but I'd have to take all the blame for everything, everywhere, throughout history and she would just be encouraged to be the same miserable cunt she'd always been. But I was beginning to see that when I was nice to her she became the most beautiful girl in the world and when I wasn't she was intolerable.

Men in the street sometimes asked her to smile and she hated it. To her it was as boorish as asking to see her tits. But she really was such a beautiful girl when she smiled.

I made no further reference to The Kiss and I was careful *not* to behave in a way that might confirm or deny that we were seemingly, in appearance at least, back together. I was too busy doing somersaults and backflips inside myself. I somehow managed to walk her back to the car.

I couldn't bear the probability of a good-bye kiss being demoted to a peck on the cheek so rather than try for it I nodded at her comically and jumped on my bike. She looked sufficiently regretful to see me go and I trembled with delight that she might just miss me if I removed myself fast enough.

But my triumphant ride home was followed by a deep, dark, echoing chasm of nothingness. For what would prove to be the eternity of the rest of that evening and the yawning void represented by the following day there would be no text, no email, no word.

Was she that cruel or was I just overly sensitive?

It felt like we were breaking up all over again. Wounds only half-healed opened anew. This couldn't go on. She had mentioned the possibility of inviting me over to watch the

DVDs and I was very keen to see what would happen since the unsolicited kiss/smile combo had to be indicative of sexual imminence. And I was aware that the following week, she would be mixing with all manner of potential suitors so this was not the time to reject an invitation to her apartment. She would be less susceptible to new advances if I could reestablish myself as a romantic possibility.

I heard nothing until 9:50 PM.

I was hoping to be already ensconced in her place by then since her roommate had left two hours earlier for the weekend. But no. When she finally did call she said she'd been looking for her phone for two hours and that when it eventually turned up there was a message on it from someone I hadn't heard of before, accusing her of not being a good friend, so she felt she had to call her back and having done that she now felt terrible. I was hearing all this on my way to a ten o'clock AA meeting, the beginning of which I would now have to miss because it was already 9:55 PM.

She was accusing her friend of being self-centered. This was rich coming from her. I wanted to hang up and go to my meeting. I could say my phone died. But this was Marian, I couldn't do that. But then because I had answered in the street I had to ask her to repeat what she'd said and this was dangerous because I knew she moved the receiver away from her mouth and this had always infuriated me. But it couldn't be mentioned. It was mind-boggling that I now yearned to hang up on the very person I'd spent the entire day hoping to hear from because she was keeping me from the meeting I needed to console me for the fact that she hadn't called.

If she didn't let me fuck her soon I'd walk away.

She had studiously omitted any reference to my coming there until the end of the call.

"Okay see you around eight PM . . . and if you have any laundry, bring it with you. I can do it for you."

It was a strange afterthought but endearing.

Like she was being maternal.

Was this a cultural thing? Maybe there was an American tradition, like studying together, where a mention of laundry was shorthand for platonic? Or maybe it was a precursor to cohabitation. I looked around for some token items to fill a bag. I intentionally didn't shave or shower in case she'd think I was expecting to get laid.

Which of course I was.

The moment I entered her apartment she asked for the laundry, the reasoning being it would take at least an hour to wash and dry while we ate and watched a movie. It also set a convenient time limit on my visit. At the door to the basement where the washer-dryer was located she paused.

"Hmmm, I don't recognize this one."

She was holding up a black-patterned knee sock like a dead snake. I had no idea how it had gotten in with my socks and jeans but I immediately felt robbed. I had never seen it before. And why was there only one?

"I've never seen that before," I said, sick with myself for being trapped in such a cliché.

67

"It's okay," she said.

I might have been her little brother whom she'd caught having a wank. It was obviously a deeply embarrassing moment for me but she'd be gracious about it. It was none of her business. But I wanted it to be her business. It would have been the perfect opportunity to clear the air if I hadn't been forced to be so defensive. Where the fuck had it come from? I had honestly never seen it before. I would have loved to see it on her but I couldn't even allow that thought in.

After we ate, she stretched theatrically, yawned, and removed her shoes and socks before settling onto the couch beside me. The opening credits were already rolling on the DVD but my attention was required elsewhere as I felt her bare heel in my lap. It was so pleasurable and unexpected I almost cried. It seemed unfair to be subjected to these extremes.

Deep-fried to deep-freeze and back again.

A knee sock inferred I was sexually active, which should have meant I didn't have a hope with her but now my poor confused cock was starting to get hard in response to the outwardly innocent movements of her naked heel in my crotch.

She pretended not to notice and so did I.

Instead, pronouncing the film *not very good*, she offered to walk on my back. This was something she knew I loved not just because it was highly therapeutic for the tensed up muscles in my back but because it had often been a prelude to sex. I was almost in tears as I lay facedown on the carpet and she stepped onto my lower and middle back and shuffled around up there, occasionally shifting her weight onto a buttock, effectively crushing my hard-on into the carpet. This was disconcerting enough but then she jumped off and invited me to stand. Surely this was it.

She waited until I was fully upright so I could register her nod at the door.

"I need to get up super early tomorrow but it was lovely of you to come out and see me."

Had I blown it because I smelled bad? I knew I should have showered. Outside on her stoop, just before I got on my bike, she leaned forward and brushed the front of her hand against the subsiding cock in my jeans. This was an unprecedented gesture from someone who had until then made a point of avoiding even the abstract suggestion of such a thing. It was as if she needed to confirm that it was in fact still vaguely hard. The fact that she used the outside of her hand was significant in that it demonstrated her interest was purely analytical.

I must have looked anguished.

"I know, I know . . ." she said, nodding sympathetically.

"You know? What do you know?" I said, almost sobbing with lust. The enigmatic smile again as she handed me my laundry.

"Have a safe ride home," she said.

And yes, the knee sock was included.

• • • •

Was it her?

The girl approaching my table looked like Marian when we first met—before I happened to her.

69

She was about to sidestep a man taking a photo of the Tourette's sign when she stopped, and after reading it broke into an easy smile. The same bangs, same height; the body wasn't as lithe but from a distance it could have been her. I tried in vain not to stare as she touched my books on the table.

Her voice was calm, soothing even.

"So what's all this?"

My throat tightened. There was a possibility I might start to sob. I was capable of it. This seemed unnecessarily cruel. I was being shown how fresh-faced and unaffected Marian was when we first met. She looked at me, looking at her, intrigued if not a little unnerved. I pointed at the blurbs on the back of the books. I didn't dare speak.

It was obvious she felt my eyes on her as she read because she nodded slowly, telegraphing that she understood. Our eyes met again as she handed me a crisp $20 bill and I signed her book *The Oxygen Thief*. In an unexpected lapse of inhibition I wrote my number on the inside flap.

I gawked unashamedly now because I was sure I'd never see her again. Her large ass, as she walked away, should have been disappointing but for some reason it didn't seem to matter.

The following week she texted.

It's Audrey. I met you on Prince Street and bought your book. I read it in one sitting. I have so many questions—

And then in a separate text, *Did Aisling ever bring out her book?*

I called her.

Toward the end of our relationship, Marian's phone manner grated on me so much I avoided answering when she called. So there was something healing about the idea of talking so easily on the phone to a girl who looked so much like her.

Audrey's voice was definitely silky, but even more alluring were the silences she allowed when she sensed I was about to speak. So wholehearted was her faith in my acuity she closed down her own. This was new to me. And deeply flattering. It was seduction on a spiritual plane.

But it was becoming obvious that anyone who liked my book was far from normal. Or maybe there was no such thing as normal. She'd had a crazy upbringing where her parents were almost always drunk or high and frequently arrested. She took the brunt of her father's beatings even when her more feminine sister had been the cause.

"Well, someone was going to get it and I thought it might as well be me."

She learned to "poke the beast" so as to control the timing of the outbursts if not their savagery. It was important to her to be the normal one in a fucked-up family but her sister, whom she described as needy, might have been the smarter one since she managed to avoid being beaten altogether.

She felt her recent election to the zoning board of her local district of Westchester was completely undeserved since the full extent of her preparation for politics consisted of watching one episode of *House of Cards*. As a child she hid behind books. Shields against the madness. In one of them she came across a new word and after looking it up she realized it was what was missing from her parents' life. The word was *divorce*. Amazingly they agreed.

She was nine years old.

By the time they actually separated she was eleven and at that age, children of divorced parents were required by law to see a counselor. These sessions were quite cheery since she was delighted her parents had taken her advice. She was proud of them. She saw herself as their parent and now that they had grown up she could concentrate on her own life goals. No surprise then that she became a divorce lawyer.

She also felt that she'd been born with the powers of a matchmaker. On three separate occasions she had dreams that friends of hers, still unintroduced at the time, would later marry. They scoffed when she mentioned it but in time they ended up together.

I was delighted to hear her say that at conferences men often walked right up to her and asked for sex. It meant she was physically attractive not just to me but to complete strangers. She said she enjoyed playing with these guys' expectations, letting them think she was going to have sex with them but saying good night at the last moment.

She said she had a married friend who was worried because her husband liked to fuck her from behind and she thought it might mean he wasn't attracted to her or that he had something to hide. This might well have been the case for all I knew but I didn't want her to think that if/when I fucked her similarly it meant I didn't like looking at her so I lied.

"Maybe sometimes it's just nice to change things up a little."

This was rewarded with a little giggle and I suddenly realized I was being interviewed for sex. She didn't drink or take drugs.

"I don't like to have any distractions when I have sex. I like to be present and aware of the other person."

"This makes me think of a theory I have but I think it's best saved for our second conversation."

"But we've already talked for what could be considered the duration of two phone calls."

She wanted to hear it but I didn't want her seeing me like that just yet. (My theory involved a dildo being inserted in my butthole.) But I was happy she wanted to know.

I ended the call against her protestations.

Satisfactory of course since it left her wanting more.

A quick google of "Audrey—Zoning—Westchester" revealed that she had been married to a guy from Belfast with a shaved head who if you blurred your eyes could have been me. Not that I was Northern Irish but my continued use of British-isms must have evoked memories in her. And according to an obituary, she'd given birth to a stillborn child. *Born sleeping* was the term used. I imagined a grave where her vagina should be.

There was no mention of any of this in our three hours of conversation. Somehow it meant I was exonerated from behaving like a gentleman. Also the word *tragedy* was used in connection with her husband. If she didn't want to talk about any of it then neither would I. I had decided I would come loudly at the end of our second call and then disappear. It would be my unannounced revenge for her unspoken insult.

I would come *at* her.

Prnnnnng

"This is Audrey."

I could clearly detect an excited tremble in her voice. It was obvious from the moment she answered she'd been waiting for the call all day. Her wifely silence insisted on nothing less than monologue. I began.

"Because a woman is actually penetrated during sex, she needs more information about the perpetrator. A man remains outside and therefore relatively aloof during the act but a woman is actually intruded upon. I realized this first when I slipped a dildo into my ass for the first time and felt an emptiness filled that I hadn't until then realized was there. A cavity, not just physical in nature but emotional too. I felt completed. Like a missing piece from a puzzle had finally been slotted into place. If this was even vaguely what it was like when a cock entered a woman, well, then I understood why they, meaning you, always want to know as much as possible about the person attached to it."

She waited. After all, I might not be finished. This marvelous man might have more to say.

"That's very astute," she said after a respectful pause and then perhaps feeling the need to offer something similar in tone she continued shyly.

"And there's that lamentable need for the man to get an

74

erection while for the woman there are so many other levels of pleasure."

"I'm sporting a rather lamentable erection as we speak."

"It would be even more lamentable if you weren't."

I hadn't actually been hard at all but now, suddenly green-lit, my cock surged into being. I imagined aloud that my hands were her hands and from there on it was plain sailing.

She didn't say as much as I would have liked (her smooth voice was so fucking sexy) but her breathing had an enormous effect on me. She began to exhale quite heavily but somehow it was still ladylike. She remained civilized even in her primal state. Unlike me. I started to pump my poor enraged cock holding the phone up to it so she could listen to the obscene squelching as I fucked my own spit-filled fist. This had a tremendous effect on her and she began moaning and sigh-ing prettily, which only fed my lust more and my confidence further and I began to tell her not just that she should imagine I was fucking her at that moment but that I was going to *actually* fuck her when we met. She might have wanted to stop and deal with this prediction in case it sounded too much like an ex-pectation on my part so I decided to up the ante by telling her she should lick her fingers to taste the juices from her already sopping wet *cunt* and then slip them back in there and hold the phone to it so I could hear it as it happened. It didn't seem like she was going to come in any climactic sense so I thought it might be time to take matters into my own hands.

Show her how it was done.

I started moaning and groaning and pumping on my cock

and letting her hear what that sounded like and demanded she say *I want your cock* and *fuck me* and at one point she ad-libbed and said *split me in two*. This was unusual. It almost gave me pause. It inferred that I might need a bigger cock than the one that was at hand. Split me in two? Was this what it felt like to have a cock thrust into your pussy? Like it was the thin edge of a much larger wedge? That opening her legs ever so wider would in fact have the effect of splitting her from cunt to throat? I decided to change the subject.

"Get down on the floor and lie on your belly."

Whether she did it or not was not important. It allowed me to think of her with her ass raised in the air. I told her I was now licking her out from behind as she fingered her-self. This received load moans of approval. I said I was now spreading her ass cheeks and tongue-fucking her gaping butt-hole. The idea was to introduce all manner of taboo before we even met. The lack of resistance to these imagined sex acts gave unspoken permission to their three-dimensional counterparts.

• • • •

I thought he was another one of Françoise's jilted suitors coming to fuck with me. To avenge himself on the smartass who duped him into buying his shitty book. The guy with him looked familiar. I knew his face from somewhere. Was he in AA?

"Wait, why does it say '*I don't have fucking Tourni-quettes*'?"

He was obviously pretending to misunderstand. First he'd mock me, then he and his friend were going to stab me right there in the street. He looked into my frightened eyes. He seemed upset with me. Oh fuck, he was Alpha. Undercover cops. I suddenly remembered I'd seen the other guy helping a handcuffed vendor into the white van.

They were partners doing their rounds.

Should I correct him and risk embarrassing a police officer and perhaps awaken a need in him to avenge himself? Stone Cold Joe dipped in and out of my peripheral vision trying to warn me with his face. Difficult, since I had only ever recognized one expression there and that was of patient endurance. The Alpha cop was now actively frowning at my sign. Was I about to be arrested for use of profanity in a public space? The frown deepened when he looked back at me. Had he just realized the sign was attached to the lamp pole? An offense that carried a $1,000 fine. I'd seen the white van summoned for less. The fact that they put the handcuffs on so carefully was in itself scary. It showed the professionalism involved. How streamlined the whole procedure was for them. It wasn't personal. There was no passion.

And it was a Friday afternoon.

They waited till Friday to make these sweeps because the judge didn't come back to work until Monday morning. This meant that if you were arrested on Friday you were going to spend three nights in the Tombs and have your table and merchandise confiscated. It would take months to get them back, if ever.

"Hahahahaha, oh now I get it," he said at last. "Haha . . . that's hilarious . . . I'm the one with the issues."

He showed me his badge like he was ashamed of it.

"And you have your tax ID right?"

"Yessir." I lied and bent down as if to retrieve it from somewhere under the table.

"No that's okay. Good luck, buddy."

They were already walking away.

But this was not such a good result for me. It was like being shown preferential treatment by the prison guards. None of the other vendors would have ever gotten away without producing state ID, tax ID, and a street-vending license appropriate to what they were peddling. In fact our long-suffering leather bags and belts vendor had earned his nickname from just such a situation. Arrest-Me-Dante would rather be choke-held and tasered than shown this sort of preferential treatment. I once watched him beg police officers to take him in. It had been a routine inspection probably initiated by a phone call from one the local stores. They were irked at having to compete with street vendors often selling the same or similar merchandise as themselves without having to pay the crippling monthly rent that is the cost of doing business in SoHo. As soon as the cops arrived at his table he greeted them with crossed wrists.

"Arrest me . . . arrest me . . . go ahead . . . arrest me."

The cops smiled at each other sheepishly.

"I come home after serving overseas and now I can't even earn a living to feed my family?"

The nearest he'd been to overseas was the Staten Island Ferry and I knew for a fact he didn't have a family. But it was important to be seen to resist *the man*. Your status was proportional to your defiance. I could try to explain my good luck to each vendor within ten blocks but even at that they'd still see what they wanted to see. A white privileged little bitch. What I didn't know was that they were happy having a white guy among them since it meant they were all less likely to be harassed. In the end they did cuff him and he spent the night in a holding cell. I know this because it was all on YouTube. He doubled his amount of followers and even more customers turned up at his table.

Meanwhile I couldn't even get arrested.

Drinnggggg

I waited until Audrey had taken at least one sip from her tea before joining her on the couch. Since our phone conversations had already progressed beyond the need for small talk we melted into an embrace that was surprisingly affectionate. She felt comfortable and deeply erotic at the same time. Those cushioned lips pressed against mine.

This was a new combination for me.

I was benefiting from skills she'd developed in the arms of her husband where intimacy, affection, and sexual generosity merged. I felt guilty knowing as much as I did about her past and I imagined she was only able to hold me so affectionately precisely because she thought I knew nothing. I was reminded of Marian's initially innocent affection for me before she found out what I was capable of. Meanwhile, cushioned kisses impacted my undeserving face.

We were both liars now.

We practically levitated off the couch and floated to the bedroom.

It was obvious a large transaction had taken place in the vicinity of her groin. It was strange knowing she'd had a baby die inside the vagina I was now stroking through her soaking wet panties. And I couldn't help but notice, while waiting for her to turn up, that the phrase "fatal car accident" described the fate of someone with the same name as her husband. The car had driven off a bridge. My fertile mind began to wonder if he had taken his own life. A stillbirth is a hard knock to recover from. Her oral talents suddenly evoked the determination of a dutiful wife's attempts to reinflate a marriage. Most girls didn't need to get that good at giving head because they were just providing one half of an equation, the other half being that the man would go down on them with equal fervor.

But this felt different.

This was a woman doing what she believed her man wanted *before* he asked for it. It felt important. If he had to ask for it then it was valueless. She should *want* to suck his cock and so this is what she wanted to want to do. But even as those Scarlett Johansson lips slipped up and down my shaft and her thick tongue, so tentative when we first kissed, now strafed the tip, I found myself unable to come. I took my cock from her and wanked it almost to the point of no return and then fed it back into a mouth so hungry it was already sucking and swallowing before it was even entered. When she did finally coax it all out of me I almost cried. My entire body weight seemed to shove itself through the eye of my cock as I leapt out of myself into a thick warm pond of darkness and didn't wake until I heard the girl's soothing voice whisper in my ear.

"I came four times last night."

This was so much better than *good morning*.

It removed any need to perform.

Was this a Jewish thing? The matriarchal softness, the maternal bosom, the ease with which she was prepared to let the man take charge. Or at least seem to. The unconditional silences preceding your every utterance. The unwavering support, the preagreement.

It was deeply seductive.

Gale force winds shook the trees outside and branches bashed against the window. I wasn't missing anything on Prince Street. Of all the weather conditions to contend with wind was the worst. Books flapped and signs collapsed. As I woke I felt her body shivering against me with lust. It may well have been what woke me. And at first I was flattered, thinking she was waiting politely for me to wake up so we could resume but when I asked her about it she said that this was how she was every morning. That sexual desire was a constant state for her.

She brought an extra pair of panties to work every day because she soaked the first one through. She was always, as she put it, "in heat." Over the years she'd learned to suppress the yearnings only because giving in to them would require more sex than was physically available. But didn't this mean she couldn't be satisfied? Having felt like a stud only moments before I now felt inadequate. The fact that she'd come four times meant nothing.

Snowflakes to a furnace.

She'd married in her early twenties and before that she'd only had a few partners. Early into the marriage there was unspeakable tragedy. Twelve years later I was the nearest she could get to fucking her dead husband. Maybe it was okay to unleash her limitless libido at me because I was somehow channeling him? Was it *his* cock she was sucking so ardently? Or was she so insatiable no amount of cock could ever satisfy the sexual famine inside her? I was happy I hadn't had to hear about it all, but it was still weird she'd kept it from me. It wasn't as if she hadn't had ample opportunity. For instance when I mentioned I'd never lived with anyone she reacted as if I had stumbled on a cute coincidence.

"Really? Neither have I."

It ceased to matter because due to an unforeseen mishap I never saw her again. She was taking so long to arrive I began flirting with a twenty-year-old mother just to kill time. It was quite a luxury playing with this young thing imprisoned as she was in her apartment while I waited for my sexual virtuoso to arrive preceded by those nipples and lips. She texted to say she'd bought pillows because she had decided mine were some-what questionable. I normally preferred a girl to be fucked and disposed of within a few hours but Audrey was timing her arrival so late that an invitation to stay the night was guaranteed. In fact this was probably the real reason she was taking so long. And now she was buying me pillows?

Even so I couldn't wait to get my cock back inside that mouth. I had felt unplugged all week. When she sucked and rolled her tongue at the same time she somehow managed to evoke abstract images in my mind as if she had administered hallucinogens. She likened it to playing in a jazz band saying she "listened" for what worked. At one point with my cock already deep in her throat she began to hum on it so that resulting vibrations rippled up and down my very being, causing me to moan so deeply we performed a tuneless duet of sexual song. She loved my apartment and joked that she'd soon have me out of it and herself installed. This couldn't have been less funny and I tried not to let the fear affect the cock momentarily out of her mouth. I had noticed that she liked to juxtapose deeply practical if not unpalatable utterances like this with the soul-soaring joy of a sucked cock. How devious. But if you can summon joy then you can also deny it. None of it mattered in the end because of a misfired text intended for the single mom in Flushing.

So what do you paint? Landscapes? Portraits? Nudes hopefully?

And that was that. No more cock-baths. I didn't even get the new pillows.

I hope you'll be happy with your painter.

It was probably just as well since there was nothing tangible there to begin with.

Her husband's ghost fucking Marian's memory.

. . . .

Hats-And-Socks-Tom told me he'd once rolled away from the kicking feet of an assailant not just to avoid injury but so the event could be captured by security cameras a few feet away. His agile mind was already thinking ahead to the court case even as the skull that contained it was being kicked.

I never actually saw him handle any contraband but he was almost always high. He claimed he was on a combination of prescribed medications because of a back injury he'd sustained "over there" and that his doctors were perpetually adjusting the doses trying to get the balance right. Meanwhile he wasn't complaining. He referred to himself without irony as an amateur anesthesiologist. So much so he was able to advise each new doctor assigned to his case which drugs and what dosages he responded best to. A table full of socks had to be a front for the drugs he must surely be selling. Occasionally he'd turn up with strangers. For $100 a day you could rent a veteran to sit with you and render your operation legal. He could ask for a percentage of sales if he thought you had a good product but this was rare. He usually took the $100 up front. But spending a day with someone suffering from PTSD exasperated by fluctuating doses of medication could be fraught with politics.

Hats-And-Socks-Tom got very pissed at two ultra-cool-looking black dudes who hired him to lend legitimacy to their fashionable T-shirts. They were far too cocky for his liking. He turned to me to celebrate the fact that they hadn't sold even one in over three hours and then to my absolute delight he jabbed his thumb upward and said, "And I'm not at all happy with the use of negative space in their logo."

One particularly slow Sunday when only three people walked past, loathed and laughed at him, Hats-And-Socks-Tom decided to share how he'd received the injury for which he now received a lifelong military pension. He'd been defending his position when his team came under attack. The opposition were well organized and relentless and though he fought hard to defend his position he just couldn't hold them off. Before he knew what happened he went down.

I was reverent.

It seemed so generous of him to use the term "went down" as if he knew to spare me the horror of the event. Or maybe he had learned over the years to streamline the telling of the story so that it could be related without upsetting himself or the listener. I secretly idolized him. Here was a real veteran. This guy had actually been in combat.

"I could show you the medal." He squinted into the middle distance, presumably at the memories he saw there.

"My back has never been the same."

I didn't agree with the politics behind his being over there but it was hard not to respect someone who had seen action.

"I hardly ever play now," he added.

He'd been injured in an soccer game and was sent home with the rest of the wounded.

"So you know the author?"

A tall dark-haired girl presented me with dog-eared copies of both my books.

"You could say that," I said, smiling way too widely.

She studied my face.

"No way," she said at last.

She handed me the books.

"Okay, now you have to sign them . . . Catherine."

In the first one I wrote, *"Hi Catherine, It's so nice to meet you—The Oxygen Thief."* And in the second: *"We should have coffee some time—The Oxygen Thief."* After reading each inscription and replacing the books in her bag she straightened herself and responded quite formally.

"I would love that."

It turned out she was the personal assistant to Pulitzer Prize–winning author Terrence Holt. She said she wanted to show him my books. Then she said she was in AA. This gave me pause because I had never been with a girl from the rooms. Far from being noble it was a self-preserving tactic. I'd seen many of my peers fall on that sword. All I had to do was imagine myself with a vagina and it was easy to avoid. But this girl was not only gorgeous, she was a possible stepping stone to New York's literary elite. Maybe she was a gift from my higher power. She could be my big break into mainstream literary success and as such, a road back to Marian. And if I got to fuck her all the better. She was telling me that her sister had recently married a Canadian and moved to Toronto where that weekend she was due to visit to "meet" her newly born niece . . . "You should show your books to Mr. Holt."

I looked at her, incredulous.

Had I somehow audibly inserted those words into her mouth? Was she in fact still talking about Toronto and babies and I, out of boredom, had re-synched her mouth with words of my own choosing? Or had she recognized the same glaze in my eyes that had so often infuriated Marian and changed tack to see if I was listening. Listening? I was riveted. Of course I should show my books to Terrence Holt. But how the fuck was I going to do that?

"Easy," she said. "I'll bring them to work with me."

When we met in Cafe Fiat the following Monday she was coming straight from work.

Assisting Mr. Holt meant she regularly attended all manner of celebrity-infested gatherings. She dropped so many names with such nonchalance I had no choice but to pretend I was unimpressed. Harley James, Francis Swynn, Emerson Gray, Kevin Donaldson. We had what felt like an amazing chat. Mostly because every word she uttered now needed to be doted on in case there was another mention of my books. She was studying psychology and was able to ask all manner of searching questions relating to the AA program and recovery and whether this affected the voice in my books. She grew up in Switzerland in the nineties. Her father was an economist from Ohio attached to the American embassy. Her mother was a translator from Portland sent to Geneva to improve her French and German.

"My parents didn't really get along."

"It doesn't show," I gushed.

She was the product of a beautiful liberal mother and a

right-wing father. The most thrilling part of her biography, apart from the literary name-dropping, was the plight of her restless breasts as they fought heroically against the confines of her constricting blouse. A clause written into her father's will insisted that she and her mother drink a glass of bourbon to see him off. She joked that it was just as well she wasn't sober at the time or she would have been disinherited.

Oh how I laughed.

He became an international tax consultant. A booming business in Switzerland. They moved to the U.S. when she was fifteen. She was sent to a succession of boarding schools as her father moved from city to city. She didn't have sex until she was twenty-five but until then she loved to dance. She charmed her way into clubs and bars where she reveled in being the eccentric-looking, long-haired girl who danced alone with her eyed closed. She never had to buy a drink. She was a regular at the Williamsburg AA meetings that I barred my sponsees from attending. Too many hot chicks and not enough sobriety. She said she liked older men because she had daddy issues. I nodded carefully. She'd had a boyfriend until two months earlier who used to "stuff her turkey"—the term seemed so self-flagellatory it slashed the portrait she'd painted of herself.

She quickly changed the subject.

Was I familiar with a recent article titled "Has Modern Marketing Invaded Our Morals"? Apparently it listed countless ways we could now legally sell ourselves. For instance tattooing a company's logo on your forehead would earn you

$10,000. Fighting in Somalia (no experience required) paid a thousand a day.

"It would be unfortunate," I said, "if after having Target's logo tattooed on your forehead you signed up to fight in Somalia." Oh how she laughed.

• • • •

Diary of an Oxygen Thief—The Walking Tour

You'd take in some of the more notable locations featured in the book. Sit in the same seat where Anonymous squirmed as he was photographed by the dastardly Aisling. Exchange your printout for a pint of Coca-Cola just like his. Visit Cafe Drill, the Cat and Mouse bar, the Chess Cafe. Your charismatic tour guide, billed as possibly being Anonymous himself but probably not, but maybe, would intercept the Sex and the City Walking Tour and with the help of a few prebriefed provocateurs, an Instagrammable skirmish would break out. For those less willing to participate in the communal tour, a map app with an accompanying podcast featuring the voice of Anonymous would narrate your tour.

I could dream, couldn't I?

I watched the asshole across the street make so much money I wanted to cry. In fact one day, when I was feeling particularly vulnerable, I did cry. It was the day the girl in culottes shouted back at him, "Yes, but that isn't art."

He had obviously referred to himself as something other

than a vandal since she looked far too cultured to volunteer an opinion without provocation.

His amateurish silhouettes of hip-hop characters Sharpied onto splayed-out New York City subway maps sold consistently well from the moment he arrived until he reluctantly began to pack up. Theatrically bending and stretching over his trestle table he produced his *art* while tourists and even some locals shuffled reverently past. Here was a real New York street artist in his natural habitat. You might be looking at the next Keith Haring or Basquiat. In summer he stripped to his emaciated waist, revealing badly rendered tattoos that only served to authenticate his claim on street cred. Twenty dollars bought you Essence of New York Street Artist available in travel-friendly cardboard tubes.

Families took selfies with him as Dad's first and last fist-bump was immortalized. Girls secreted for him and young men all but genuflected. Jabbing the air with splayed fingers he punctuated his pitch. Meanwhile something so serpentine lurked inside his visible-above-the-jeans boxer shorts it required constant and delicate adjustment. The result was that he simply could not keep up with demand. Or at least not on his own. He oversaw an empire of three, sometimes four tables placed end-to-end by his casually employed acquaintances.

The law allowed one six-foot-long table per vendor but there was nothing to say you couldn't display the same art on multiple tables as long as each was manned by a different person. And since his franchise occupied so much more surface area than the rest of us, his commercial presence was more forcibly felt.

His response to the girl in culottes was to wave a fat sheaf of cash high in the air after her. There had to be at least $2,000 in twenties. He was too clever to shout anything at her, that would end in handcuffs. He knew that and so, on some level, did she. He just wanted her to understand that he was making thousands out there.

That was when I dry-cried.

• • • •

You're good company but I have no other motives. It was a clarifying text from Catherine in case I thought there was any chance of fucking her. *But I'd love to pick your brains about publishing and writing.*

She was being responsible. Making her position clear. Probably following the suggestion of her sponsor. A disclaimer removing my right to object when she refused me sex.

But try explaining all that to a half-hard cock.

I would soon find out that what she was really looking for was far from literary.

She was interested in her ex turkey-stuffer. In getting back at him and or getting him back or maybe both. Having recognized some of his behavior in my book she felt sure I'd be able to help her navigate him. Okay, so there was no chance of fucking her but she could still give me access to her Pulitzer Prize–winning employer. A quote from him would be better than sex with her. She said she'd be my pretend therapist. As if it was so obvious I needed one. What a cunt. And yet as I thought about it, maybe it wasn't such a bad idea. With the possibility of sex out of the way I could at least be more honest with her than I had been with Courtney. And it occurred to me that from the protected sanctity of a therapist/patient arrangement I could freely insult her by inferring that I didn't find her attractive and that I had only feigned a desire to fuck her because of her literary connection. A lot of effort just to get a few jabs in. Much more efficient to just walk away. But that's not what happened.

I had been asked to speak at the Rehab Center in Williamsburg and I decided to let her know since she mentioned she was a regular at the meetings there. My intention was to lay the groundwork for a weekly therapy session, maybe in her place, which would at least provide me with continued access to her. If I couldn't fuck her maybe I could fuck *with* her and in the meantime get my books seen by her boss.

I was surprised to receive such an enthusiastic reply.

"Yes I'd love to, let's grab a coffee before the meeting so we can go there together."

I wasn't going to turn down the chance to be seen around Williamsburg with such a strikingly beautiful girl and even better to be seen at an AA meeting with her. It would send out a strong message to the newcomer: sober guys get hot chicks.

When she texted to say she was having "wardrobe problems" my ego jumped to the conclusion that she was dressing to impress me but later I would realize she was agonizing over precisely what to wear to evoke the maximum amount of regret in her ex who was also a regular at that same meeting. She even arranged to meet me in a coffee shop whose interior was plainly visible from the sidewalk just around the corner from the meeting. This would provide the guy with a *tableau vivant* of the two of us together seemingly engrossed in a tête-à-tête. And even though I'd been told she wasn't interested in me sexually there was sunshine in my chest when I looked at her. So when she arrived at the café it was impossible not to make much about her oh-so-cool spent-bullet pendant or the turn-of-the-century graphics tattooed on her newly exposed forearms.

She wore a pale blue expensive-looking short-sleeved sweater and faded and torn ultraskintight jeans. No coat on a night that was reputed to be one of the coldest on record. I felt it would be rude not to compliment her on how cool she looked because after all she might have put this outfit together for me. She looked like a rock star who had somehow been separated from her entourage. The impression you got was that you had about five minutes to impress her before they burst in the door and reclaimed her.

She had obviously overcome the wardrobe problem.

On our way to the meeting she saw someone approach in the distance.

"We should make out under that streetlight so he'll be jealous."

As soon as she said this I began to see what was happening. And all the more insulting now because she didn't even care how I took it. I was as functional to her as a shovel. *Let's make out so he'll be jealous* was already manipulative enough but *under the streetlight* inferred a clinical Germanic efficiency. It was as if we'd already discussed the plan at length and I was fine with it.

I suppose she thought I'd be up for this sort of manipulation because of the books I'd written but she can't have known how shocked I was by the suggestion coming as it was from an AA member with three sponsees and a respectable sponsor.

But mostly I was pissed about being used as a decoy to get the guy she really wanted. Not the best situation to unfold around you before speaking at an AA meeting.

Once inside, she sat in the front row, looking straight at me, which I found unnerving.

I felt kind of dirty about the whole thing because she was using my talk at an AA meeting to make her ex jealous.

So there I was, sitting at the lead table watching people take their seats when she leaned forward and handed me her phone. I was painfully aware of her ex's eyes on me as he selected a chair and sat down. He couldn't really look anywhere else but at me since I was the speaker. She smiled widely and nodded at her phone indicating that something on it needed to be acknowledged.

(It looked like an unsent text.) *Lots of people here tonight.* She looked so happy. She really was very beautiful.

It didn't make sense. Was she being supportive? Maybe she was just happy to be at a meeting. I was too distracted with what I was going to say to realize that the phone had been a genius move because it inferred to an onlooker that we were

94

undeniably close. That she was comfortable enough to show me the contents of her phone. If not the contents of her panties. Maybe he had even sent her a text and now it would appear as if she and I were laughing at it.

At him in fact.

I nodded. Yes, there were a lot of people here. She laughed far too knowingly and shoved the phone into her tight jean pocket as the chairperson announced me.

"Tonight to share his experience, strength, and hope with us is . . ."

Her ex would probably already assume we had shagged and if he didn't he would after she put up her hand and shared during the actual meeting itself.

"Great to hear your message and it's been really wonderful getting to know you . . ."

Her breasts were aimed not at me but at the long-haired guy to her left and my right. She held her shoulders back and blushed and played with her hair. I blushed involuntarily. One of my sponsees had come in late and I saw her nod hello to him too. Christ almighty this had the potential for disaster. It was the first time my solid center of AA had become vulnerable to attack from my own actions.

It was just too close to home.

Her ex also shared and to my chagrin he sounded like a pretty decent guy. She had to be very much in love with him. He was lucky. Tall of course and humble looking. Not handsome in any conventional way, more like a hangdog type. Having initially agreed to a casual relationship he ended it when she began to want more. I was disgusted. I had just been used by a girl in AA. This was the first time it had happened to me (that I knew of) and if I was honest, the reason it had happened was due to my own ego and lust. I shouldn't have told her I was speaking there in the first place. But I couldn't help but admire the skill with which she had performed her part. I wondered how many times I'd fallen for classic traps like this. I was reminded of all the times Marian had "bumped" into me as we walked so that I might get a head full of her scent and be back under her spell. And of how willing I was to be subsumed.

After the meeting as I was being congratulated for my talk, I caught a glimpse, between the handshakes and shoulders, of her elegant frame leaving with the hangdog guy.

MAN'S GREATEST OBSTACLE TO SEX—WOMAN
#TheOxygenThiefDiaries

I'm in a PMS-related abyss of loneliness.

I was insulted. Why tell me how lonely she was but exclude the possibility of my absence being the cause of it? Because she only wanted me as a friend, that's why. A confidant. So be it.

Marian was confiding in me. Showing me her vulnerability. I should be flattered. She needed a friend and she had chosen me. I had managed to raise her spirits in the past and I could do it again. At least I'd be of service. Of some use. I vowed as I pressed *call* that whatever happened I would avoid being needy, cloying, or self-pitying.

Five long, sneering ringtones later she answered.

"Hah . . . so you were debating whether to answer," I said, and it went to shit from there.

"Well, Deidre doesn't think you're a good influence."

Her roommate had become my competition. Had I been blind to this all along and not seen that she and Marian were basically a couple living together? She freely admitted to having been a lesbian when she was younger but that just seemed to me to be something girls from Williamsburg said to appear cool. And yet her overgrown bush had been quite a shock. No straight girl would ever let that happen. Plus she drew attention to that girl's ass on the beach.

Like I was her wingman.

I knew I should walk away. There was no winning this. But I couldn't. I was actually enjoying the sensation of spiraling. It was in itself a mild form of high. And she was too much a part of me to just eject. I wasn't even looking for sex anymore. Sex would have seemed too much at this point. Confusing of course because that body and those tits contradicted all of the above. I was not myself and I was about to prove it.

"I don't just miss *you*," I said, "I miss *us*."

Silence.

It was the sound of secondary embarrassment.

Instead of getting over her I was merely finding new ways to self-immolate. She knew better than to laugh but it must have been satisfying to witness my decline. She knew that a line like that coming from me was a betrayal of everything I claimed to stand for. A tactic perhaps, but a desperate one. If I was feigning defeat then she wasn't falling for it.

This was how the English lost the Battle of Hastings to the French. The English defense was strong and would have held had they stood their ground and maintained their shield-wall. The attacking French had to find a way to break through or they'd be starved into submission on foreign soil. They had developed a strategy that succeeded best against enemies lacking discipline. The idea was to attack with as much force as possible once, twice, maybe even three times and then basically behave like they had collectively lost their nerve and decided to run away. The commanding officers feigned panic and shouted orders to retreat while the foot soldiers threw away their swords and ran for their lives. The English, confident of their reading of the situation, gave chase.

But pursuing the French meant breaking their ranks and this was what the French needed to penetrate and massacre the entire English army. Those who "ran away" were rearmed at the bottom of the hill to wait for the English to run into their swords. Meanwhile a murder squad was assigned by the Duke of Normandy to find King Harold and basically fillet him so that there could be no question of competition for the throne. The Bayeux Tapestry has him receiving a neat elegant arrow into the eye but it was much more Tarantino than that.

All's fair in love and war.

Anyway I wasn't faking it, I actually meant it. When we

first met I could clearly remember thinking she'd never let me fuck her. I was sure she'd just string me along until she built up enough contacts in the city to ease me out of her life. I was just someone to hang out with while she looked for someone more worthy.

Now that we were broken up the same fear repositioned itself. She would dangle the distant possibility of sex in front of me while she looked for someone new. The difference being that this time I'd be denied sex I'd already sampled as opposed to some abstract future possibility.

At one point, back when we were together, she was deeply in love with me. I remembered feeling the tickle of girlish kisses on my shoulder as we walked. Somehow I could feel the love even through the fabric of my jacket. Kisses that, even as I received them, I knew I didn't deserve. And now there was something sweetly twisted about the idea that she should watch me suffer the spasms of pain I inflicted on myself by pushing her away.

More crying followed.

Primal guttural keening. Unbelievable sounds emanating from unknown nooks. Like cockroaches scurrying from broken furniture. An AA meeting cooled the smoldering embers in my chest but an hour later it began all over again. That carsick feeling. I decided that all it wanted to do was pass through me and I was blocking it.

I sat still and tried to let it do exactly that. But I was too terrified to let go in case I'd lose all trace of her. Surely the cavernous depths of my pain was just the inverse measure of how dizzyingly high we had soared. And with her gone I had total control over my memories of her. I rewound them, edited them, played them with the sound down, watched only the dirty bits.

I repeated a mantra I'd learned in the meetings. "Let go or be dragged . . . let go or be dragged." And slowly I felt something begin to budge. It was like exhaling an enormous rain cloud. The memories, the treasured keepsakes began to crumble and dislodge. How pitiless that I should be expected to let go of these valuables. They were of no use to anyone else. But maybe that was the point: God is the ultimate jealous lover.

● ● ● ●

"Dude, did you write this?"

"Oh hi . . . so yes, thanks for stopping . . . I—"

"I loved this."

"Oh, you read it?"

"Yeah, I got it at St. Bernard's Bookshop."

"Oh yeah?"

"Yeah!! But wait . . . you wrote it?"

"Yes."

"I loved it. I thought it was really good."

"Thanks."

"You know I write too?"

"Oh yeah?"

Here we go, now I'd have to listen to him pitch his book to me.

"Yes I'm . . . Junot . . ."

"You're . . . 'you-know'?"

"No Junot."

"I know, you just said that."

"Haha, no seriously dude I loved this, and you can say that. I mean you can say I said that."

"Thanks man," I said, unimpressed.

As far as I was concerned he'd already given my money to St. Bernard's Books and they never paid me. The only reason I supplied them with books at all was because it was a good endorsement to be seen on their shelves. "Saint Bernard" himself had actually stopped and attacked me one day for selling a book that was being featured in his window. He assumed I'd stolen my copies and was brazenly selling them a block away from his shop.

Apparently it was something junkies did all the time.

Bellowing at me in front of everyone he became even more agitated when he found out I was selling *signed* copies. How could I sell signed copies? Of an anonymously written book?

"On whose authority?" he roared.

"On my authority," I said.

This was too much for him. He actually made a motion to upturn my table but seemed to think better of it when a passerby stopped to take a photo. This seemed to bring him back to his senses. When I contacted his assistant to see if they needed more books she told me he had stormed back into the store after his lunch break that same day and personally removed all my books from the window and shelves. She also told me it was Junot Díaz who had stopped at my table and I should be very proud that a Pulitzer Prize–winning author had praised my book. She even remembered him buying it. I had never heard "Junot" pronounced out loud before and even if I had I would have thought he was joking.

Meanwhile I watched the Latino "artist" roll up another one of his subway maps and hand it to a delighted customer. He had this habit of pretend-drumming after he made a sale. A sort of shave-and-a-haircut rhythm that culminated with him mimicking a cymbal crash. I trained myself not to look in his direction but it was useless because someone would saunter past with his cardboard tube protruding from a tote bag and it'd sting all the more for being unexpected.

At one point I risked a sidelong glance only to be greeted with an empty patch of sidewalk. He'd had such a good day he had knocked off early. Usually he waved good-bye to everyone but I was so intent on not looking his way he had slipped away unnoticed.

People constantly asked if I had T-shirts. I could have sold hundreds of them with my various headlines on them but I wasn't out there to sell T-shirts, I was out there to sell books and to slow-drip their titles into mainstream culture. And to get Marian back. Yes that was it. Selling the book would get Marian back. And her ass. Wouldn't it? The money, the real money would come later. But in the meantime there was no harm in charging a little more. It was a question of self-esteem. In fact I quickly began to see that you weren't taken seriously if you asked for too little. If they balked at the price it was easy to come down and make them feel like they were being cheap.

"That's a lot for a paperback," one guy said.

But when I offered him a reduction he shook his head.

"No, I want to support you."

He was making it clear he didn't care about my bullshit book, he was just giving me a handout. A donation. I was merely a charity he could bear to give to. My role was to advertise his wealth while he demonstrated he could afford to throw away $20 on a book he had no interest in. He purchased self-respect at the expense of mine. The book was just the receipt.

But he would spend the rest of his afternoon in his fashionable clothes strolling around the Lower East Side and Nolita visually condoning my nonsense. He had just paid me $20 for the privilege of wearing a micro-sandwich-board.

"Thank you, sir, I appreciate it, I can use all the support I can get."

I was his bitch but he was my ambassador.

WEARING ENOUGH IRONY TO ALERT AIRPORT SECURITY
#TheOxygenThiefDiaries

While traffic wardens competed for cars and the homeless fought over trash cans, photographers pounced on the fashionably dressed. The success of apps like streetwawker and strut_street meant that any magazine worthy of mention now had to have its own street-style section. Long lenses protruding from midriffs made it difficult for street photographers to mingle with pedestrians. Striking-looking girls dressed in faultless outfits would stroll past two or three times hoping to be noticed.

I had begun to photograph my customers posing with their new purchase. As far as I was concerned they were photobombing pictures of my books but it was a good way to get the cover art into circulation. I started out by photographing only those who bought the book but when it became clear that the more attractive people got more likes I began asking strangers.

Beautiful female strangers.

It was surprising how malleable they were. I only asked the prettiest, most stylish girls because I realized I could harness their hope that a real photographer might notice if someone else was already shooting them. I was encouraged by the sight of dowdy, sometimes middle-aged photographers approaching granite-faced beauties who immediately cracked up laughing at the enormity of the compliment.

They fucking loved it.

Ordinarily these girls had to be subtle about how beautiful they were. Play it down. Pretend they didn't actually get a better deal than the rest of us. Unleashing the full force of your good fortune only invited retaliation. It was the equivalent of having a rent-controlled two-bedroom apartment in the East Village: you had to tell people it had cockroaches and loud neighbors.

But for a photo the gloves came off.

Now they could pout shamelessly at the camera and the attention it promised.

Pulling their hair forward or pushing it back, teasing it up or letting it down, it was obvious each girl knew exactly what her best look was. The shape of the face changed, the mouth grew smaller, the breasts stuck out, the eyes grew wide. One girl licked her lips to make her mouth into an obscenely wet O. Another shook her hair so that it fell over her apparently just-fucked face. Another laughed spontaneously again and again and again until eventually she nodded grimly at what she considered acceptable.

The more beautiful they were the more they insisted on seeing the photo. They deleted what didn't work for them. One girl simply handed me her phone so that there was no chance of an image existing that wasn't under her control. Once they were happy, they wanted it sent to them immediately, which meant I was given their details. It also meant there was a pretty good chance they'd post the image on their Instagram. I didn't write captions saying these beautiful girls bought my book but anyone looking at the images would be forgiven for thinking they had. I began to notice a phenomenon in passersby. Already three yards past my table their feet received the order to stop. The cover was starting to be recognized.

"There was an interview about this on NPR."

I knew for a fact it had never been on NPR but who was I, a mere street vendor, to argue with a well-dressed, gainfully employed resident of Nolita? One guy insisted he'd met the author. He confided that the misogynistic author was in fact a woman, a lesbian no less. Suffice it to say the cover was recognized, the writer was not. One girl, having stopped abruptly, composed herself and approached me reverently.

"My friend bought this book."

"Oh really?"

"Yeah, he bought it because he wanted to meet the French girl you created."

I was careful not to nod.

She held me in her gaze, enjoying my discomfort.

"It's okay," she said at last, "he's cool with it and so am I. In fact I think what you did was bloody brilliant." When Americans used Britishisms you knew you were safe. She wasn't trying to investigate me, she was merely trying to introduce herself. It turned out her fiancé was an actor and her childhood friend was a well-known theater producer and she felt sure a stage adaptation of the book would be a smash hit on Broadway.

"Confessions are all the rage right now, Mike Tyson just raped Broadway."

She watched me again, savoring the controversy in her delivery. I felt better about what I was hearing but I was still unwilling to confirm or deny.

"I'm having a little get-together next week and you're invited."

She proffered her card. *Mackenzie Tote, Dramaturg.*

"See you around eightish."

Dramaturg sounded to me like one of those American mashup words, like *staycation* or *humblebrag*. I looked it up; a *dramaturg* was someone who generally assisted in the writing and producing of a theatrical production. It was the kind of vague, ill-defined title that was perfect for the daughter of rich thespian parents, which is what I imagined her to be. Correctly as it turned out. My definition? *A gossipy little cunt who routinely got credits as cowriter and producer on quality plays just for being the type of chick who is willing to fuck the contents of her parents' Rolodex.*

But I imagined Marian and me at the premiere, ducking camera flashes, deflecting compliments. Of course I would attend.

Marian . . . I think it's great that we were able to re-find our affection for each other even after all the weird confusion/pain/anger that led to our breakup last May . . . but it's also been a source of confusion because I must confess I've been nurturing hopes of us getting back together . . . the question now seems to be, can I continue to enjoy our time together in the knowledge that we will never be intimate again? . . . this is where I am right now . . .

XOXO

• • • •

Mackenzie's mother owned an apartment on West Seventy-Fifth Street. It was one of those places you only ever saw in Woody Allen films, where the elevator opens directly onto wooden-walled interiors. Before the doors had fully opened, her boyfriend, Carlton, greeted me like an old friend. In this sense he wasn't a bad actor at all. Or perhaps since I wanted it all to go well, I was a gentle audience. He was all grace and charm as he regarded me with clear blue eyes and I remember thinking I'd be happy to have him play me. After all, this was why I'd been invited. To ascertain whether they were worthy of collaborating on a stage adaptation of my book. And as they began to talk about it I got the distinct impression that he and Mackenzie were of the opinion that I should play myself.

He would direct and she would produce.

Rich, rich, rich.

Bookshelves rising from parquet floors to corniced ceilings held so many books it was intimidating. I ran unworthy hands over expensive-looking volumes of Kafka and Steinbeck, first editions of *Heart of Darkness* and *Tender Is the Night.* This was obviously a literary family.

Or at least one that wanted to be perceived as such.

I felt flattered she thought me worthy of being introduced to these rare editions but tricked too because being a writer, I had no choice but to show interest in them. If I didn't, then surely I was a sham. And there was an unspoken hope that I'd somehow bestow a blessing on her gathering. Plucked as I was from the gritty realism of the street, I represented purity.

"I know how to make poor-people food," she said, holding a tray of sausage-rolls wrapped in bacon. Why was I being welcomed into this enclave? Meanwhile she was already teetering from the impact of what I supposed were too many cocktails.

"Spoken word is all the rage now," she informed the room.

Confessional one-man shows were playing to packed theaters and they wanted to approach the same producers who had turned Mike Tyson into a Broadway sensation. Mackenzie, who had gone to school with one of them, showed me his number on her phone.

I was being sold to.

Anonymous starring in his own story written by Anonymous and delivered on stage by a nameless man who was supposedly the guy who had written the book.

"Hi, I'm the actor who'll be playing Anonymous tonight."

It had never been done before. Or were they just playing with me? It did sound like they were talking about it in the right way. But then a nineteen-year-old girl in a combat jacket and jeans stepped out of the elevator and stood nervously in front of us like a mouse among anacondas.

"Oh look everyone, it's Celeste."

Did she get off on the wrong floor? Her tits were huge for her age and her skin was pale as milk. I could see her eyes dilate and her paper-white cheeks stain with color as those impossible breasts heaved inside her tight open-buttoned army shirt. I wanted to push her up against the Viennese yellow walls and pump my seed into her so that we might beget a child.

"Celeste . . . this is Anonymous."

And then to me.

"She's been dying to meet you, she loves your book, read it three times, isn't that right Celeste?"

Celeste nodded once and blushed.

What was happening inside me at this point was beyond lust, it was menopausal.

The fact that she was so young and therefore fertile seemed to summon my seed from its dustier nooks. Her flushed, interested face forgave sins I hadn't even committed yet. No longer the miserable, cynical little shit I supposed myself to be, through her eyes I saw an interesting, nuanced bon vivant, a human culmination of experiences gleaned from a world she had yet to visit. It was obvious she was up for adventure. And that sex with an anonymous writer could be something she'd need to strike off her list, somewhere between bungee jumping and her first tattoo. Oh to fill that slot. Mackenzie toppled back into the room as if someone had pushed her from the kitchen and teetered backward for a second before somehow popping up out of the floor beside me.

"Carlton has the hots for her," she whispered, "just go along with it."

She'd met "the poor thing" at one of his performances. Seated together in the audience they'd begun to chat. Mackenzie sounded like a drunken Marilyn Monroe for a second until I realized she was imitating Celeste.

"Ah've been foraging in Central Pawrk all day." And then in her normal voice: "She took out all these leaves and pine

cones from her adorable little backpack. I'm giving her to Carlton as a wedding present."

She and Carlton were engaged but she was unperturbed by his lust? While I secretly reveled in all this delicious decadence the elevator doors let a bearded heavyset man with chiseled features into the room and the conversation. This, it turned out, was Everett, the guy who'd fallen for my online impersonation of Françoise. He and Mackenzie had dated some time previously and he was now being introduced to me as someone I'd already met.

"And this, as you know, is Françoise," said Mackenzie, nodding delightedly at me.

She was in her element. Carlton smiled knowingly.

"You got me fair and square sir," said Everett, offering me his hand to shake.

I managed to get past a moment of high-octane paranoia fueled by the notion that they had concocted this entire evening to avenge Everett's bruised dignity. But no. He was already half-drunk or stoned before he even turned up. This was what convinced me they were for real. These people got drunk before meeting for a drink. Meanwhile a seriously right-wing-looking fucker sitting in an antique armchair with a crystal whiskey glass began to look like he was moments away from becoming deeply unpleasant. He had the gait and bone structure of a well-bred WASP and when Everett and I were slagging off the CIA and the NSA he began to speak, to no one in particular.

"Yes, well, I have family in some of those institutions . . . I can't say which ones . . . but . . ."

I wanted to suggest that he couldn't say which ones, not because of national security but because he was too shit-faced to risk the pronunciation involved.

Instead I prepared to leave.

The lovely nineteen-year-old had already left and had been replaced by a drunken hag who was desperate to get fucked by anyone. As I heard her refer to God as The Universal Orgasm I politely made my apologies and smoothed over any possible crevices caused by my departure before being shown out of the building by a surprisingly intelligent-looking doorman in a silly green uniform. He had obviously been warned of my departure while I descended in the walnut-walled elevator because he referred to me without irony by name.

"Good night, Mr. Anonymous."

I decided I'd write a great play for these members of the American moneyarchy.

You can read it here—02thief.com.

• • • •

Marian pleaded with me to meet.

My email had freaked her out. I was elated that she couldn't bear the idea of not seeing me ever again. And yet she was offering nothing new. She went as far as to suggest that she had never given me the impression that we might get back together. The enormity of this statement seemed so untrue to me that I wanted to smack her. There was no way I would have continued seeing her for what turned out to be an entire year if I'd known we'd never get back together. But there is no logic when the emotions are involved. Love is not only blind, it's hard of hearing and has no short-term memory.

Of course I'd meet her.

My email had been an attempt to get some sort of declaration out of her and in a way it had worked; after all, she was now the one asking to meet me.

It was raining pretty hard and she texted that she'd ducked into a drugstore on Eighteenth Street and so maybe I could meet her there. When I saw her in the aisles looking like a tastefully dressed, very sad stranger, my heart leapt and then sank. Here was everything I'd ever wanted in a girl. She knew exactly what to wear and how to wear it. The artsy-looking bangs collaborating with the upturned collar of a raincoat framed her sad, pale, pretty, pouting face. The raincoat stopped just short of a pair of thigh-highs that continued dizzyingly downward into gun-gray Wellingtons. All of this arranged so that two rectangles of maddeningly smooth, milky-white thigh could commandeer what was left of my reason. Again she had stage-managed the meeting perfectly. I was so affected by the way she looked I couldn't speak until we sat at a little table in a shitty little pizza place where I bought a bottle of overpriced water just so we'd have a reason to sit there. I couldn't resist producing a sheet of paper that listed all the areas where I felt I had improved in the time we'd been hanging out together *as friends*.

I pay my way in restaurants
I don't use the word cunt
I don't interrupt you as much
I listen when you're speaking
I don't look bored because I'm not
I brush my teeth more
I text you back within ten minutes
I pay my share of the gas for our road trips

"Cute," she said. "That is so cute."

In response she took out a large hardbacked notebook and opened it in such a way as to prevent me from seeing into it.

"I have a list too," she said, unleashing the smile. With her thighs under the table she needed to hypnotize me by other means. I was overjoyed to hear this because it seemed to mean we were both, in our loveably geeky ways, doing our best to repair the relationship.

Half-standing, I peered over the top of her opened notebook almost perpendicular now to the table and I could just make out a pen being maneuvered across the pages as if she was adding a new entry. I caught a glimpse of parallel squiggled lines before sitting back down again. Was she hoping I'd mistake those scratchings for actual notes? Surely she wasn't that naive? I looked at her, incredulous. If this was the level of self-deception involved there was no hope for me, or more worryingly, us.

She was losing my attention.

Time for another smile.

I felt my pupils dilate. So much so I hardly noticed her slip the notepad back into her bag or that she was saying something.

"I thought about us . . . maybe, you know . . . just dating from time to time, and wondered how that would be."

Surely she was just trying to change the subject. The subject being: *Marian is a lying cunt.*

But on hearing this my cock took over.

"That . . . could work," he ventriloquized.

Dating from time to time would mean sex with Marian without the need to feign commitment. I'd be able to do whatever I liked and still get my hands on that ass. And those tits. It might have been her last-ditch effort to keep me around but I didn't care. I'd earned it.

She smiled, embarrassed by her own idea.

It was so unlike her to suggest something like this. Neither of us spoke. I was afraid to discuss the details of such an arrangement in case it disintegrated under the weight of realistic scrutiny. I called for the bill, happy to pay now that there was a possibility of casual sex. Ill-defined figures waiting for tables parted to let us out. We strolled with no destination in mind. There was the thing about Marian. Even when I hated her I wanted to fuck her.

I was imagining that body naked. Those tits. I enthusiastically led the way to the subway station in the hope that I might have an excuse to kiss her good night.

But when we got there she twisted sideways to prevent me from hugging anything of value. All I got was a cold, hard cheek. Dating from time to time? But from what time to what time? It was just more bullshit to keep me fluffed. It was more enjoyable for her to keep me on probation. One misstep from me and she had the right to throw up her hands and walk away forever. It was like being under one of her glass vitrines, airless and scrutinized. She had already decided we'd never have sex again but it would never be said out loud.

That would be too merciful.

"Let's think about it," she said, accepting a cheek-peck.

I thought about nothing else.

•　•　•　•

I further insulated myself against the long lonely nights by corresponding with CamGrrlJameson. She had contacted me through my website and after rummaging my snout in her digital feed I couldn't help but notice the marketing potential of having a cam girl read passages from my book to her thousands of regulars. I also couldn't help but notice her beautiful little ass and her perfect tits. She was much more homely than I would have expected from such a genre.

In fact she was very charming and verging on demure.

Jameson and her peers were doing the same thing in front of webcams that women generally did in our culture. Shaking their covered tits to excite male interest before exposing them for monetary gain. Once a rapport (and a price) was established you were invited to participate in the ultimate goal: *The*

Private Chat. This was where you were encouraged to pay extortionate per-minute rates to "hang out" one-on-one with an increasingly naked girl who masturbated with a dildo.

But leading up to the private session she needed to be polite and amenable even to those who weren't paying. Getting annoyed at the guy who kept asking to see your tits might put paying customers off. The more you seemed to love the idea of being on camera and fingering yourself in front of strangers, the more money you'd receive. Which would be fine if you made serious money but Jameson said she made between $50 and $200 a night. Yes, she was getting paid to masturbate, but even so. To me this meant she had to be getting something else out of it. All that attention was a form of low-level fame. She said she couldn't wait to get back to it after the Easter break. Her kids were getting in the way. Apparently her four-year-old boy had been "an asshole" since the day he was born.

You can't divorce a kid, she said.

I couldn't believe how good her body looked after three kids.

But she plummeted in my estimation when I heard how little she was willing to fuck herself for. It seemed to indicate that she had to be doing it for some sort of validation. But was it really that empowering to have fat old men in Florida wanking off to the sight of you naked? Most of her customers were in Florida. Statistically that was where most webcam users resided.

Her ex-husband tried to use the fact that she was a cam girl to show she was an unfit mother. She in turn used the fact that he had repeatedly punched her to show that he was an unfit father. There was video footage of him doing it. He countered by saying there was a BDSM element to their cam work and as part of their "performance" he regularly whipped, spanked, chokefucked, and yes, punched her. Her defense countered by saying there was a difference between rough play during sex and being punched in the face. It was also announced, in front of a full courtroom, that he had ejaculated on her face without consent.

This she believed was what won her the case.

A facial was no big deal as far as Jameson was concerned but the female judge seemed to think it was indicative of a wider lack of respect. In the eyes of the law, coming on her face *without* consent was worse than punching her in the face *with* consent. It was interesting that Jameson knew how to play this card. She gambled that spurting sperm on a mother's face would be deemed more villainous than throwing punches at it. Video footage of both types of assault were played for all to see. It must have been an interesting day in court.

She'd been on a few dates and when she told one guy she was a cam girl he freaked out. And she was on the verge of fucking another guy until he took his jacket off and revealed a Nazi tattoo on his forearm. She had been "ready to get some" until that moment.

"Plastic dicks will only get you so far," she said sadly. "If you get the train to White Plains I'll pick you up at the station."

In her soccer mom SUV.

"You can sleep on my couch," she said.

I would have given anything to watch her camming and coming. Apart from money, that is. She said her ex-husband couldn't be relied on to keep to a schedule. He sometimes turned up unexpectedly to pick up the kids but she never knew when. He usually came the same day so I'd need to be able to jump on a train with little or no notice.

They had been married fifteen years.

It had originally been his idea that she start stripping so they could make extra cash. He had intended for her to strip in bars and clubs but Jameson preferred to do it online. As an experiment she posted a topless picture on Girlsnexxxtdoor and it got so many hits she felt confident enough to appear live. But then Jim insisted they appear together. Jameson had already set up a separate account featuring some of her more tasteful nudes and this proved to be the more popular site by far. They had some success together but her solo effort received thousands of visitors.

Visitors who were willing pay for a "private chat."

Up to this point they received money while they had sex together. But there was a much bigger demand to watch her insert dildos in herself and even more if she inserted the type of dildo that received Wi-Fi commands. Prostitution is defined as selling a sex act for money. Stripping didn't come under this heading since it was a visual experience. Even lap dancing was still considered adult entertainment because no physical sex act took place. Lap dances aren't legally supposed to culminate in orgasm, not just because it's illegal but because the money stops once the guy comes in his pants. But now that digital commands could be sent to a dildo buried in a girl's twat you could text her brains out.

The host website took 80 percent and there was no vetting process. They didn't care. If you attracted a million followers it was as good for them as it was for you. All they needed was a valid driver's license to prove you were over eighteen. There should be no visual evidence of a pet, i.e., a dog leash or cat litter. Or of a child, i.e., toys or diapers.

Jameson lived in a three-story house. Her children were restricted to the first floor. Whenever she was online she cranked up the stereo on the second floor so that the events on the third went unheard. She had a very homely look about her. Her voice was wonderfully soothing in an American sweetheart sort of way, and she had a great sense of humor.

She told me this joke over the phone.

A man is being interviewed for the LAPD and just as the interview ends the HR guy hands him a gun and says: "Everything looks good here but I just need you to do one more thing for me." The man agrees enthusiastically. "I want you to go outside and shoot five black guys and a rabbit."

"Sure," the man says, "but why the rabbit?"

"Excellent attitude. You've got the job."

And she had a great laugh.

She was thirty-six but looked much younger. And to look at her body you'd never think she'd had three kids. In fact it was after the third kid that Jim began urging her to strip. I didn't get the sense that he wanted her to do this for money or that they were hard up but more that it was an attempt to inject some thrill into their sex life.

Anyway he began to get jealous because she was getting all the attention even when they were both on screen. He was seen more as the human dildo. Not surprising really since almost all the customers were straight males.

She looked so wholesome. The sort of proper girl you'd fantasize about seeing naked. I felt drawn to her as one would to a mother. Maybe it was the big tits and the sheer openness of her attitude. I found the whole encounter intoxicating. When I first found out I let an entire pot of sweet potatoes burn on the stove because I couldn't contain the information and cook at the same time. I told Jameson I was impressed.

"Why? Because I fake orgasms for a living?"

"So you hate what you do?"

"No. Mostly, I hate that I don't do it enough. But that's misleading."

This showed a sophistication I hadn't expected from a cam girl. It showed she was willing to open not just her legs but her psyche to me, which was flattering beyond belief. Here was a girl who had thousands of male worshippers willing to answer *my* questions. Why? At first I thought it was a scam to get more guys interested in her but she had already shared quite a bit of personal information with me.

". . . and to be fair I'm not always faking it . . . sometimes I completely love it."

So there she was waiting for strangers to tell her what to

do, basically masturbating and getting paid for it. I found my-self getting jealous, not that other people were ogling her but jealous of her ability to attract that kind of paid attention. After all it was a form of approval. Paid approval and the pleasure she had to be getting from it on so many levels. Not to mention that she was putting her kids through school. She was paying her rent. She was avenging her husband. ("He's an awful per-son.") It had to be addictive.

"Plus I know he's looking and that always gets me off."

Now it all made sense.

FROM CROW'S FEET TO CAMEL TOE SHE'S ALL WOMAN
#TheOxygenThiefDiaries

At first I was thrilled to see her name in my inbox but the businesslike tone of *details on my Facebook page* indicated I was only one of many people invited to the open house at her workshop. It was insulting to be blank cc'ed. And unnerving because I had until that moment forbidden myself from look-ing at her Facebook page for fear of what I might find there. Namely, pictures of her with men or any indication of some-thing similar. But after convincing myself there would be noth-ing more emotionally taxing than an informational poster or a map of how to get to her exhibition, I summoned the courage to click on her page.

And there she was.

Gazing out at me from the letterbox format with some of

her pieces evenly spaced on a shelf in the background. Her eyes looked marshy to me. From crying? She seemed sadder. Dazed, but smiling heroically. I cried because this was obviously my doing. She was the repository of my misdeeds. Not only did I owe her the opportunity to punish me, I owed her my happiness too. In the email, under the invite, there were two lines meant for me only. *I don't hold out much hope, it's a long way to come for something so goofy.* This was so guilt-inducing I shivered. And yet it seemed to indicate that what she was going through had to be at least as bad as what I was having to endure if not worse.

I don't hold out much hope

My newly acquired capacity for crying was frightening. I could cry on top of crying. Like retching after having already puked. I heard someone say that crying is prayer in liquid form.

Later that same day I got a text. *WHAT THE HECK!! I'M BEING SLOWLY DRIVEN MAD*

My first reaction was to run across the Manhattan Bridge, scramble up Park Slope to her apartment, and gather her to me when she opened the door. I'd protect her. From what though? Me? How could I shield her from what I'd already done to her? By staying away. And then I began to wonder if the text referred to me at all. I remembered her saying her upstairs neighbor moved furniture around in the middle of the night. She might have been referring to this. Her next text did little to clarify the situation.

!!!!!!!!

That was it. Nothing else. No wink to inflect the tone. No annoying emoticon. Nothing. Was it an admonishment for not responding? Or was it the sort of thing you sent before committing suicide? On the way home with my packed-up cart parked beside me I pored over the possibilities on a bench in Washington Square Park. I had abandoned myself to the act of crying when two teenage girls seemed to just materialize on either side of me.

"Would you like us to pray over you? To our Lord Jesus Savior?"

I blinked at them.

I would have felt more comfortable if they had tried to sell me drugs. I waited for the shrieks of cynical laughter, but they couldn't have been more serious. Kneeling beside me, right there in the park, they began to pray aloud.

"Lord Savior, please bring peace to our brother's soul and if it is your will, Lord, ease his suffering."

Ping.

I miss you to pieces . . . big misshapen pieces.

Even I couldn't call this a coincidence.

Well, not immediately.

I wanted to just call her and initiate arrangements for our wedding but after the initial flush of euphoria subsided I asked myself, *Why*? Why would it be any different than before? She'd already done this so many times. Hooked me back in only to find that what she meant was she just wanted to "hang out." Still, I was glad she was actually saying something tangible.

It meant she was feeling the same sense of loss as me.

Didn't it?

I hid the text, and my glee, from the visiting angels.

I wasn't about to give them a cute story they could tell their brethren that Sunday.

• • • •

"I admire your balls."

A ridiculously fashionable journalist from a supposedly cool underground magazine stopped to say she wanted to do a piece on me. She talked about the death of the bookshop and how self-publishing was the future and how cool she thought it was that I was "out here doing this." I wanted to respond that I admired her tits but the moment had passed and it would have been unnecessarily provocative. Plus she didn't have great tits.

The theme of the next issue was *obsession*.

"We'd want to put you on the cover."

The amount of people who stopped and made these sorts of promises was staggering. From the security of their day jobs they masqueraded as film producers, artists, musicians, directors, and actors. Most of the time they didn't even sound like they believed it themselves. In a way we were both pretending. I'd pretend to believe she was a journalist if she pretended to believe I was a writer.

"Sure," I said, waiting for her to buy a book.

"Great," she said, waiting for me to give her one.

Awkward silence.

"Oh by the way, when is Aisling bringing out her book? My editor wants to interview her."

Did she really think I was going to contact that cunt?

"Oh yes of course, I'll ask if she's interested."

The rest of that day was dreadful. I felt so pointless and lonely and old and beaten. I kept thinking I had cancer. There was a crick in my neck that felt like a lump and I couldn't massage it away. It seemed like there was no point in planning the rest of my life until I knew there was a rest of my life.

Being out there on a sunny day was forgivable, enjoyable even. People didn't need to be embarrassed on your behalf. But in January the book was the only thing between you and begging. It wasn't just the absence of cash that stung, it was the implied comment on your choice of career. If no one wanted to buy your bullshit book you were obviously not going to make a living at it. And having established that, it was safe to assume no one would want to buy your second book either. A shipment of which was halfway across the Pacific Ocean in the hold of a container ship bound for New York where it would spend three weeks in customs before being delivered in five hundred boxes, each containing sixty books, on four separate pallets to the sidewalk outside your apartment. If you couldn't sell the few books on your table what the fuck were you going to do with ten thousand more?

Potential customers-readers-critics hugged themselves as they passed. I fantasized about leaving all this behind and bringing Marian to Ireland with me.

Oh how we'd cry and sigh and laugh and blush and after long silent meaningful windswept walks on frosty beaches gathering firewood for our cottage hearth we'd rest our tired eyes on each other gasping at our good fortune.

We might even have a kid.

Why not? It'd be the ultimate depth charge to drop into the world. A human dirt bomb. A leaving gift. It might actually be fun to watch my son fuck with you all. I had never really thought of it like that before. I was too busy making sure I would never have to be father to the sort of slithering soulless gargoyle I was at fifteen. But what if I could equip him with the ability and resilience to do all the damage I could no longer inflict?

"Son, I can't go out into the world and fuck with people anymore, but you can."

Or better yet, a daughter. A beautiful devious daughter to exact revenge on the planet. A highly trained undercover operative dropped behind enemy lines. This advanced the case for having a child with Marian. If my genes weren't too insistent the likelihood of the resulting progeny being attractive was very strong.

My mind in the body of Jane Birkin.

There's no Kevlar for that.

Daughter of an Oxygen Thief.

But that was before Marian read *Chameleon in a Candy Store*. I had hoped that the best way to encapsulate everything I felt about her would be to just send her my second book and let her see for herself. This would achieve two things. (1) She'd approve the content thereby preempting any fears of legal proceedings and (2) I'd woo her back into my bed. Her review was nothing if not succinct.

I HATE THAT THIS EXISTS
—Marian

2

The irony is not lost on me, that my limp was caused by a lack of oxygen at birth.

This was an email from a very pretty girl who invited me to go for a drive in her car. Why was the idea of a girl with a limp such a turn-on? Was it because the normal rituals could be dispensed with? If she was damaged I could be my unadorned self. Pictures on her Facebook page confirmed that she was creamy-skinned, long-limbed, and ladylike—but with a limp. And as far as I was concerned, a car was an upgrade from a wheelchair.

We began to correspond.

She had married impetuously because she felt lucky to be

asked and she was now in the process of getting divorced. I allowed this to mean she was desperate to get fucked.

Don't ever get married.

I made her wait an hour before responding.

We're seated opposite each other in a café . . . peering over your copy of my book you hold my gaze while you provocatively lick your fingers . . . but instead of turning a page your hand descends . . . under the table . . . under your skirt . . .

If she replied even halfheartedly to such overt filth she was effectively agreeing to sex. She responded almost immediately.

I love the idea of holding your . . . ahem . . . gaze under the table. I have an assortment of tables at my place. I mewed.

I don't doubt it, she replied, but remained adamant we go for a drive.

I mentioned I wanted to post some flyers around Williamsburg and that maybe if she didn't mind we could head out there. The readiness with which she agreed to this betrayed a sense of relief I was only able to make sense of later. She'd pick me up on the corner of Avenue A and St. Mark's at seven PM. A night drive seemed promising. But making photocopies in a nearby deli took longer than I'd anticipated and I sensed frustration in her next text.

I had to park!! I'm waiting for you on the corner.

She was easy to pick out among the early evening flux of East Villagers on Avenue A and St. Mark's because she was standing so incongruously still. Any movement on her part would require a demonstration of her disability and somehow I understood this as I approached fifteen minutes late. If I hadn't taken so long trying to figure out the copier she would have been able to pull up beside me and remain seated for our first encounter. I had unintentionally wrong-footed her and I blushed on her behalf.

We shook hands.

She asked about my writing and I provided boilerplate answers aware that she was intentionally delaying the inevitable walk to her car.

"You look so much better than your photos." I lied.

We stood there.

Her not wanting to move, me not knowing which way to go. When the moment could no longer be postponed she nodded gravely in the direction of her car. I made up my mind that her first twisted step into my life would go unnoticed but in my peripheral vision it was obvious that the act of walking required her to raise herself up and lower herself down with each new step. I filled the silence with waffle about the streets in Williamsburg most suited to self-promotion, the idea being that she'd surely be aglow with gratitude to be in the company of such a considerate man. One who didn't point at her leg and run off in disgust.

Once inside her immaculately clean car, a paused punk track resumed on ignition and she opened her coat to reveal a ridiculously skimpy dress that showed more of her lovely pale body than was necessary or even advisable in November.

As the Black Flag track exploded into its chorus she began to shimmy right there in her seat.

In this environment she had no limp.

It seemed to me like she was enjoying herself *too* much.

As we took off up Avenue A, flash frames from David Cronenberg's *Crash* and Quentin Tarantino's *Death Proof* illuminated the inside of my mind like lightning.

My paranoia leaned in close to counsel me.

Okay so you're being driven where? And by whom? What do we know about this freak? Maybe she gets off on crashing cars. Why is the interior so clean? Is it a rental? Is it because of forensics? Will you soon be sporting a limp like hers?

The aggression with which she handled the gearstick and steering wheel seemed to confirm that she was some sort thrill-seeker. Was she going to drive us into a wall? Or the East River. Why not? If anyone deserved to be drowned it was the self-confessed misogynistic Oxygen Thief. Her first message took on new resonance. *The irony is not lost on me that my limp was caused by a lack of oxygen.* We hurtled across the Williamsburg Bridge into the unknown.

The dress she'd selected to meet the weird Irish writer might as well have not been there at all. It was a token dress. And from the way she pushed herself around within it she looked like she was already having some sort of solitary sex inside it. As she checked her mirrors our eyes met for an instant and far from malice or madness what I saw there could only be described as a kind, delighted lust.

Relief gushed into my groin.

The glimpses of her barely covered breasts and shameless handling of the gear shift now conspired to produce a rigidity in my jeans that I made no attempt to conceal. I saw her glance at my bulge. I blushed with pride. I was not going to be a crash victim after all. She leaned forward offering me a view of nipples erupting against the thin fabric of her dress.

I was being rewarded for not noticing her limp.

We were now on Bedford Avenue and she made a show of checking the mirrors not for cars now but for prying eyes and having satisfied herself no one could see she reached beyond the gear stick to scratch the hot bulge in my jeans. I gasped with delight and after some impressive maneuvering on her part we were parked and tonguing each other with an urgency that would normally have culminated in the most uninhibited rutting.

Only it didn't.

She broke away dramatically and between uneven breaths somehow managed to speak.

"Not"—she panted trying to regain composure—"tonight."

I was left in no doubt that we'd go much further next time. But for now she needed to tell herself we hadn't done it on the first date. There was a loud *clunk* as she pressed the button on the center consul to unlock the doors. They were locked? Just as well I hadn't realized this or I would have begun scraping at the windows.

But the sooner this date ended the sooner the next one could commence. I found myself in Williamsburg and suitably enough preceded by a hard-on. Memories of happy times spent with Marian in these same streets began to insinuate themselves into my already lust-clouded mind and threatened to overwhelm me.

I was glad I had something to do.

I set off up Bedford Avenue taping my photocopies onto lampposts and scaffolding. It was satisfying to get A4-sized photocopies of the snowman and angel onto spaces already occupied by some of the city's most recognizable brands: Vans, Gucci, Levi's, Me.

One or two photos of well-placed flyers was all it would take to give the impression they were popping up all over the city. In this regard Instagram was the ideal accomplice. I was busy attaching one such piece of propaganda when a cab pulled up beside me and the passenger stuck his head out of the rear window.

"Illegal bill posting," he said.

"Correct," I said, shaking my head at the interruption.

I thought he was the vehicular version of the sort of asshole who stopped to ask how he could get a table on Prince Street. Given encouragement he would pester me for tips about flyer-posting. Best to just ignore him. A shadow fell over my work and looking over my shoulder I saw the same guy was now standing behind me. Oh please. A blue-and-gold NYPD badge glinted on his belt as he filled out a pink form on a mini clipboard. Looking up from his administrative duties he addressed his latest case.

"See some ID?"

Undercover cops drove around in cabs?

When he learned my age and occupation he seemed embarrassed for me. Would he take me in his cab to the police station?

Meanwhile wasn't someone getting murdered somewhere?

He gave me a ticket and by the time he'd turned the corner I had taped it over the offending photocopied image of my book and uploaded a photo of the entire ensemble to Instagram. I made sure *illegal bill-posting* was legible. I warmed my scofflaw hands on the amount of likes received.

Since I was already in the neighborhood and it had been a month since my last visit I thought I'd drop by the Williamsburg Bookshop to pick up a check. I had at one point loved going there to resupply them with books, but since one of their staff members had landed a publishing deal I tried to limit my visits to times I knew he wouldn't be there. He got fatter and fatter every time I saw him as if his body was expanding at the same rate as his career. The last time I'd been there I was consumed with jealousy and self-loathing to see him brandish a proof of his book, which was soon to be launched. Marketing, publishing, editing, cover design. He didn't even have to get off his fat arse, it was all done for him.

He had been almost embarrassed to tell me how he was being flown out to LA to meet with directors to talk about making a movie out of his book. And he really looked like he would have preferred not to have to tell me that he'd already been guaranteed great reviews in *Publishers Weekly* and *New York Review of Books*. As if it was a great burden, one he would try to bear with some measure of dignity. But then he snapped out of it, as if suddenly remembering why I was standing there.

"Oh sorry, remind me how much we owe you."

My lips smacked open to utter the paltry sum.

He paused to calculate as if he thought I was trying to rip him off or perhaps was astounded at how low a figure it was and then, shaking his head, as if deciding to let it go, out of charity, began writing. Millennial girls, waiting to be served, held art books against their chests and looked away to save my embarrassment. I was in the fucking way as usual. Pen poised over my check, Buckley Harriman turned to me, genuinely annoyed at himself.

"I should remember your name after all these years."

I never felt more anonymous.

PANIC BEAUTIFULLY
#TheOxygenThiefDiaries

Drinnngg Dringg Dringggg Drinnnnnngggggggg

Ursula commanded my doorway in a pair of thigh-high stockings and very little else. Far from being a disability, her limp only enhanced her attractiveness. I arranged her into a position that best suited my sexual needs and while I was doing this she clamped her mouth around my cock, suckling on it like it was life-giving. She stopped only once, to look up at me I think, so that I could register the anxiety in her face that I might take it away from her. As she resumed slobbering on it so noisily, I felt compelled to offer up a prayer of thanks.

"Ohhhhh Holy Fuckkkkking Jesus Christ Almighty."

Her moan-laugh caused new, even more welcome, reverberations. There was a sort of retarded sluggishness to her tongue that seemed out of sync with its owner's commands; this gap in transmission between order and act was exhilarating since neither of us knew what to expect.

I was having sex with a gimp, how edgy of me.

We talked for hours afterward. Mostly about how she should never have gotten married and how her divorce was progressing. She said she'd hired a private detective to follow her ex and that this was how she found out he'd been unfaithful. Hoping to hear a New York detective story I encouraged her to elaborate, but seconds later she confessed she had only said that because she was embarrassed to admit she'd copied the passwords from his phone and used them to track his GPS. I was impressed first by the effortlessness with which she had lied and then by the speed she had recanted. I flattered myself that the lie was what she told others but the confession was for me only. She trapped him into lying about being en route to see his mother in Brooklyn as she watched the indicator crawl in the opposite direction, across the Williamsburg Bridge to Manhattan. Even more damning was the call she made to his mother, who had no knowledge of his visit until minutes later she called back to say he had just arrived.

Meanwhile the indicator showed him still on the Williams-burg Bridge.

"Don't ever get married," she said.

There was an element of therapy involved. I think she liked talking to me because my thinking was at least as twisted as hers, or as she put it: "*Your* limp is on the inside."

It was the perfect arrangement in that we each saw the other as the charity case.

But I would soon regret having been so vociferous in my sexual release because it gave her the impression she had earned enough leverage to negotiate a proper date. Having mentioned earlier that she had always wanted to see Shake-speare in the Park, she made her pitch.

"You can stand in line for the tickets, you like me," she said.

I said nothing, preferring instead to watch her squirm.

She couldn't help but try to groom me for a relationship. It was conditioning. And it fell to me to keep things casual. To de-flect her attempts at domestication. This, I told myself, was why she liked to visit me in the first place. I was safe to like because I'd never want anything more than sex. And she was perfect for me because her limp ensured I'd never see her as a girlfriend. If I agreed to wait in line for tickets to Shakespeare in the Park the impossibility of us having any sort of relationship other than sexual would be thrown into relief. Meanwhile the combined gestalt of her shapely body, demoted by the limp and then com-pensated for by that filthy mind, continued to intoxicate.

The limp just made everything dirtier.

And her repertoire of endlessly inventive sexual techniques made me realize how lazy and unimaginative other
girls were in comparison. If they put your dick in their
mouths they expected a fucking medal. At one point I
couldn't figure out what she was doing so I opened one eye
and peered over my chest hair. The sight that met me immediately ignited an explosive ejaculation that leapt from me
into the air as I bayed at an imaginary moon. It was the image
of a pretty girl brushing her teeth with the exposed tip of my
cock. The sensation caused by the constricting pressure of the
interior of her cheek on one side and the corrugated ribbing
of her teeth on the other brought such friction to bear on the
tip I was released from earthly concerns. This sort of dental
dexterity could almost be viewed as a more chaste alternative
to the traditional blow job since the inner mouth wasn't even
entered. It didn't even require the use of a tongue. I think she
practiced her ideas on me so she could decide what would
work best on her Indian boyfriend Indra. I was glad to be of
service.

I insisted on walking her back to her car so that she could
see I was proud to have people realize I just had sex with a disabled girl. Passersby nodded at us, compensating for their own
embarrassment. A limping girl in torn thigh-high stockings has
no easy definition in our culture.

• • • •

I was always happy to receive an email from the Williamsburg Bookshop looking for more copies but I was more than

a little annoyed to have to ask the new guy behind the counter for Buckley by name. As the only one authorized to write checks he would have to be faced.

"You haven't heard?"

Was I about to hear how he had been flown first-class to LA to discuss the screen adaptation of his book?

No, I was not.

Buckley, it transpired, had been relieved of his duties after it was discovered that—wait for it—he had plagiarized huge chunks of his much-feted spy novel.

Allow me a moment here.

Researchers observing audience reactions to Broadway musicals discovered that at certain climactic peaks in the narrative an ecstatic demonstration of emotion was produced in males reminiscent of that seen at sporting events. Both arms thrust involuntarily upward. This phenomenon became such a reliable indicator of a show's success, night-vision videos of men succumbing to "Superman Arms" began to be included in packages sent out to investors. Hearing about Buckley's plight I held on hard to the counter lest I be recorded on the security cameras punching and repunching the air above me.

But the feeling soon passed as I began to fret that maybe he had intentionally choreographed the situation so that he could Tweet how he had tricked the publishing industry into exposing the reshuffled plots and storylines that passed for originality. He'd be celebrated as a cultural ironist and canonized by the millennial elite. He'd be even more of a success than he had almost been as a spy novelist. I knew he wasn't that clever but he might have hired a publicist who was.

The guy behind the counter turned his screen toward me.

"Just type *Buckley* and *plagiarism*," he said.

And indeed there it was, all over the Internet. How he'd shamelessly lifted entire passages from existing books and passed them off as his own. This would attract a version of fame but not necessarily the kind you wanted. I had certainly wondered how he managed to write something that was getting such good responses. The answer was simple.

He hadn't.

Compared to Buckley I was pure of heart, extremely talented, and very very slim.

> ### *I WROTE* DIARY OF AN OXYGEN THIEF
> —Buckley Harriman, plagiarist

I was in exactly the right mood to meet Marian.

She stood outside her apartment looking taller and more majestic than I'd ever seen her. She didn't want me to come in? The body was still tight and her lovely upturned breasts were clearly defined under a French polo neck. Yes she was wearing a bra but not much of a one. I'd never seen her in a polo neck before. Jane Birkin in Brooklyn. But there was a marshiness around the eyes that I forbade myself from looking at for too long because I wanted very much to like what I was seeing. We were obviously happy to see each other.

I had the feeling we hadn't been apart for very long, like we'd seen each other the previous week as opposed to three months ago. We slipped back into each other's rhythm. I had read, reread, and almost memorized the second email she'd sent where she said she'd shown *Chameleon in a Candy Store* to a friend who helped her see it wasn't so bad after all. That there were some very sweet parts in it. She was big enough to admit she had mostly reacted to the fact that so many other girls were mentioned.

Jealousy.

This, I decided, was a very good sign.

She'd done something with her hair that seemed to indicate that she at least *wanted* to appear nice for me. She wasn't dressed as stylishly as she might have been, but then this was a difficult "date" to dress for. She couldn't go too far or she'd appear presumptuous and she couldn't not try just in case. I would have given a testicle to know if she was wearing matching underwear. Well maybe not a testicle, a toe maybe.

On her suggestion we ended up in a Mexican restaurant nearby and though I immediately hated the place (the acoustics were awful) I wasn't going to be churlish.

After all, this was our first outing in months.

I managed to remain quiet while she ordered for us but the moment the food arrived I began to blurt. As the words spewed out of me, something caught my eye proceeding across the table—it was my hand, creeping toward hers. At the moment of contact a gush of emotion surged around inside me as if my bloodstream had suddenly become carbonated. I regarded her email as a bold proposal to start seeing each other again and I wasn't going to make her wait for an answer any longer than was necessary.

She made no effort to retract her hand but something wasn't right. This didn't feel like the homecoming I had hoped for. I began to wonder if her email had just been a last-ditch attempt to see me under any guise. I took a breath and leapt into the void.

"In all the time we were together I never said I . . ."

I held her eyes, half hoping she'd stop me.

"Well, I'll say it now."

There was still time for her to stop me.

"I love you."

I immediately regretted it.

Her eyelids closed at the key moment so that I found myself looking lovingly at two flesh-covered bumps. And presumably hoping to avoid my desperately cloying look she opened them again only to inspect my chest. The panic-inducing silence that followed was broken by the excruciating sound of her chair scraping the floor. I was listening so hard it was like the screech of feedback from a mic.

She spoke quietly.

"I have to . . . sorry . . . it's not an escape."

But that's exactly what it was. I was shown a glimpse of what this was really all about as she twirled out of her seat in the direction of the restroom.

That ass.

I sat there, pretending this was normal for me but it wasn't. I had never said those words to anyone. Not to my father and certainly not to my mother. I had never uttered those words out loud before. When she returned and settled into her seat I energetically resumed my self-laceration.

"Being without you is like being in prison."

I wanted to cry, partly because it would lend credence to my performance and partly because it would prove it wasn't a performance. I yearned to tell her precisely how I had suffered. How many times a day I'd broken down and wailed like a clubbed seal. The inhuman sounds that had emanated from me. The exquisite bottomlessness of my grief. But how could I? It might flatter her but it might also just be pathetic.

She was silent. Sadistically so. A little embarrassed smile played over her lips and it was clear she had decided to sit it out. She'd weather this unexpected onslaught of secondary embarrassment. Surely it would go away if she didn't acknowledge it. The check arrived. She must have asked for it when she went to the restroom.

So that was her response.

Unable to bear the agonizing mechanics of splitting the bill I placed a twenty on her ten and got up. She looked relieved it was over. We somehow managed to make some sort of uncomfortable small talk while she walked me back across the street to my bike. I offered her a ridiculously ironic fist-bump that she probably felt obliged to match with one of her own. I mounted my bike heroically and cycled in the general direction of the East Village, doing my best to avoid the fur-covered cars and trucks thrown out of focus by my tears. The energy required to continue pedaling seemed to subtract from the sincerity of the emotion but it was important to put distance between myself and the source of my woe. And even at that it seemed tragic to have to increase rather than decrease the space between us. More than one pedestrian looked nervously over his shoulder to see where the whimpering was coming from.

It was two days before she texted.

Bad battery . . . all's well . . . check in soon.

But her need to punish me translated in my mind as confirmation of her love. Of how deeply I must have hurt her. I'd gladly offer myself up for more of the same until she decided I had suffered enough.

No problem . . . it was lovely seeing you the other night.

ONLINE NO ONE CAN HEAR YOU SCREAM
#TheOxygenThiefDiaries

To say that I used to get into a lot of fights is misleading.

Fight is far too collaborative a term.

I just got beaten up.

And though it had been years since I'd been within arm's length of a fistfight, something instinctive urged me to look across the street just as Forgive-Them-Ron was shaping up like an eighteenth-century street fighter. His arms were raised in what looked like a comical imitation of a boxer as he shifted his weight from left to right, ducking imaginary blows. It took me a moment to realize he had assumed this persona for the benefit of an alarmingly elderly man who was now starting to respond with gyrations of his own. This lurch and sway continued until Forgive-Them swung his right arm diagonally upward to connect his balled fist with the side of the old man's head. On contact a sound rose collectively from what I could now see was a clutch of spectators already filming the scene on smartphones.

"Oooooooooh."

Laughing happily and looking relaxed and young, Arrest-Me-Dante was among them with his phone extended in front of him, soaking it all up. The older combatant, bewildered as to where he was or what was happening, continued to mimic someone who had a chance. He stumbled somewhat drunkenly although I don't think he was drunk. Forgive-Them was more confident now that he was winning.

"I warned you bro, I warned you."

The next day he turned up in a jacket with a huge floral design on the back. In contrast to his normally somber attire, he looked like he had blossomed overnight.

"A girl I met in a bar wouldn't talk to me unless I gave her my opinion of this book."

I turned to see an intense-looking young man with my book held open in his hands.

Another one?

I stifled a yawn.

This was gratifying of course, but he wasn't going to buy another copy and I couldn't sell him the second book because he'd only come back to attack me when he read his own attempts at wooing Françoise in it. Plus his insistence that he met the girl in a bar sounded like a trap. Was he hoping I'd correct him and say something about a dating profile? He was just another disciple of Marian's perfect ass.

A character in search of his author.

"Really?" I said feigning surprise. "And what *was* your opinion of it?"

"I loved it."

"Oh really? Did you tell her that?"

"Yeah, but I never heard back from her."

I didn't ask him if he'd told her this in the same imaginary bar, I just wanted him to go away. But he just stood there commandeered by the logic-melting promise of a fragrant French pussy and adjacent derriere. Nodding at my latest sign I let him in on a secret. He took a step back, but even as he read it he continued to look this way and that, hoping she was going materialize.

"That's cool," he said, as if he understood.

REALITY IS JUST SUCCESSFUL ADVERTISING
#TheOxygenThiefDiaries

Drinnggg Drinnggg Drinnggg Drinnnnnnnngggggg
It was indescribably wonderful having certain sex arrive

at your door once a week in the shape of an unpaid prostitute with a limp. Mind you, I wouldn't have had to go down on a prostitute, paid or otherwise. But when Ursula told me that in Indra's culture it was considered degrading to pleasure a woman in this way, I realized it might be in my interest to provide her with something he wouldn't. Plus I loved hearing her bleat and moan like a wounded deer. She had no inhibitions when she orgasmed and I tried my best to be for her what she was for me. A sexual trash can.

Even so, I was beginning to think that for her, the services I provided were more cerebral than carnal. She loved talking to me. This time I was to hear all about the Polish man she described as *the love of her life*. This guy couldn't get hard unless he punched and kicked her while calling her a whore and . . . she hesitated here before continuing . . . "He also liked to spit on me."

I winced when I heard this, not because I sympathized, but because it meant my attempts at choke-fucking her must have seemed so vanilla in comparison. Somehow her father found out that the guy had "heavy hands" and made it known he'd happily go to jail for what he might do to him. This was when he left town and broke off all contact. Ten years later she still loved him. He was apparently very good-looking and she would therefore do whatever he wanted as long as what he wanted was her. And knowing that he got off on punching her, she would purposely and repeatedly infuriate him. Turn up late, ask relationship questions during sex, and most successful of all, accuse him of being gay when he begged her for anal sex. In this way she enabled his habit.

After he disappeared she married the first guy who was nice to her. She didn't think anybody would want a girl with a limp who mistook punches for kisses.

Ursula sucked on my cock so convincingly it was like an extension of herself. It was amazing that she knew to keep altering the rhythms and movements of her mouth, tongue, lips, and hands so that no pattern was discernible. My cock and I were constantly kept guessing.

A prerequisite for any successful narrative.

And because she sucked so beautifully I didn't need to worry on her behalf. There was no need to convince her she was doing a great job. I didn't need to fret about whether she was enjoying it. Or whether I would come. I knew she'd deliver. This wouldn't be just another exercise in frustration. She was like a wizened washerwoman whose every move was dictated by experience. A factory worker so effortlessly capable of performing her allotted task she could allow herself the luxury of thinking about something else. Knowing the eccentricities of the conveyor belt she could give it an occasional slap whenever it shuddered.

"Oooooooohhhhh arggghhh."

Once the nasty business of making me come was out of the way she couldn't wait to tell me her news. The Polish pugilist had texted her that he was back in town. Given his sexual eccentricities, Halloween seemed the perfect time for them to re-connect. She arranged to meet him outside the hospital where she worked. This is when she mentioned she was wearing a highly sexualized Goldilocks outfit. And she had also arranged to meet Indra at exactly the same place.

At the same time.

Was she hoping to ignite a brawl? Enjoy the sight of two men fighting over her? When the Pole turned up on a skateboard (a skateboard?) looking not nearly as handsome as she remembered, she told him her father was on his way over to pick her up. This was sufficient to send him skating energetically away just as Indra pulled up in his SUV. He was told the GPS in her car wasn't working, so she needed a ride to a work party in Williamsburg, which, in reality, was a date with another guy she hoped would be a better long-term option than either of the two men she already had in play.

"Well, the outfit had to go back the next day. I had to get my value out of it," she said, defending herself against an accusation I hadn't made.

Or at least not out loud.

She related all this to me wrapped in a towel with her bad leg folded up under her after ingesting my molten soul.

She showed me the outfit on her phone. (She was still wringing the last few drops of value from it.) Standing there in her miniskirted Goldilocks outfit, flanked by children of all races, I suddenly saw the genius of the outfit. For the children and the other nurses it was a fun fancy dress, but for a succession of three adult males—four if you included me—it was cock-stiffening cosplay . . . with a limp.

Good value indeed.

The disabled permit in the corner of her windshield afforded her an unheard of luxury in the East Village. A parking spot in front of St. Catherine's Church. This resulted in an instinctive tingling in my balls whenever I passed. While others blessed themselves I readjusted my cock. Such irreligiosity only increased my desire for her.

"Didn't you say you went to Catholic school?" I said, still flushed with my orgasms. She opened the car door and leaned in close darting her tongue in my ear.

"I did and I can still fit into the uniform."

WHERE HAVE ALL THE GO-GO DANCERS GONE GONE?
#TheOxygenThiefDiaries

Back on Prince Street I began to notice a group of guys stopping girls, attempting to talk to them.

A cluster of three or four guys, one of whom seemed to be some sort of leader or coach who egged the others on. Because of their proximity to my table I worried that visits and sales might be affected by their antics. If girls were being harassed I wasn't going to sell them any books and more to the point if anyone was going to do any harassing I wanted it to be me.

So I kept an eye on them.

They huddled together, obviously discussing the merits of

passing girls and every now and then one of them detached and ran past his target until he was well ahead of her before turning around and performing a sort of jump-and-plop in front of her. Each guy who broke away from the group in pursuit of a girl employed this same strange piece of choreography. Some girls walked directly past or dodged to the side, hardly breaking their stride, but a surprisingly large number stopped and engaged in conversation. From my position I could read each girl's face as she was accosted. Polite interest morphed into mild disgust or undisguised delight depending on the success of the presenter.

His cohorts watched intently, turning to each other at various points, exchanging knowing looks. By now, he had either been told to fuck off or he was thumbing his phone. Whatever the result he would return to his buddies for a conspiratorial huddle. I thought at first it was a group of drunken guys out on the town chatting up girls between pubs. But they were much more organized than that. A very stylish girl walked past them. If they hadn't been there I would have definitely asked her to stop for a photo. But this time a small stubby-looking guy waddled on ahead of her and jumped/stopped in exactly the same way the previous guy had done. The others looked on with interest. They might have been watching a sports event. I only saw them on the weekends from noon until five PM. Never any later. Never any sooner. The girl, who looked very intelligent, blushed as the little gnome took out his phone.

I was intrigued of course.

They were obviously experimenting with ways to meet

women and this was something I was always interested in. Also there was an element of competition involved since I was mining the same terrain. After all, if a girl had already been stopped by these assholes I didn't feel I could insist myself on her for a photo. When one of them was left red-faced after an aborted attempt to talk to a tall, tough-looking, expensively dressed model who swept past my table like a yacht, he looked around desperately for his teammates. His embarrassment beamed outward from him and perhaps because he was happy to see a face that expressed interest rather than more rejection he stopped at my table. I blurted out questions that had been building up in me since I'd first noticed the phenomenon weeks before.

"Oh I can't really say," he said, but it was obvious he was dying to talk about it. "We're not supposed to say."

"Oh come on, who am I going to tell? You've seen me out here, I'm just a street vendor. It's interesting to me." I changed tack. "Well okay, how about this. Can you tell me if you got her number?" At this he blossomed.

"Yes," he said, hardly able to believe it himself.

I looked at him.

A fat fucker really. Certainly not the type of guy who you'd think would approach a model in the street. He was obviously lying. Wasn't he?

"Really?" I said, genuinely surprised. "Well listen, man, tell me what this thing is, because I might want to join. I mean no offense, but if you can get chicks like that then maybe there's hope for me."

He paused. Had I insulted him? He looked left and right before leaning in close and whispering behind his hand.

"It's called Streetmeet."

Of course it was.

On Streetmeet.com I learned that members were issued with pens housing tiny cameras, enabling them to record conversations for later analysis. I watched one session on their website featuring the leader/coach I recognized from the street, talking to a girl in a bikini top like she was an inattentive child. There were videos from all over the world: London, Chicago, Los Angeles, Paris, Barcelona. This one was from Rio de Janeiro. After he said, "Can I text you? I'd like to invite you out some time," she gave him her number.

As far as I was concerned the term *invite you out* already implied expenditure so fuck that. Plus I knew that a phone number meant nothing because even if it *was* her real number she could still always block you. In a separate video he's sitting behind a desk wittering on in a clipped English accent trying his best to suggest that just getting a phone number and a promise of a date was the equivalent of getting a cock-bath. Nonsense. You couldn't afford to congratulate yourself until both balls had been dredged. Until that happened you still couldn't be sure if she was using *you* for sex. You'd find yourself owed five orgasms after spending an hour eating her out. This was obviously aimed at sad poor bastards who had never encountered a woman outside of Pornhub.

But it was a huge operation. Global even.

The tutorial kept returning to what they considered to be

154

the most important part of the process: "Perfecting the stop."
This referred to the moment you ran ahead of your quarry and
arrived in "a friendly yet masculine way that attracts her attention." Having arrested her pedestrian progress you could then
unleash the rest of your amorous arsenal on her.

"The more masculine you are, the more feminine she be-
comes."

The premise for Streetmeet was built on surprise.

The subjects (meaning *single females*) were accustomed
to being approached in clubs and bars. Their defenses were already up. Their skills at rejecting men like you honed through
years of practice. Not so in the street. Here they were vulnerable and unprepared. It sounded like we were being trained
to hunt deer. To leave a trail of metaphorical crumbs that
culminated at your crotch. On Prince Street organized groups
of three or four men practiced and recorded their attempts at
stopping and chatting up women and posted the results. Weekend workshops cost $1,500. You found your own accommoda-
tion and it was hinted that you should try to book somewhere
decent because this might well be where you repaired to with
your catch after a successful day's hunting. Streetmeet col-
laborated with certain high-end hotels in each city so discounts
could be arranged by quoting a password.

In other words, serious money was being made.

And you didn't even have to take part in the street sessions
to benefit from your membership. The spy-camera content was
uploaded and broadcast on a live feed where experienced com-
mentators from all over the world could critique your game

in real time. There were freeze-frames and slo-mo replays as strategies were discussed and scenarios reenacted. A panel of ridiculously attractive women analyzed your efforts and invited you to try your luck with them on their social media.

Grades were given, dates awarded, winners congratulated. It was comforting to believe that mastery of strategy and employment of guile was all that was required to distract and subdue the timeless Might of the Vagina.

IS YOUR BED HALF-EMPTY OR HALF-FULL?
#TheOxygenThiefDiaries

I had come full circle.

From being sick of the sight of Marian to feeling high at the thought of her.

But wasn't this just the recoil of a spent relationship?

The air displaced by its discharge.

Absence makes the heart grow fonder but unavailability makes it pound frantically against its rib cage. I emoted freely at her on-screen image but when she was actually present I was not so forthcoming. That was too much responsibility. I didn't really want her to love me because I knew I couldn't live up to it. Or return it. It was like being given a million dollars. It might be given freely but the unspoken expectation of repayment hung in the air.

Meanwhile I monitored and analyzed anyone who friended her on Facebook.

A bass player.

Probably nothing to worry about. Musicians, like writers, needed to build an audience.

But he was sensitive-looking. The type she'd go for. I imagined them making love and shuddered. Next up was a newly approved friend, a mousy looking guy from Montana. Probably nothing to worry about. A wannabe. Willing to play the long game. Just a platonic friend waiting to be promoted to lover. Like me? Neither of them seemed to have girlfriends from what I could see. A short-haired, stylish-looking older woman. A client? A mentor? A dyke? Had Marian retreated into lesbianism? I investigated each newly added friend and scrutinized their profiles for signs of interaction with Marian. This ritual could occupy an entire evening and if nothing else it gave me the illusion of having spent a few hours with her.

And where did all the tears come from? On more than one occasion the sound of someone crying woke me. It was me. Being out on the street was an effective deterrent but the moment I was alone it was a different matter.

Was that really love?

I was reminded of a guy in AA who had obsessed about his ex for years until one day he saw her on a bus and didn't even recognize her. He wasn't even remotely attracted to her. But even as he sat there looking at this stranger he yearned for the version of her he had created. He suddenly realized it was the yearning he was addicted to.

My biggest fear was that I'd have to watch as she sauntered toward me with her new man all happy and cuddling like we used to be and be introduced to him right there in the street as I scavenged for handouts.

And these days, meeting Marian was like being given a guided tour of a city I'd bombed from ten thousand feet. There was nothing left of a culture that had once been alive and bustling. The tragedy was all the more heartrending because the reason I'd bombed it in the first place was to protect myself from being attacked. But now there was nothing left for anybody. I had exceeded my brief. A weed killer that exterminates the flowers.

Meanwhile I was haunted by memories of her arriving up the stairs looking so achingly beautiful I almost shut the door to remove the pressure of having to deserve her. Such images and emotions came and went like days and nights inside me. Her emails had become so clinical. *If you have any interest in meeting up* . . . There was nothing about missing me or even hating me and then just in case I might glean any satisfaction from rejecting the invitation: *If not, that's okay too.*

The crying had become a regular bodily function. I learned not to resist it. I'd feel it approach. It would begin. I'd let it pass through me. I'd be relieved. Each onslaught was like an enormous sneeze in extreme slow motion. It would have been easier if she had died. At least then I wouldn't have had to think about her being so . . . available. I brewed up a new batch of water and salt over the phrase "loss of life," which for some reason persistently presented itself. The road trips, the breakfasts, the exhibitions, the days spent in bed. How easy it would be to just press *call*.

We'd catch up.

We'd agree that the previous two years had just been something we had to go through to realize how much we needed to be together. We'd put it down to inexperience and panic on my part. We'd plan trips to Ireland. We'd live together. Anywhere. I'd let my place go in the East Village and go to couple's therapy. (Yes, it was obviously a fantasy.) I'd insist on not using condoms to demonstrate my willingness to have children (definitely fantasy). I'd even pay off her student loan (babble from the sickbed). Why not? Hadn't she been instrumental in selling hundreds of my books? If not thousands? Daydreams such as these were sandbags against the desolation of never seeing her again. Or going to the other extreme there were more macabre imaginings, where she, unable to bear the idea of living without me, committed suicide. Her note forgiving me for dumping her culminated in a coup de grace in the shape of a postscript.

ps. feel free to use this note in your next book, it might provide some dramatic irony.

Oh how the briny tide would rise within me.

SPOONING IS GOOD, WOODEN SPOONING IS BETTER
#TheOxygenThiefDiaries

Isabel was incensed when a huge black woman threw one of Yoko Ono's onesies back in her face.

"Trash," the woman declared.

An exchange followed where Isabel invited the unfeasibly large woman to apologize.

"Why? Whatchew gonna do?"

The expectant gaze of abruptly stopped pedestrians fueled the tension.

"She's my friend," said Isabel.

"Okay then, why don' you do somethin'. Whatchoo gonna do? *Fat ass!*"

An onlooker groaned. Another tittered.

Isabel, looking overly pleasant in the way people often do before the fighting begins, casually reached under her display to retrieve a daggerlike pair of scissors that she now held low by her leg as she strode casually toward the bigger woman.

"I will cut you a new cunt."

She didn't sound angry so much as informative. Helpful even. And though the big black woman responded with a warning that she was a member of a gang, her body language was that of a very frightened member of a gang. A well-dressed girl browsing at my table had at first shrugged off the altercation as mere bravado. Her eye-roll inferred it was the kind of thing she had already seen so much of in her event-laden life. But now she began to slide imperceptibly sideways as if the sidewalk had lurched into life conveying her away. I increased the volume of my pitch as she diminished into perspective.

My phone writhed on the table.

FELLATIONSHIP

It was my screen name for Courtney. It had been at least a

month since I'd heard from her. As the alleged gang member raised a one-finger salute and the small crowd dissolved in disappointment, I was to learn of an altercation a different kind.

A third date with Courtney's Wall Street guy had gone terribly wrong when he mentioned that a French girl on datemedotcom had recommended my book to him. Courtney felt duty-bound to explain that someone she knew had created a fake profile of a sexy French girl in order to sell his book. The impression she hoped to impart was that she had been aware of the creation of this marketing idea and had been so uncomfortable with it she'd cut off all ties with its creator. On the one hand she'd associate herself with a notorious writer and on the other she'd distance herself by rejecting him.

But as soon as the Wall Street guy grasped the implications of what she was saying he simply got up from the table and walked out. She didn't need to tell me he'd bought the book because I remembered his messages very clearly. He was very much looking forward to meeting Françoise. He had invited me/us/her to dinner at Soho House. Courtney's intention had been to inoculate him against my disease but he saw her involvement as duplicitous. She began to cry as she related the story and I somehow understood that her fortieth birthday had come and gone. She went on to say that a week before this she'd met a journalist who had bought the book in the same way. I beamed with pride. I remembered him too. So keen was he to get into Françoise's pants he not only bought the book, he wrote a review of it.

A good one.

But presumably he wasn't worth exposing her involvement with me. Anyway, the reason she was confiding in me now was because she hoped the Wall Street guy had contacted me through Françoise's profile to vent or verify.

When I reminded her the profile had been shut down she begged me to reactivate it so that she could dictate a message to him. I usually stopped all communications the moment a book was bought because well, what else was there to say? She must have had high hopes for this guy because she wasn't thinking clearly. Realizing I wasn't going to be of any use to her she changed her tone.

"You need help, you know that right?"

She said it as if she suddenly remembered her responsibilities as a therapist. I was beginning to think she might have a point until she mentioned that she met the guy in the Cat and Mouse bar on Bleecker Street. This meant that when she let him know she was an acquaintance of mine and that I was the one who'd been fucking with his head by posing as Beautifullylit, she did so in the same bar featured at the end of the book.

His hopes of a tryst with an apple-assed French girl were dismantled in the most psychologically devastating manner possible. And by a trainee-therapist no less. He would be forgiven for thinking he was the subject of an underground experiment. Surely he was being secretly filmed. In fact the scenario was not unlike the last scene in the book. Was he in fact providing the raw material for a sequel, where he'd be humiliated in a similar way in the same bar? If he didn't end up shouting at traffic I wanted to read his memoir.

I might even publish it.

Of course I mentioned none of this to Marian when we met for dinner that night. She looked great in the way that girls do when you can't have them.

Fish and chips and black currant crumble pie in a London style café in Brooklyn. I'd brought along a Barry's tea bag because I preferred it to the British equivalent but when the well-intentioned waitress came back with two mugs of hot water instead of one, Marian waved hers away.

"Oh sorry," said the waitress, "I wasn't sure if you'd reached the tea-bag-sharing stage yet."

Marian looked at me pleadingly as if to say *please don't say anything embarrassing*. It was an unexpectedly heart-breaking comment. It suggested we looked like a couple on the brink of a romance as opposed to two exhausted partici-pants at the negotiating table.

But I was happy we at least *looked* like a couple.

She was still a little bit marshy-looking around the eyes. From crying? It was so good to see her. And more importantly it was so good to see that she was happy to see me. Her be-havior when she was with me was of a girl in love. Blushing needlessly, holding eye contact, giggling. I was very careful to keep my hands to myself and if she touched me even ac-cidentally I made sure I didn't respond. After all, we were just friends now, weren't we? And yet there was a torrent of emo-tion built up just off-screen waiting to be unleashed. Or at least there was for me. The relationship we'd had before no longer existed but we still shared a basic history.

There was something correct about being with her. It wasn't even sexual, it was, dare I say it, better than that. We'd been fused together. It was comforting and terrifying at the same time. And yet her body contradicted the notion of two friends just hanging out. Having a guy around who wants to fuck you had to be the best kind of friend a girl could have. He'd never argue, he'd never disagree. He'd always be subservient and pleasant. He'd listen to your every utterance hoping for clues to how to get in your pants. You'd never need to worry about him being unfaithful because all he thought about was fucking you.

Like having a man-sized pet.

She suggested we take bicycle repair lessons. This was something I'd benefit from too because I spent a fortune on repairs but it would have to be in her neighborhood. Of course it would. Everything would have to go her way. Her topic of conversation. Her every word intensely listened to. She got pissed when I couldn't understand what she'd said. Like there was something bigger at stake. As if her reputation as a great communicator had been slighted.

There were times when I couldn't help thinking that she just didn't *want* to be happy. But there was a sound she made when she was being unselfconsciously loving. It was like something I remembered her doing with her cat when she didn't think I was watching. It was a kind of baby language mush-mush sound that required the pursing up of her lips in mock kisses.

"Modge-modge-modge."

It was my reward for not talking.

• • • •

"Nah. That's okay . . . here you go."

A stressed-looking tourist tried to hand back the "free" CD he'd just been given by one, then two, then three, ultracool black guys who suddenly seemed to surround him. The CD was presented as a handout but as soon as it changed hands the recipient was encouraged to make a donation.

"Show me some love, bro."

It was at this point that futile attempts were made to hand it back. All three wore urban uniforms of backward baseball hats and skinny jeans worn ridiculously low across their buttocks, revealing brightly patterned boxer shorts. If the victims were a father and son the CD was handed to the son so that Dad had to pay for it. If there was a wife she was assured it was true what they said about black men.

The intention was to unnerve.

"Dude that's my shit right there, I put a lot of love into that."

The tourist smiled weakly.

"I've only got a twenty-dollar bill."

"Oh you need change? I gotchoo, bro."

Now it was just a question of how much you got back, if anything. I was watching an auto-mugging, self-robbery.

"Oh that's okay, just keep it."

"Aww thank you, bro . . . yo dad's gangsta."

And if he objected?

"Oh it's because I'm black? . . . Das okay, I get it."

Did the tourist really want to get into an altercation with a group of black males on a New York street? One of them noticed me watching him and waddled over.

"See how it's done, bro."

I was reminded of the manifesto of a famous ad agency in London.

> **WE DON'T SELL. WE MAKE PEOPLE WANT TO BUY**
> —Shearling, Woolcott & Simon

Hi Mr. Anonymous

My name is Lucretia and I wanted to say your book touched my deepest emotions. I read it in one sitting. I identified with the events in it and I saw myself in the main character's actions. Have you ever considered adapting your story for interpretive dance? If so, I'd love to show you some ideas . . . by the way did Aisling ever bring out her book? ps I attached a photo so you'll recognize me if we ever meet

Laughable of course but the perfect little ass suspended in midleap forgave the notion of a dance troupe from Nebraska attempting to communicate pub-brawls and self-loathing in

South London. One phrase in particular jumped out of her bio: *I'm serious about Christianity*. This required urgent clarification since it could seriously affect my chances of getting into her leotard.

I responded that I'd be interested to hear what she had in mind but I was far from devout and that she should know this before we went any further. Almost immediately she responded saying Midwestern theaters were often dependent on deeply conservative patrons and that her reference to religion was merely her way of ingratiating herself with them. I need not concern myself, she'd spent time with my books and had thoroughly enjoyed herself and she would very much like to meet me if that was at all possible. She would of course respect my anonymity.

She'd be in my neighborhood rehearsing the following week if that was convenient.

An ass like that on a body so flexible?

Drinnnnnng

There had been plenty of time to get ready but I intentionally cultivated a sort of feral nonchalance since opening the door shaved and showered would infer I gave a shit. But I immediately regretted my decision because standing there waiting to be asked inside was a very young girl with luminous white skin and a magnificently taut little body. There was something well-bred about her. Had we been in London I would have said she was of aristocratic stock. It seemed suddenly clear to me that this beautifully poised dancer was on a mission to mock me. In some corner of her hugely successful future I'd be relegated to an amusing misstep in an otherwise perfectly choreographed career.

She exuded such grace I felt the need to apologize.

"I'm sorry . . ." I said, referring to my very existence. "I just got back here myself."

She performed a faultless chassé into my apartment.

"Why? Where were you?"

Unsure if I was being scolded for not having made more of an effort, my answer emerged untrue.

"I was at an AA mee—"

"Good for you," she interrupted.

There hadn't been enough time to extract meaning from what I was about to say but she was already congratulating me.

She fist-bumped me with white knuckles.

"Oh," she said, noticing my laptop on the coffee table, "are we going to look at your reel?"

Again I was caught off guard.

She would have gleaned from my book that I had worked in advertising but only an insider would refer to a copywriter's compilation of commercials as his *reel*. I logged onto my advertising website and as she oohed and ahhed at how I'd spent my twenties and thirties, I fought heroically against an urge to ogle her blindingly white thighs while somehow managing to list the awards I'd won and the agencies I'd worked for.

She nodded vigorously, shaking herself for my benefit. Aware of my eyes on her she placed a theatrical open palm over her left breast as if to still her beating heart. Clasping her imaginary pearls. Satisfied with my qualifications as an adman she was ready now to hear about my literary achievements. But first, as if to incentivize me, I was given my first live look at what was on offer should my application be successful. Using the three strides it took to get to the bathroom, she made her ass wobble, shudder, and bounce.

A dancer indeed.

I feverishly googled my books and by the time she returned, a menu of results lay open for her inspection.

"Ooooh, you have a Wikipedia page."

"That's a good thing right?" I said, as if I had no idea how all this modern media stuff worked.

She turned to look at me. I could almost hear her count the ways I might be useful to her. Not wanting to give me a big head or perhaps amazed I didn't already have one she shrugged like she didn't know either. My silence encouraged her to project on me, project all over me. I heard my mouth go dry as I feigned interest in her job as an assistant to a high-end insurance company that investigated the veracity of claims.

"That sounds like an HBO series waiting to happen," I lied. The words crackled in my mouth, the saliva having evaporated in the heat of erotic anticipation. Or disappointment.

Her body language invited an approach.

How to close the gap between us. I was telling her that the stage adaptation I'd written, based on my book, was being read by the guy who won a Tony for his choreography of *Blackwatch* at St. Ann's Warehouse. She held my eyes, unblinking, inviting. *Blackwatch* being the name of a Scottish battalion deployed in Iraq. She smiled as if this was charm itself. Somehow I had started to blabber on about France's refusal to get involved in the Iraq War. She was a little perplexed by this but tolerant. I dry-mouthedly explained that supporters of the war campaigned to have the word *French* removed from the US vocabulary by popularizing terms like *freedom* fries and *freedom* kiss. Hearing the word *kiss*, those alabaster cheeks were invaded with color.

"Freedom *kiss*," she repeated as if remembering the name of an old friend. But her pronunciation was as dry and fear-filled as mine.

"What would happen if I moved a little closer?"

"Dunno," she said, watching me do exactly that.

She offered no encouragement but she didn't look unhappy about it either. Before I knew what was happening we were kissing very softly. Respectfully even. I began pecking on her lovely white neck and she cocked her head to allow me better access. Would she just tolerate me for a few more moments before announcing she had to leave? She had alluded to a dentist's appointment the next morning.

"You have a lovely neck," I whispered, trembling now with lust.

"Thank you," she said politely. "It's nice to have it kissed."

It was an invitation to continue.

Pushing her hair aside I nuzzled against her neck and continued to peck and nibble and even introduced the tip of my tongue. This was welcomed with a barely audible moan.

No more encouragement was needed.

I pulled her head back and planted my mouth on hers. This time it was much more open and soon we were tonguing away at each other as she began to undulate inside her clothing.

It was time to try for a tit.

Placing my palm over the breast pocket of her denim jacket I squeezed hard and she moaned with approval as her tongue stiffened against mine.

Opening a button of her jacket I slipped a hand inside her blouse, and nestling in a padded bra I found one and then two pert breasts peaked with expectant nipples. I squeezed one and to my delight she began bucking against me as if she was already coming. I allowed myself a secret moment of congratulation. I couldn't believe this was happening. If a nipple hadn't already erupted between my forefinger and thumb I might have pinched myself instead.

"Oohhhhhh."

We had unhurried gentle sex for the next two hours and it was fucking bliss. Her body was amazing; pale clean skin with no freckles anywhere. And believe me, I looked everywhere.

A snowscape with shrines.

"I can tell by the way you touch me that you appreciate my body."

It was true. I was hardly able to believe she was in the same bed as me but I hadn't realized she could tell. I caressed her like porcelain. Her ass especially.

She touched a clear droplet of precum emerging from the tip of my cock and blushed.

"See how wet you make me?" I said.

"What is it?" she asked shyly.

"Precum," I said, and her face fell open. Apparently it was a new concept to her. Was she playing innocent? She'd never heard of precum?

"It only happens when a guy is seriously . . . oooohhhh fuck."

She spread it over the head with her fingertip. Pleased with my reaction she placed her palm over the tip of my cock and began to agitate her closed hand over it until I stopped her. I wasn't ready to come yet. She smiled as if she understood and began again until I stopped her again. I liked the sensation of being brought to the edge and as she gripped my cock like a stick shift about to go into fourth, I stopped her again. Mock-exasperated she sighed and placed both palms flat on my chest, and straddling my left thigh began to grind her clean-shaven pussy against it.

She did this until she came.

It was my turn to learn a new concept.

She said it made her feel like the guy and the girl at the same time.

It made me feel like an onlooker.

As she lay beside me absentmindedly stroking my still-hard cock a thought occurred to her.

"That's definitely one way to make sure you get a second date. You know for sure I'll be coming back here tomorrow night."

I hadn't said I didn't want to come *at all*. And who said anything about tomorrow night? She was sure I was saving myself so that she'd return for more. So be it. I could wait till the next night. She was probably worth the wait. But now, perhaps because she had convinced herself we had embarked on something more than just a one-night stand, she felt the need to fill me in about her previous relationship.

As if I needed to be properly briefed.

She had been reluctant to move in with her wealthy, older boyfriend but his insistence seemed to make up for it. Five years later she was desperate to get out. Her preferred method for ending a relationship was to be unfaithful with a mutual friend. This technique had proved to be surgical in its efficiency since it removed two relationships at the same time. No one wanted to see any of the others ever again.

She probably felt comfortable telling me this since I had been such a self-confessed cunt in my books, she was always going to seem angelic in comparison. I thought she might have at least offered to feel guilty but it didn't even occur to her. Anyway all the men she met through the wealthy, older boyfriend were either too loyal or too afraid to betray him.

Her solution?

"I suggested we go to a sex party."

• • • •

Trundling my cart into position I noticed a mustachioed man occupying the spot usually occupied by Arrest-Me-Dante. He stepped back from his easel the better to regard his creation: an impressively accurate line drawing of Cafe Drill no more than a few strokes from completion. All manner of sophisticated cross-hatching and line-work conspired to produce this effortless impression of the pub's facade.

I had only just arrived but could see this guy had talent.

As I set up my table and positioned my signs I was interested to see if anyone else appreciated his level of artistry. He was an eccentric-looking man with a walrus mustache, not given to banter. He made no attempt to be social even as I made repeated attempts to catch his eye. He appeared foreign. A young couple approached and after shuffling around viewing both the artist and his drawing, nodded at each other before introducing themselves. After some gesticulating the artist removed the drawing from the easel, rolled it up, and handed it to the girl. She placed her hand over her mouth as if overwhelmed by the enormity of the gift but her other hand was already closed around it.

The artist held his palms together in a namaste gesture and the boyfriend took out his wallet. A just-drawn image like that, fresh from an artist's easel would probably fetch hundreds rather than tens of dollars and though it was impossible to see how much he received it didn't look like enough. The couple walked away very pleased with themselves and the boyfriend looked over his shoulder to confirm he really was going to get away with robbing the poor sad bastard.

The artist, satisfied that they were gone, reached into a folder and took out another drawing identical to the one he had just sold. The only difference was that the bottom right-hand corner was still white. Placing the photocopy on the easel he began scratching away at the unfinished corner just as he had done before. Tilting his head from side to side and squinting professionally he stepped back the better to regard his creation.

"Ha ha your knees, right?"

I looked around and there was Arrest-Me-Dante. He thought Tourette's was something to do with your joints. He pretended to get the joke and laughed knowingly at the good of it. I didn't have the courage to explain it to him since it would have exposed his lack of education to such a degree my attitude would be again called into question and I didn't want to contaminate the atmosphere around my table any more than I already had. The real reason he'd stopped by was to offer me a business opportunity. His idea was to lock bikes to lamp poles around the city with FOR SALE signs on them. When people called the number I would come and meet them with the key to the lock. He himself was too busy to do it because he had other tables to attend to but he thought this might be a cool thing for me. It was presented like he was doing me a favor. Like I needed something proper to do.

It was left unsaid that the bikes were stolen and that my phone number would be posted above them. Arrest-Me-Anonymous. Before he walked away I saw him take some money from the artist. Rent presumably for the location that matched the angle of the drawing.

• • • •

Ping

"Hope you like lingerie."

Lucretia had promised to return that night and *perform for me* but I was to be repeatedly cock-blocked by circumstance. First there was an email to say she was running late and it would be more like eight PM and then another at 8:35 PM: *I don't know if you've been getting my texts but I sent you this.*

Attached was a JPEG, not, as I had hoped, of her milky-white self reclining in thigh-highs and garter belt, but a glossy looking promotional photo of a toilet disinfectant. The clear plastic pack displayed two navy spheres under italicized letters announcing the brand's name.

BLUE BALLS.

Ever since my French ex-girlfriend Yvette had made it clear that coming before her was a crime punishable by castration, death, exhumation, and recastration, I had trained myself not to ejaculate prematurely. I became convinced that lasting longer meant more pleasure for all concerned, but the moment Lucretia thought I was doing it deliberately she seemed insulted. After all, if she was the cum-summoner she believed herself to be, how could I possibly refrain from erupting all over the vicinity?

Drinnnnng.

In the end she turned up at ten thirty in a lime-green dress that looked like something out of a Doris Day movie. She was probably wearing the mind-melting lingerie underneath.

"You probably think I'm wearing my outfit under this but there was no way I could do that."

She had promised she'd come and *perform for me* and now I was starting to see what she meant. This would be a sort of audition. So much so, I might have been a theater employee admitting her through the stage door. It felt like I was there to facilitate her performance, not to benefit from it. It didn't help that the bags she carried, brimming with fabric and cosmetics, gave her the impression of a girl moving in. I watched stupefied as the bathroom door closed behind her. Something until that moment, I wasn't even aware it could do. Within seconds she was out again and handing me something.

"This goes under the mattress in an X shape. You'll see what I mean."

She disappeared again. I was holding an interwoven mass of black canvas straps, each culminating in one of four Velcro cuffs. It was a harness for tying a person to a bed. She was going to tie me down so that my wrists and ankles were akimbo like a confused, stumpier, bald version of the famous Leonardo da Vinci drawing. She popped her head out of the bathroom and I must have looked completely confused, still standing there in the same spot staring at the harness in my hands. Her slow, deep, patient inhalation would have resulted in a disappointed sigh if she hadn't used the captured air to speak.

"Come on, I'll show you."

Snatching the mass of straps from me, she led the way into my bedroom. I could have been a sulky uncooperative child as she lifted my mattress into the air and suddenly we were both staring at neat formations of cardboard boxes where six thousand yet-to-be-sold copies of my books were stored.

This was unexpected.

Maybe the harness was a ruse to investigate the horrors lurking under men's mattresses. A quick way of airing subjects that might otherwise remain dormant for years.

"Why are there boxes under your bed?"

The question was asked without judgment.

"They're books."

"Your book?"

"*Books* plural," I corrected her. I had written two books, I was not about to have one of my children snubbed. It obviously hadn't occurred to her that I was self-published. She had just assumed that if I had been reviewed online and had a Wikipedia page, then I must be a proper writer worthy of her best game.

"Oh," she said, visibly disappointed but still not ready to be distracted from the matter in hand.

She remembered herself.

"Okay, this goes here and this goes down here, it should make an X under the mattress."

I think she hoped I was bright enough to handle this while she got on with the most important part of the show, her appearance in it. But I was still confused. Was I going to tie her up, or was she going to tie me up?

"Oh, and I'll need that robe you were wearing the other night."

This too was unnerving since it meant she'd been taking inventory. She had imagined herself in the comfortable embrace of my robe? In my apartment? My fur-lined lair was already part of her entitlement? I felt invaded. Lifting the mattress was like looking up my skirt. I didn't want her touching anything in my place apart from my cock.

Meanwhile I was the stagehand, dresser, background artist, and audience-to-be.

"And I need you naked," she added matter-of-factly before closing the bathroom door again.

I was happy at last to hear the word *naked*.

Up to that point she might have been a neighbor requesting the loan of a shovel. It was the first indication that something sexual was imminent. She popped out again, this time wearing my bathrobe, and seeing me naked on the bed carefully closed the Velcro cuffs around my wrists and ankles and as easily as that I was rendered limbless. It was already eleven thirty and I was so exhausted I was afraid to close my eyes in case I fell asleep. Lifting my head to look for her I was just in time to see my favorite black towel land over my face and everything go black.

In the darkness I felt the ice-cold water of paranoia trickle down my back. Was she quietly letting her accomplices in to torture me for my PIN? I'd heard that they withdrew the maximum daily amount moments before midnight and then the following day's maximum amount again just after midnight. It would explain why she arrived so late . . . What was taking her so long? It wasn't so much the darkness that gnawed at me as the uncaring way the towel was thrown.

No caresses or coos as she did it.

I began to worry in earnest. I mean there I was naked and tied up in my own apartment by a complete stranger. People were murdered in situations more pleasant than this. From somewhere inside the blackened pit in which I found myself I heard the wail of a lone clarinet. It was joined by the nasal voice of a thirties-era singer crooning ever so politely about flowers. Presumably it was coming from her iPhone. I felt the mattress shudder beneath me as the towel fluttered away to reveal, stretching upward into perspective, a living breathing alabaster-bodied monument to Lucretia standing astride me in black nylon thigh-highs, garter belt, and corset. The long green stem of a red rose clenched between her teeth. Her paper-white thighs all but glowed between the dark stretches of black lace. Her panties were just see-through enough to show the vertical line of her hairless pussy. Suddenly being tied down was the perfect excuse to savor the mirage that hovered above me.

She turned sideways more professionally than I would have liked and tilted her head with a half wink as if this was taking place on a bed in Nebraska. A place where female sexuality was funded and informed by the Patriarchy. Where the man was not supposed to know that the girl probably had some serious daddy issues or that she was a terrible actress. Even in normal conversation her eyes opened far too wide with mock interest, her concern ridiculously disproportionate for someone she'd just met. And now here she was giving her man everything she had. Her dance skills, her acting skills, her body, her very self. It might have been an act of domination or an act of submission, but it was still an act.

It was also a wet dream come true.

She folded herself in half so I could more fully under-stand the perfectitude of her ass. She took the rose from her mouth and sprinkled its petals over me, making sure a good proportion of them landed teasingly on my nodding cock and groaning balls. The routine that followed was like the dream sequence in a Midwestern musical where the mild-mannered bank clerk fantasizes about the virginal school mistress. The bit in the romantic comedy that had to be inserted to give the men in the audience something for their ticket price.

And yet, there was nothing vulnerable about it. The lin-gerie was like body armor. I didn't even feel naked because I knew it was all just playacting. She sat astride me and yes, I was hard, but she was so focused on getting her movements right and bending so carefully and stretching so eloquently I felt like a prop in one of her YouTube videos. The ones she used for auditions. My poor stiff cock was just another ver-sion of a "thumbs-up" on Facebook. She then thrust her pant-ied pussy right up to my face, and though it was marvelous to witness that pouting girlish pudendum through the basque, no heat emanated from it. She dangled a lace drawstring that held the sides of the panties together, letting the ribbon fall across my face, presumably to tempt me with the possibility of catching it between my teeth and unwrapping the prize. But then she took it away again. This was intended as a teaser for what was yet to come but I couldn't shake the feeling that I was being shown around the interior of her previous relation-ship. Was it her ex she saw when she looked down on me from behind her half-hidden treasures? She scooched backward now until she was sitting rather heavily on my embattled balls.

The awful music continued and her routine now demanded she lean so far back her head was between my feet and the only thing visible was her panty-veiled slit. She held this position for a few beats, crushing my balls with the lovely hard mounds of her ass until she began the slow athletic return forward with another long-stemmed rose between her teeth.

Her arc continued uninterrupted until it culminated petals-first on my lips in a romantic scent-infused kiss. I would have wiped my mouth had I not been tied up. Still with the rose between her teeth and still with the imitation Charles Aznavour playing she now arranged herself into a very painful-looking position that required her right ankle to be placed somewhere beyond my right ear while she leaned so far forward that it seemed as if we both should listen very carefully to that same ankle. Her hair cascaded, unbearably ticklish across my face. I could feel her entire body shudder as she held this position for one, two, three, four, and five seconds before using up what must have been the remaining dregs of her stamina to inhale enough breath to whisper two words.

"The splits."

So this is what it felt like to have a tight-assed little dancer do the splits on you. She was showing Daddy what she'd learned at school. Here was proof the tuition fees had been put to good use. You see? Dance wasn't just some useless waste of time and money where gay men and girls pranced around in tutus all day, it had its functional side too.

The music ended.

If I'd been sitting in the front row of a Nebraskan theater I'd have understood that the climax of the number was the image of her aesthetically pleasing body in provocative lingerie, performing a technically perfect iteration of the splits on a tied-down male. It had all the elements of what would have been scandalous to a theater full of locals but I was just waiting on her to finish so I could resume thumbing her butthole. Its little beige mouth had been cooing to me all day.

Without the music she was scriptless and free to ad-lib. So, pressing the rose against my balls, she trailed the petals over the tip of my cock. This was maddeningly wonderful. It felt soft and cool like the lips of a pussy, but a pussy with more lips and folds than normal. She lay alongside me, comfortable that I couldn't resist, and began to flick her fingers over the head. Her open mouth hovered over mine, not kissing it, just hovering over it; the only freedom afforded me now seemed to be gathered in my tongue and I wanted to fuck her face with it, but each time I tried she pulled her head back, taunting my efforts. This was more like it. She *was* an evil little cunt after all.

Now I was rock hard and very fucking happy.

How had I managed to get this wet dream to happen? Why was she here doing this? I couldn't see what I had done to earn it. What app had I inadvertently downloaded that enabled me to 3-D print this scenario? There it was in front of me. My ideal. This is what it looked like. This is what it smelled like. Roses. This was not a dress rehearsal. This was all my hopes and dreams condensed and suffused with life.

She licked a finger and used it to drip spit onto my shuddering cockhead. I stared at her in disbelief. The corny theater act had thrown me off guard. It was as if a cynical little Russian whore had pushed the Nebraskan out the door and taken over. And this little fucker was *bored*. She even checked her messages while lying pussy-down on my smashed cock. I was speechless. I felt so incapable of artifice at that moment, if she had asked for my PIN I would have happily given it up—no need to torture me with jump leads and pliers.

I felt all responsibility leave me in those few moments. My self had been spirited out of me. I had never let go of control to that degree before. Was this what it was like to be a submissive? I had to admire the sleight of hand involved in creating the corn-fed diversion. It led me to believe I was dealing with an amateur. As I laughed up my imaginary sleeve she picked my metaphorical pocket.

The vexing little bulge of white flesh over the rim of her thigh-highs, the sidelong glances through strands of black hair monitoring the accuracy of her intentions, confirming her hits. And then as I lay there with the eye of my cock crying real tears she uncuffed one wrist and left the room.

"I'll be out here looking at your porn."

This stunned me of course, because now I wanted more. Much more. Again I was being shown what it would be like to be with this girl. How a relationship could be stretched out over years with techniques like this. If it was Sunday night in Nebraska and I had to work the next day, I'd be malleable for the following week hoping for a repeat of what had just happened.

What *had* just happened?

She was experienced enough to know that I only needed one uncuffed hand to free myself. I was impressed and perplexed by this. Should I follow her? Was she pissed at me?

Had she just received a text that changed her opinion of me? I imagined she had asked her high-powered detective friends to look into me, and even as she lay on my balls received the news that I was in fact ten years older and millions of dollars poorer than I purported to be. Was it because I hadn't applauded? My hands were tied. Should I have gushed with appreciation? Ejaculated even? What sort of a man retains control in the face of such eroticism? I undid the rest of the Velcro straps, ensuring the ripping sound was loud enough for her to be in no doubt as to what was happening.

But she already knew. She was completely in control. When I appeared around the doorway she was sitting rather demurely on the couch, her face lit respectively by the dark and light of the on-screen fucking. Her expression was anything but lustful. Forlorn maybe.

"I brought a dildo in the brown bag," she said as if it was a pint of milk she'd forgotten to put in the fridge.

Seconds later I found myself holding a friendly-looking dildo no bigger than my own modest-sized cock. I was grateful she hadn't brought a twelve-inch monstrosity to dwarf anything I could muster. I wanted to thank her for her consideration but it came out wrong.

"This would look great in your butthole."

I was trying to regain some sexual currency.

185

"That was the idea," she said without even looking away from the screen. It was as if this had all happened to her before somewhere. She actually wanted it in her ass? No shock, no embarrassment, no feigned resistance. How was I to show up on this girl's sexual radar? There were various sections to choose from on the website and I invited her to click on one. She sat straight-backed in perfect debutante's posture as if waiting to be offered a candy.

As if reaching for it herself would be unthinkably rude. So mannerly and sluttish at the same time. Without hesitation she said:

"That one, that one, and . . . that one." She was voracious.

A bonfire requiring all the wood in the vicinity.

My best idea was to bring her back into the bedroom and tie her up so I could provide her with some semblance of what she'd done to me. Meanwhile she might have been shoe shopping. This girl was going to require a lot of sex. Not just my usual two-handed, fingers-at-the-front and thumb-from-behind routine that probed her G-spot and got me out of having to fuck her. For her this would merely be an appetizer. In her corset and garter belt she looked like a turn-of-the-century prostitute in an American TV movie. That is to say the sexuality looked cosmetic. Not emanating from within her but pasted on the surface. There had been a moment where she'd gone off-menu and I witnessed the arrival of the very bad girl within her. But she had now reverted to automatic. How could I summon that nasty little cunt again?

I led her back to the bed and cuffed her like she had cuffed me, only now the cuffs had shifted and she was able to reach her left hand with her right.

"That's no good."

She was obviously annoyed. Like I was the understudy who could never grasp the subtle pressures of being an erotic deity. The basic realities required to tease a fantasy into existence were beginning to weigh heavy on us both. As her annoyance began to interfere with my hard-on I felt more like a manservant than a lover. Was it a Nebraskan thing? The result of the Midwestern class system? Once she was suitably restrained I stroked and teased her unbelievably smooth young body.

Reddish-purple hues morphed and merged just below the surface of her milk-colored skin like she was a human lava lamp. I could have lingered there all night doodling on her with my fingertips. She was less poised now with her hair unkempt and slightly glistening with sweat. She strained and wriggled against the cuffs as I began to tickle her. She obviously hated this but I couldn't resist because the more she wriggled the harder it made me. There was no way for her to correct the maddeningly ticklish wayward strands of hair that fell across her face and there was no way I was going to help. I was in control now. I reveled in the idea that she was being forced outside the norm she'd built for herself. Her completely bald pussy showed no evidence of hair having ever been present. It looked like she'd spread her legs too wide and the skin there had torn.

I inserted a finger and contrary to expectations found she

was sopping wet. It was like dipping a finger in warm honey. She didn't moan in acknowledgment so much as sob quietly, like this was the final humiliation. Her legs began to kick almost comically, frog-like, trying to swim away from each new thrust of my finger. Two fingers caused the swimming to increase in intensity as her arms pulled downward against their restraints and her legs spasmed and kicked against theirs. No more convoluted choreography and no more frozen smiles, now she was filthy, feral, and unguarded. She looked like a vicious little bitch capable of murder if that was what was required. A dirty-minded clever ambitious pretty twenty-one-year-old little whore.

And I liked it.

This was the real Lucretia. The girl whose dad disappeared when she was twelve. Who admitted to fucking best friends to get out of relationships. Who was amazed and didn't really believe me when I said I didn't find it awkward not to drink. Who openly rejoiced when I made references to her ass. Who had a reservoir of sexual lava bubbling inside her waiting to erupt.

It was humbling though because I knew I couldn't satisfy this. Not with fingers and not with tongue and not with anything else I could summon. This girl, the one darting sidelong glances at me as if to inquire, *You really want to wake this up?*

I heard myself asking about the sex party.

I couldn't help it.

She was tied up and interrogation seemed apt.

I told myself it would excite her too but the truth was I wanted details. Did it take place in someone's home? Was everyone naked? Were there more men than women? Was there a fuck machine? I would have asked for pictures if I hadn't thought it would totally freak her out.

"I've only been to the one," she said as if this meant she was hardly qualified to speak on the subject. But it was one more than I'd been to. The layout she said was like a nightclub with couches and a bar in the front. There was a curtained area at the back marked NO CLOTHING. Once entered you were basically consenting to the idea of being approached by strangers for sex. Couples were already fucking when she and her ex walked in. There were others present, all of them men, standing around watching. It occurred to me that even at a sex party there was still a very real possibility of being rejected.

Rejected naked.

"I'm not going to come," she said matter-of-factly, and I knew without being told that I was expected to uncuff her and stop.

Within seconds she was sitting on the edge of my coffee table still in her lingerie but any flush of orgasm or passion had been replaced by a pale normalcy that I should have been more attentive to. This line of questioning was not doing anything for her. I knew I was testing her patience but since she'd made so much of my not coming the night before I was confident she'd at least want to witness the phenomenon before she left.

"So you started having sex with your boyfriend while these other guys watched?"

"I invited one of them to join us."

"So while you were having sex with your boyfriend you invited one of the naked guys to come over and join in?"

She nodded.

"I had already told him I wanted to see what it would be like to be double-penetrated."

It must have been devastating for the incumbent boyfriend. After all, it hadn't been his idea. She had decided to go to a sex party ostensibly to get fucked by two guys at the same time but in reality planning to dump the guy she'd been with for the previous three years. This way she'd not only be unfaithful to him, she'd make him an accessory to the act.

"And was it fantastic?"

I should have changed the subject but somehow I needed to know more.

"Well, it was a relief to be fucked by someone else."

She said this as if it was what she had been resisting saying all along.

"But then I only went to that one, so I don't know how they normally work."

"And how come you were so confident the stranger wouldn't refuse you?"

She looked at me, the naked and doughy middle-aged man sitting beside her, to see if I was joking.

"There's no way a guy is going to refuse," she said with the confidence of a beautiful young dancer wearing lingerie.

"I should warn you, you better get moving because all this talk is . . . well, the balloon is losing its air."

She stood up and strode into the bathroom and then into

the bedroom and before I knew what was happening she was standing there completely naked.

"So are you going to fuck me?"

She was acting like I had deliberately avoided fucking her. Which I had but I was only holding out because I thought the longer it took me to come the more pleasure there would be for both of us. Because when I came it was all over.

"Yes of course, are you kidding me? But I'm just afraid that as soon as I put my cock in that tight little pussy I'll come immediately."

"You're holding back for you. Not for me," she said, the flush returning to her cheeks. "It makes it better for you, not for me. I need you to fuck me."

She thought for a second.

"Why *won't* you fuck me? What's all this . . ." She made a disgusted face as she mimicked my fingering movements and caresses. She was standing there naked, dancing almost, mimicking me.

"Is it because of all those years of drinking? Is that it? It makes sense."

She was inferring I couldn't get it up but she wasn't going to say it.

"Well let's try again then," I said, determined to be engaged in the act of *trying* to have sex rather than standing around talking about it. But she was already shoving a foot into one of her sparkly flat white ballet shoes and the enormity of what this meant exploded inside me.

"You're leaving?"

"Yes. I'm sorry. I'm not in love with you, I broke up with the last guy because he was not the man I'm going to marry. He was seventeen years older than me. I'm trying to improve on that. You're in your forties right?"

I nodded warily. She was fully dressed now and I was naked and flaccid.

Not a good look for me.

"I was kissing you in there and I realized I don't love you."

There was another pause now before she continued: "I only broke up with him two months ago."

My only hope now was that such a vulnerable revelation might lead to more sex.

"That's . . . very recent," I said.

But she was merely offering it to me as an escape route. She was willing to take the blame for the tension between us but the truth was I had been unable to give her the fucking she required and she wouldn't stay where she wasn't wanted.

The idea of me holding back from coming was insulting to her. If I was really attracted to her I wouldn't be able to control myself. It shouldn't be so easy to resist her. I was negging her, inferring she was less sexy than she actually was. It was like acknowledging a joke was funny but refusing to laugh. Something for which I would judge a person very harshly. It was a form of stinginess. I had become an emotional as well as financial miser.

She had probably decided to leave well before she announced it because she'd already managed to gather up her harness and cuffs. How had she managed to do this without me noticing? It had been a two-person job to get the fucking thing installed but presumably retrieving it was easier. All the sexual paraphernalia squirreled away well in advance of her announcement and when she did announce it she did so in a way that preempted debate.

After a heavy sigh she decided to clarify.

"I wanted to get double penetrated but one of the guys went soft."

"Oh," I said, terrified she was going to accuse me of the same thing. "That's actually insulting, considering how beautiful you are."

But secretly I understood what her ex must have been going through. He was expected to continue fucking her even as he felt the cock of a stranger nudge against her butthole and yes, his balls. Their cocks would have been separated by a membrane no thicker than a heavy-duty condom. I'd go soft at the very thought of such a scenario. And having established that he had lost his erection are we not to assume she went ahead and fucked the stranger not just in front of him but *instead* of him.

How humiliating. How vicious of her to have set that up. She had already told me the intention behind the sex party was to find a guy to fuck that she could use as emotional leverage to end the relationship. But now it was beginning to sound like she had sprung a sexual ambush on him. The sex party was the perfect scenario to achieve a number of goals. Try out some new cock. End her relationship. Wordlessly demonstrate her reason for ending the relationship.

"I'm sorry, I know you're a writer and you like to talk

about things and we can meet for a coffee later if you like, but I can't do this right now, I'll take my Mormon self out of here."

The Mormon reference threw me.

"I'm not as wild as I pretend to be, I was brought up very conservative. I can't do this. I thought I could."

My mind raced trying to think of something that would at least encourage her to stay and talk about it.

"Can I at least have a hand job?"

I was incredulous at the idea of all that sex being taken away in bags and ballet shoes. She looked at me standing there naked and nervous like I had just stopped her in the street.

"I don't think so," she said kindly. "Especially since you seem to like not coming so much."

She twirled once in the open doorway and when it closed she was gone.

I SUFFER FROM PREMATURE EJACU . . . OH SHIT SORRY
#TheOxygenThiefDiaries

Burrrrrrr

Later that night I was busy trying to externalize the frustration sown by Lucretia when my phone vibrated on the bed beside me and my poor embattled hard-on twitched instinctively at the name on the screen.

MARIAN

She had some fucking nerve calling me after ignoring me for . . . was it two months? I summoned one or two of the more sexually explicit memories we'd created in the same bed on which I lay and took great pleasure in letting her go to voice mail. For an ill-informed millisecond I thought I might call her back and convince her to have phone sex but I somehow made myself hear sense over the roar of my midriff—we had never been compatible on the phone.

Instead I selected from my mental library a memory of her knelt astride me with her apple ass basically in my face letting me caress it while shamelessly showing me the open seam of her carefully curated cunt. Meanwhile my remembered Marian stroked and teased my cock in the same way I was now stroking and teasing it. Ahh yes it was a classic moment. And all the more erotic for her knowing the effect the pose had on me. She always knew *exactly* the effect she had on me. Sometimes when I couldn't come she'd take my hand and just place it on her ass knowing from experience that this would finish me off in seconds.

"Ohhhhh arghhhhhh arghhhhhhhhhh . . ."

An obscene montage of freshly occurred Lucretian moments superimposed themselves onto some of my favorite moments with Marian to inspire an eruption from somewhere deep behind my balls, releasing what felt like a startled flock of doves into the night. In my just-come state her voice message was more soothing than I had a right to expect.

Fittingly enough the first word out of her mouth was *Sorry* but then her voice trailed away into something muffled and half-said, which, after not hearing her voice for so long, was mildly panic-inducing as it seemed I was to be robbed of my moment, but then she returned as if breaking surface from underwater: ". . . I was traveling for some of it, but anyway I don't have a lot to say for myself, I just wanted to call and apologize and I miss you too. Hope you're well."

I miss you *too*? This was her reply to a voice mail I'd left four months earlier.

I wanted to be elated.

I felt like I should be.

But this was just the same old bullshit. Wasn't it?

Within seconds I was able to convince myself that the reason she hadn't contacted me for so long was because she found it too painful to hang out with me. She didn't need to apologize, I was just happy she called. But I decided not to respond because I couldn't bear the idea of getting her voice mail and then the agonizing countdown to her response. If it came at all. I was sick of being rejected by her. I resolved not to fall back into it all again. I would find someone new. Maybe I could still salvage Lucretia. But then, rather eerily, as if sensing my reticence a text arrived reiterating the sentiments in the voice mail: *I mean it, if you have an inclination for dinner some time, fish and chips, on me, if not, that's okay too.* It was such a luxury to hear from her twice in the same day. It felt significant. It *was* significant. Wasn't it?

Even so, I savored the luxury of snubbing her. I so rarely got the chance.

• • • •

On one particularly cold and miserable day the sky was the same color as the pavement and just as empty. I was hopping from foot to foot to try to keep warm. Appearing from around the corner a vaguely familiar-looking man accompanied by a stylish-looking Asian girl. When they got closer I could have sworn it was Val Kilmer. He was presumably staying at the Laurence Hotel.

He squinted at my signs.

"So what's all this about?" he said, picking up my book and flicking through it.

As I began my spiel he looked everywhere but at me. It was as if he was waiting for me to recognize him. I stuck to my pitch until he interrupted me, probably out of boredom.

"A friend of mine had a pottery stand like this in New Mexico, where I live, I sat out with him one day and he made five thousand dollars in an afternoon."

"You're very welcome to sit out here with me," I said.

It was the first time his eyes met mine. For a moment I thought he might say something like "You wish," but he just looked away, offering me a new angle of his famous face. Like I was a camera. He was undeniably chubbier than I remembered him in *Heat* and *The Doors* but it was him all right. The Asian girl looked longingly into her phone as if she would have preferred to climb into it rather than wait for Val to finish up with his latest distraction.

"Anonymous, huh? I get it. What would you want for something like this?"

"A mere twenty dollars," I said, already feeling the heat of self-laceration that I was actually in the process of selling a book to Val Kilmer and I had let the battery in my phone die. If all I ever got from being out on that fucking street was a photo of Val Kilmer buying my book it would have all been worth it. But no, it was not to be. I would have preferred if he hadn't stopped at all. Now I would have to spend the rest of my life regretting the fact I didn't get a photo of what was the equivalent of a UFO landing to ask for directions.

"Bit steep for a paperback isn't it?"

But even as he said it he was already turning to the Asian girl, who was fishing out a $20 bill from her anime-festooned purse. I couldn't even muster a smile, I wanted to leap out of myself, depart the flaccid casing I referred to as myself, and leave it there on the street deflated, crumpling, evacuated. But I had nowhere to go, no one else to be. I had been handed a gift from the universe only to have it snatched away by an asshole that looked very much like me. *Look at what you almost had,* I heard a sarcastic voice say. A trolley of delicacies trundling past a starving man. Maybe I had hallucinated the entire thing. A celebrity mirage brought on by attention deficit.

Val handed the book to his friend and walked away.

Opening her bag and slipping the book inside gave her the perfect excuse to wait till he was three paces ahead before following him. The moment they disappeared around the other corner I felt an urge to shout. I should have at least pitched my *Beowatch* idea to him. I could have dressed it up as a movie if he was even slightly interested. Relocate it to the Gulf of Mexico. As Greenwald terrorizes the American holiday-makers it's up to the local team of lifeguards to step up. Couplets that borrow from LA rap. Set it in a post-apocalyptic future. Surreal. Kitsch. Timely. Educational. Kendrick Lamar. Donald Glover. Rooney Mara. Dakota Fanning. Michael Fassbender. Marion Cotillard. Val Kilmer. Hoffa would have a cameo of course. Like the wizened Robert Shaw character in *Jaws*, he'd seen it all before. Hats-And-Socks-Tom, who was packing up early, had a question.

"That was whatshisface right?"

I nodded.

"Tell me you got a picture?"

I looked at him as if to say, *Do I look like a fucking idiot?*

• • • •

I had to hide how happy I was to see her.

After all, it had been a while and I still didn't know if there were going to be any surprises.

Carefully, we told each other how we were doing.

"I'm not going to pretend I didn't see that award you got," I said, and instead of acknowledging the enormity of the compliment, i.e., that I was willing to admit I'd been checking her Facebook page, she began to complain about how horrible it had been creating a series of sculptures for the Holocaust Museum. How she'd had to work on-site four floors below ground, and how there were no toilets and once down there she'd had to listen to recordings of survivors describing the horror of what they'd been subjected to over and over and over again. Within minutes of us sitting down she was on the verge of tears. Compared to her, I felt so healthy and happy I might have been Californian.

She said she'd made $30,000 out of it.

"I know you make much more than that, but for me, I've never had that kind of money."

I hadn't updated my expression since her unburdening seconds earlier, so I was still looking sympathetic when she told me how much she'd made. Suddenly I was guilty of denigrating the sum she had suffered so much to make. And not only that but she'd had to split it three ways. I didn't dare ask why. I already knew about her existing business partner but there was now a third? She seemed too delicate to withstand any sort of normal conversation. All that could be hoped for was an imitation of two people talking. And so that is was what I strove for.

"I'm a mess," she said.

But she looked pretty fucking good to me. In her artsy tweed jacket and shorts over tights she looked like a girl I'd be proud to be on a date with. I got the impression she was coming on to me but the feeling couldn't be trusted. The last thing I was going to do was make any sort of romantic overture, not after all the beatings I'd already received. After dinner we strolled aimlessly through the dappled streets of Park Slope. The fact that we were walking in the opposite direction of her apartment indicated a willingness on her part to spend more time with me than was necessary. And was she walking closer to me than usual or was I imagining it? All the other times we'd met she was overly conscious of the space between us. As she repositioned a wayward strand of hair, her sleeve brushed gently against mine, making me aware of her famous personal scent. It smelled like home.

I wanted to hide behind her hair.

A hunted animal behind a waterfall.

I realized I was happier in that moment than I'd been since . . . well, since the last time we'd met. I wanted to say something but it was too risky. I might open up yet another can of Blurt 'n' Cry. I needed to get away so I could leave on a good note. Or at least a note I had played as opposed to continuously dancing to her tune.

But she wasn't ready to go yet.

It seemed important that I be told she'd instructed her sister to forbid their mother from calling on her birthday. She didn't want sympathy for being alone on such a special night. Surely this was her way of letting me know she was still single and that there was still a chance we could get back together. She also mentioned casually that the lease expired on her apartment the following month and she'd be looking for a new place. My cue to invite her to live with me?

"Oh and Derry says hello."

This was a huge vote of confidence.

A proxied greeting from her sanctified sister was as good as a papal blessing. When we eventually got back to where I'd locked my bike she was up for even more.

"So, what would *you* like to do now?"

This inferred that up to that point, I hadn't been doing what I wanted. An accurate assessment because what I really wanted to do was paste her against the wall and fuck three years of frustration out of me and into her but there was no way I was letting that beast loose.

"I better get going," I said, grateful that I could pretend I had to get up early to get a spot on Prince Street. She shuffled her feet and stepped forward into the warmest hug we'd had in a very long time. I patted her back, afraid to breathe, in case I inhaled her mind-bending scent and begged her to take me home with her. I leapt on my bike and rode away. When I got home there was an email from her: *Sorry if I seemed a little off tonight . . . I just had a breakup that was shocking and unexpected.*

LESBIAN IN MAN'S BODY SEEKS GAY MAN IN WOMAN'S BODY
—Craigslist, BDSM/Men Seeking Women

I felt an overwhelming, self-preserving urge to put something, or more accurately, someone between me and the realization that Marian had been in a relationship. I was terrified of finding out more. If she'd just broken up with someone it meant she'd been in a proper relationship of some kind. If this was true I'd need someone to fall back on. But I wasn't going to waste time with *proper* girls anymore. It was exhausting having to pretend you wanted a relationship just to get laid. It was a waste of time. Love made the sex better but it required so much lying it wasn't worth it. I'd venture into the BDSM side of things. At least they were honest.

They just wanted sex. Unconventional sex.

I was late for a lunchtime meeting with a twenty-two-year-old stylist called Caitlin. Unexpectedly coquettish, she actually blushed when I sat down to what quickly turned into an interview to decide whether we'd have sex once a week, preferably after nine PM, in my apartment, where I'd be expected to spank, paddle, and whip her with equipment she'd provide.

Never before was I so nervous before an appointment.

In her photos she was raven-haired and pale skinned and even if she didn't live up to them in real life, the explicit sexual self-assurance of her language and the clarity of her intentions was worth investigating.

I became tortured by the idea that I'd fumble what was certain sex. On a normal date there was no predetermined menu of sexual activity. You weren't shown in advance what you might not get. But in this case, what I was being interviewed for was so clearly delineated I'd be left in no doubt what I had failed to achieve.

I was relieved she asked questions because it removed the pressure to converse. She received my answers with slow, careful nods as if wary that a sudden movement might startle me into running away. Her general demeanor inferred I was doing well. All her questions related to my writing. She was obviously not about to be spanked, paddled, or whipped by anyone who wasn't up to her creative standards. I mentioned I'd written a play and because she continued to show interest in it I ended up telling her the entire plot. I had never been so tense about pitching a story because I knew that if it was well received I would be rewarded with the sort of sex I had until then only fantasized about. When I finished talking she gave no indication that she found the twist at the end in any way clever or even interesting.

Instead she began telling me about herself.

As a freelance stylist who provided props and clothing for shoots and plays she worked mostly with theater directors and photographers. In fact she had just wrapped on a job for Creepyhehe's new line of gothic lingerie.

"I'm wearing a sample under my coat."

Her eyes held mine for a significant second before we both looked up to see that my hand was in the air calling for the check. Where had that confidence come from?

My cock was in charge now.

As we strolled across the park she repeatedly brushed against me, and each time she took longer to pull away again. I decided I might as well be rejected here as anywhere and stopped her not far from where Marian and I had first kissed. She let her coat fall open and encouraged me to maul what I found inside. Interlacing strands of black silk, crisscrossing two beautifully caged breasts.

"You live nearby, right?" she whispered.

We had excellent, nasty, sweaty sex. She deliberately gagged on my cock. Such a dirty mind. For instance she licked her own juices off my face, unthinkingly, like a human version of Barney the dog. This had a massive effect on me. And she opened her legs proudly, like a porn star, no hesitation or embarrassment whatsoever. Her girlish face glowed happily and her tongue protruded slightly between her lips like a girl who hadn't yet been told it was impolite, or having been told, didn't care. I went down on her lovely clean-shaven slit and used every trick I had to ensure she came.

"Yessss-uh." She said it like it had two syllables.

Then she made me come with her hands and mouth and giggled at the good of it as I enunciated my joy for the entire neighborhood to hear. We lay panting for a while until she sat up and actually gave me a high five before agreeing to come back again the following week.

I got the job!!

Drinnnnnng.

It was so flattering to know that a twenty-two-year-old was coming to my apartment with the sole intention of having sex. There would be no need to hear about her day, her workmates, her mother, her roommate. She politely resisted any contact with me until she had taken out a black leather riding crop, a black leather paddle (it looked like a large Ping-Pong bat), and a leather version of a cat-o'-nine-tails. I was still inspecting these items when I heard her coat fall to the floor behind me.

"What do you think?"

There she stood enjoying my discomfort in a schoolgirl's uniform complete with thigh-high stockings and heels. Without waiting for an answer she turned and climbed up on my coffee table and unhitched the little skirt. No panties. She had walked here wearing no panties. Her beautiful white ass and just-visible pussy lips, presented on all fours like this, was mute-inducing.

She had a porn-style method of waving and swaying her pussy/ass ensemble into the air as if for the attention of an imaginary camera or yes, an audience of one. Hers was the first butthole I was happy to tongue and it didn't taste of anything at all. Except maybe youth.

Positioning myself in front of her she sucked on my balls with such abandon they might have been leaking life. How flattering it was to see my cock replaced by a young girl's face. My main problem was that I didn't want to come. I had to slow her down.

After all, I had work to do.

Determined to impress her with an innovation of my own, I attached clothespins to each of her nipples. The same type of wooden clothespin my mother used to hang steaming wet clothes in the freezing Irish air only to find them frozen solid the next morning. And instead of asking me what the fuck I was doing, she moaned with pleasure, and it's safe to say, pain. She insisted on being spanked. And spanked. And paddled. And whipped. How unexpectedly intoxicating to notice the muted mauve stains appear on the white orbs of her ass and expand there like ink on paper. And the unholy wobble before the chalky cheeks repositioned themselves.

"Oh Daddy."

My cock lurched when I heard it.

Daddy?

Suddenly the schoolgirl outfit took on deeper significance and I felt like I was complicit in something that hadn't actually been made clear. Was this even legal? There were things that couldn't be said out loud because of the implications on both sides. Did she see me as her father? Had he beaten her? Was I in fact reenacting some crucial moment from her childhood?

Did I care?

One look at my cock answered that. All sorts of respectable people enjoyed this sort of thing. As usual it was just Catholic guilt trying to derail my enjoyment. Or maybe the sense of wrongness merely enhancing it. I took her by the hand and led her into the bedroom, looking over my shoulder in case I missed anything. She sashayed behind me with her outfit askew and, lying on the bed, spread her white legs like swan's wings and flapped them in the air.

I bowed in reverence and began to lap on her.

"Oooooh, Daddy, yes."

I inserted one and then two fingers into her wet gash and pushed them in and out while my other hand reached for her vibrator. Taking it from me, she ground it against her clit while I continued to finger-fuck her until all that white flesh began to look like it was heating up from the inside. Her entire body seemed to blush as if deeply ashamed of what it was feeling.

This was when she splashed.

It was as if a huge oceanic wave had crashed against her interior and what was able to make its way through the fissure did the best it could. A forceful excretion of lukewarm liquid that brought with it a strange acrid odor—not quite of urine but similar, more like seawater or extremely diluted sperm—went everywhere, propelled as it was by heave after involuntary heave launching out of her raised hips and aimed at the world in general. She contracted and moaned like she was giving birth to a water baby. In my mind's eye I froze the action so that one specific squirt stopped in midair and lent itself to inspection. It was substantial, like a liquid starburst.

My balls and midriff glistened in baptism.

She looked up at me smiling sweetly. Her hair wet across her forehead from sweat and ejaculate. She looked down at my wet waist and the widening stain on my bedspread. We had achieved something together that no normal person would ever understand. As the parents of the most avant-garde wet patch, we looked upon it dotingly.

· · · ·

I was only out there ten minutes when a couple dressed in matching pastel shades paid $400 for the Tourette's sign. The guy looked like he could give a shit but the girl wanted it so badly she kept escalating the price. She started off by offering $25 and I told her it wasn't for sale. I suggested she buy the book instead since that was where the quote came from. Or at least it would after I added it to her personalized dedication.

"Will you take fifty?"

Her eyes sparkled, she was now in shopping mode.

I shook my head pleasantly.

A haggling, white, middle-class blond wearing Ralph Lauren was a great advertisement to passersby. She demonstrated how safe it was to stop and browse at my table. She stared at the sign, imagining it on her bathroom wall or in her father's den or her friend's bar.

She would have it.

"How about one eighty?" she said without taking her eyes off of it. The polo-shirted husband could no longer contain himself.

"You fucked us with that, he would have taken seventy, he was about to say yes."

She was quite pretty in a waspish kind of way, blond hair and blond skin, even her eyebrows were beige. Her smiley-pout-face was borrowed from a little girl who knew Daddy wouldn't be mad for long. She sidled over to him in an overly cutesy manner and basically rubbed her tits against his upper arm.

He looked into her buy-me-stuff eyes.

"Aww?" she said.

It had probably worked a thousand times before but he pulled away.

"I'm a bitch?" she said incredulous.

He must have whispered it.

"Yeah . . . I'm really pissed at you," he said, taking out his wallet. Far from being hurt she was aglow. She stepped back the better to view her handiwork. She had just put the finishing touches to a living breathing irate man. She knew that blind rage was as good as undying love, maybe even better.

"I don't even know if I have two hundred here, I was going

to get you a handbag or something really nice today but now you've blown it."

She caught my eye, naughtiness itself.

Then she looked to my side.

I followed her gaze.

The scraggy-looking boy-faced woman in the tight dress shocked me when I turned and realized Marian was standing beside me. Why had she crept up on me like that? And why stand to my side instead of approaching from the front like everyone else?

I wanted to tell her to fuck off.

It was my first instinct when I realized who it was. But I couldn't let the opportunity pass. I still had too many unanswered questions. A *breakup* was something that only happened at the end of a real relationship. It meant she'd been involved in something serious. I had to know more. It turned out she had resumed seeing the guy she'd been with before me. She volunteered this without me even having to ask.

That's how keen she was to talk about it.

"How long?" I asked, expecting her to say a few months, six at the most.

"Three years," she said quietly.

I looked at her. She would not meet my eyes.

Three years.

I tried to update my information. Frantically downloading all the new data while at the same time trying not to react. I *wanted* to react. It was life-changing news but I had to hide it from my face. Something must have showed but I minimized it as best I could. This was a surprise attack. And at my table. My place of work. Actually it was more than that. I had tried to present my street vending as a form of self-flagellation to atone for my sins against her but now I was learning she could have cared less about all that. It wasn't a question of love or hate. Such strong emotions would indicate hope. She had been indifferent. I felt I was reddening but I couldn't help it. Maybe this was what she wanted. Watching me try to affect nonchalance as these muffled explosions took place within me must have been deeply satisfying. I tried frantically to recall what I knew about the guy but all I could remember was that she said he was low energy . . . and that he had a big dick.

She was getting fucked by a big dick while I rolled around in anguish . . . on my floor . . . biting on towels . . . for the past three years. Oh, and that he was Californian. I'd actually met his mother because she and Marian had still been friendly but I hadn't got the impression Marian had unfinished business with her son. Or that there was even a distant possibility of them getting back together. Percolating inside me now was the uncomfortable realization that I had merely interrupted their relationship.

I was determined not to get angry.

Or at least not to let it show.

A silence descended as she sauntered to the front of my table the better to view my display. She picked up the book that related with glee the story of how intimate photos of her magnificent ass were harnessed to sell the other book on the same table, both of them written by the guy standing in front

211

of her with the blood-filled face. She smiled to herself, eyes lowered, aware of my gaze. She might have been a little nervous but who could tell.

Her lovely long fingers that had caused such havoc on my cock tip trembled slightly as she turned the pages. With rage? Or was it the thrill of victory? Her movements were slightly theatrical as she touched one book and then another, allowing her gaze to meet mine only to make sure I understood there was more going on than casual browsing. But what exactly? I was still trying desperately to count the years backward to the day we broke up. Three years? This meant she'd been seeing him pretty much from day one.

Day one? Oh fuck.

Had they started again *before* we'd broken up?

They already had a history together so why not? We hadn't had sex for almost the entirety of our last year. Had she been fucking him then?

And why tell me now?

If it had been so important to hide it from me for all this time why was she now so keen to share? She hadn't even mentioned him when she read about herself in the second book. The same book she now held in her hand. That would have been the perfect opportunity. Had she been ashamed? Was she afraid of hurting me? Maybe she'd been waiting for this moment? Three years. Was that how she saw it? We'd dated for three years. Having had three years stolen from her she was owed three years of mine.

Jesus. Fucking. Christ.

I recalled those excruciating evenings where I tried every trick I knew to get her back only to cycle home through streets blurred by my own tears, sobbing so loudly pedestrians turned to look. At the time I had been consoled by the notion that she must surely be going through something similar but now it was beginning to look like this was not the case. She'd had her boyfriend to fall back on, his big dick to back into. She'd been able to retreat into an already existing relationship. This meant she had watched me frantically flapping around in my own silt with little more than detached interest.

The knee sock? Was it hers? Surely not? Had she just pretended it was in my bag so she could fuck with me? The pictures she posed for in the woods? *Send them to me, would you?* They were for him. New Paltz was where they'd originally met. It was him she'd dressed up for that day, not me. It was him she had taken that walk with before. Fuck.

"How was your trip to Maryland . . . for surgery?"

She looked at me. Puzzled.

"Oh. That wasn't for me, that was my sister."

Fuck.

She had been happy to meet me occasionally. I was encouraged to think I still had a chance of getting her back. Or at least the possibility was not extinguished. Torture through hope. It was beautiful. So elegant. I knew I couldn't shape these accusations into audible utterances and yet there they hung, tangible in the air between us.

I hated her now and was glad for the clarity.

At least now there might actually be an end to it. It had

stung all the more that I had to be the one who ended the relationship three years earlier. She would never have done it. I had to be the executioner and condemned in one. She had already had a man in place to console her. Actually there was nothing to console her for. She would have been relieved I ended it. I didn't dare mention any of this. An angry outburst might have felt good but I couldn't risk giving her an excuse to withhold answers only she could provide. If I lost my shit she might walk away and leave me to stew forever.

Three years of self-imposed hell.

I needn't have suffered like that.

"If I'd known you were with someone I wouldn't have felt so guilty about . . . . everything."

But as soon as the words left my mouth I realized I had no rights here. Why should she tell me? Especially after the way I treated her. I knew it had to end and the best way to do that was to negate our time together from the first day. So when I told her the entire relationship had been a ploy to gain access to her body I myself had set the ball rolling. Why shouldn't she watch me suffer now? It was justice. Yes she had stolen three years from me but when you steal from a thief there is no higher authority to appeal to.

She remained silent as if thinking about it.

"Well, we never talked about who we were with . . . and anyway what about you?"

This was her way of asking if I'd been with someone too.

This suddenly explained her reaction at one of our dinners when I told her I had become an American citizen. She had looked horrified for a split second and at the time I had no idea why. Now I began to wonder if she thought I'd gotten it through marriage. She probably thought I had been with some-one too and had kept quiet.

"It's not as if I was with anyone . . . consistent," I said.

I felt like I was being forced to concede a point. Like I was less dateable than her. But the real reason I had avoided talk-ing about other potential suitors was because I was sure we were on the verge of getting back together. New realizations impacted me like the rear carriages of an abruptly stopped train. Was she fucking this guy while we were still together? It would certainly explain why we'd had so little sex in that last year. And those freckles she always got after an orgasm—I no-ticed them on her face one day a few months before we broke up. Had she banged him that afternoon before meeting me?

Why not?

She might have wanted to keep me on the back burner, such as I was, in case it didn't work out with him. Either way she was definitely getting fucked by a big dick for the preced-ing three years (maybe even more) while I begged for crumbs. The reason I'd started selling books on the street was so I could prove to her that I could make a living from my writing without using photos of her ass. Or at least this was what I told her. I searched frantically for the moral high ground. Surely she was a cunt and I had been wronged? But even through the fact-warping haze in my head as I watched her standing there holding my books to her chest I could clearly see how I, and I alone, had brought all of this to my table. Should I give her a copy? I had only ever sent her the PDF. *Nah, I'm good*, I imagined her saying. If she did I would most certainly cry right there in the street. I wanted to run away but I couldn't leave my table.

"If I'd known you were with someone I wouldn't have felt so bad. I felt so guilty about the things I'd done while I was with you."

"What things?" she said quietly.

She wasn't trying to get away, she wanted to hear all about it. Jesus Christ. Maybe she was worried that there were other things she didn't know about. Some new atrocities on my part that could alleviate the sense of guilt she now felt for her actions.

I couldn't look at her. I daren't.

"Don't worry," I said. "There's nothing new, just the same stuff we talked about . . . like me being online and well . . . all the rest of it."

"It's okay," she said quietly. "It's okay." Like she was talking to an excitable horse. As if to say, *It'll hurt less if you don't fight it.*

She was standing beside me again so that we now faced customers together and in my peripheral vision I sensed she was looking down at the books on the table, mimicking or maybe mocking my penitent stance. I yearned to look at her. But it was too risky. I wanted to look at her. I *wanted* to gather her up into my arms like freshly laundered sheets and take her away with me to a safe place whispering and giggling as we bundled through the streets, but instead my right hand rose involuntarily and blocked her from sight. I stepped awkwardly away, breaking any symmetry that had crept in between us. I was as surprised by this as she was and I squinted now at triangles of her between my fingers. My hand would shield me from the emotional onslaught emanating from this stranger. She peered comically around my raised hand like she was trying to get through to a lost little boy.

It didn't help that she had once told me he had a huge dick. All those times I'd sat in front of her hoping for a hint that she might want me back. I was reminded of the scene where a drugged detective is dining with Hannibal Lecter. They converse pleasantly as the detective forks slivers of his own brain into his mouth. He has no idea he's been anesthetized and the top of his cranium has been opened like a tin of sardines. This was how manipulated I felt. And this in turn communicated to me how she must have felt when I told her I had only used her for sex.

Our eyes met for an instant.

I hated her.

She hated me.

My stomach churned in the same way it would in the presence of an enemy. The fact that she actually came to visit me at my table suggested she knew I wasn't ever going to respond to her email. She knew she'd never get another word out of me if she didn't turn up and surprise me. I had already dismissed her when I thought she'd only been with a guy for a few months but to hear she'd been in a relationship *for three fucking years*. And not only that but with the same guy she'd been with before me. It seemed unthinkable that I should have been cycling all the way out to Park Slope on those evenings after selling books all day in freezing temperatures and all the time she was getting serviced by a huge dick.

"So was there any overlap?"

"What do you mean?"

"Was there any overlap with him, when you and I were together?"

She looked at me quickly.

"No. I would never do that."

She'd been able to keep him secret for three years, why not four?

And why was it suddenly okay to tell me now?

Now she looked deeply uncomfortable, squirming inside her tight dress. Had she worn it purposely? Of course she had. Turning sideways she momentarily hypnotized me with a profile view of those upturned breasts. She moved with the confidence of someone whose body is capable of dissolving logic in lust. Or of a duelist presenting less of a target.

She described the breakup as *unexpected* so it was safe to assume he'd dumped her and not the other way around. At least I could take some solace from the fact that she would now, at last, suffer like I had. No wonder she'd been able to resist my advances so adamantly. There was never any question of us getting back together. That position was taken. And now that she was suffering from losing him, she thought why not spread the pain around to make herself feel better. If nothing else she'd have someone to talk to about it. Did she think I was going to sit and talk it out with her? Help her get over the fact that she'd been dumped by a guy I didn't even know she was with?

"We talked about me going out there," she'd said quietly.

Going out there as opposed to *moving out there* because *moving out there* would be too painful for me to hear. She was minimizing the blast. Muffling it for me. How very considerate. It was the emotional equivalent of lying about the amount on the check. She had been as good as married to him. All the more reason to have told me.

I was only hearing it now because she was in shock. In her reeling mind I was the nearest she had to a confidant. I could never have conceived of such a devilishly clever comeback. There I was thinking I'd dealt her a coup de grace three years earlier only to find that I had merely been a distraction from the real love of her life. The big-cocked Californian silversmith. But now that he'd ended their relationship she needed someone to talk to. She couldn't hurt him back so I was getting it instead. She probably thought I was now recovered enough from breaking up with her to be able to help her get through her breakup with him.

I had been far too chirpy the previous evening. The happiest I'd been in recent memory. Was I healed enough to hear the truth? That had been her litmus test to see if I'd be able to console her. Or maybe she was just reaching out like a drowning person. I hated that I now had to revisit the three years after our breakup under the new heading of Marian-Had-A-Boyfriend-All-The-Time. My only consolation was that she was suffering.

But why hide it for all that time? She even hid it from her Facebook. I would have thought she'd be delighted to tell me. And that previous night she'd spent twenty minutes talking about how she had begged her sister not to let their mother know she was alone on her birthday. But she hadn't been alone. Was she trying to give me the impression she was free so I'd still be interested? Or could it be that she couldn't continue to make me feel guilty if I knew she was getting fucked regularly by a guy with a good job and yes, yes, we know, a big dick. Maybe the real reason she had hidden him from me was because she didn't want to read about their intimate details in one of my books.

Too late for that.

3

To prevent street vendors from setting up outside their hallowed doors, staff members from the Laurence Hotel positioned tasteful shrubs in cast-iron urns along the sidewalk. Their black attire and economy of movement gave them the air of stagehands arranging props between scenes. They retreated one after the other through a door held open by their manager, who, satisfying himself no one had been left outside, removed himself from sight.

It was a provocative move.

At least five well-established regulars would now need to migrate up the hill and I steeled myself for all manner of territorial dispute in the coming days. The law stated that the first to arrive on any given spot had the right to occupy it for twenty-four hours. This meant that the earlier you got out there the more confident you could be of getting a spot. But I wasn't going to get up at four AM, especially now that I had learned that being out there was having no effect whatsoever on my chances of getting Marian back. I wouldn't have wanted her now even if she was available. But I had to fight the urge to isolate. Alcoholism loves a straggler. I needed to be among people and my fellow street vendors just about qualified.

And there was the small matter of ten thousand books.

They weren't going to sell themselves.

But putting those urns on the sidewalk was an illegal act so it was generally agreed the situation wouldn't last long. Meanwhile the human flotsam would need to be dealt with.

Previously, to dissuade newcomers from setting up beside me, I had invented a much-feared mythological vendor who had just been released from Rikers Island. I helpfully informed the doe-eyed novice that the spot they were about to take was usually occupied by a guy called Turk who sold leather jackets and boots. They should of course feel free to take the spot since it was legally permissible but all I was saying was *Turk* might choose that day to come out and . . . well . . . they had been warned. This was usually enough to shoo the uninitiated but it wouldn't work with the veterans.

Like the guy who sold screenplays.

Sun-Tan-Tom (not to be confused with Hats-And-Socks-Tom) had people on his payroll who kept spots for him. *Spots* plural. He oversaw a franchise of tables that served the entire downtown area. Multiple tables, manned by minions, were furnished with the latest screenplays before the corresponding movies even opened. It was reverently whispered that Quentin Tarantino had turned up at his flagship table outside the Apple Store and threatened him with legal action if he didn't stop selling his scripts. It was also whispered with equal reverence that Sun-Tan-Tom could have given a fuck. So much so, a photo of the exchange sat framed on that same table, which, taken at face value, gave the impression the great auteur had actually endorsed the sale of his scripts.

Then there was the German T-shirt merchant who you only needed to look at to know he was not to be fucked with. So fight-faced and muscly (he flexed needlessly as he rearranged the T-shirts), he repulsed assaults on his sovereignty while they were still conceptual. Then there was the dodgy-looking Iranian guy who materialized in the gaps left by others. He set up next to me once but sold so little he moved on in disgust. He managed to make it seem like a comment on my spot. Like it might be good enough for white trash like me but he had more self-respect. The closer you were to the Apple Store the more sales you could expect. And the more you needed to defend your spot.

The Laurence Hotel was only three stores away from Apple so Operation Shrub-Block was most disruptive. Arrest-Me-Dante tried to unite the vendors, saying we should form a union. He began canvassing up and down the street looking for support. He walked past me because he didn't like me. He did, however, like having a white guy on the roster since the cops were more likely to behave around white people. If this had not been the case I would never have gotten such a good spot to begin with. There were lawyers who had helped the vendors fight cases in the past and apparently they were now being consulted to get the shrubs moved. I respectfully approached a fat-backed vendor.

"Erm, excuse me sir?"

He spit out his coffee.

"Motherfucker I'm a combat veteran, you don't wanna be creepin' up on me."

But in reality he was too fat to get up off his milk crate.

Then Arrest-Me-Dante really freaked me out by actually talking to me.

"You better get here early tomorrow or they'll take your spot."

It was interesting he said *your* spot not *our* spots.

Drinnnnng

Caitlin came over again and this time I really got into it. I was shaking with lust and I could see she was loving the effect she had on me. She stood to attention this time in a skimpy French maid's outfit, arms by her side, while I mauled, sucked, bit, licked, and tongued her where she stood. From certain angles, most of them from low-down looking up, she was intoxicatingly pretty. Her milky-white thighs disappeared into black woolen knee socks that dragged my very soul after them into the murky moral complexities of a pair of glossy-black stilettos.

I was halfway through whipping her and calling her a *dirty little cocksucking cunt* when the doorbell rang. Since I was naked and holding a riding crop I decided against opening the door, but squinting through the peephole I could just make out the top half of the white-haired head of Barney's mom from the apartment below. She obviously wasn't interested in talking to me since she was already halfway down the stairs so her intention had been to stop the disturbing sounds emanating from my apartment rather than discuss them.

I returned to Caitlin's molten ass.

I blew cool air on it, providing a contrast that would be all the more startling when the next fusillade fell. It was virtually aglow.

"You little cunt . . . shake it at me . . . raise it up . . . no point in pleading . . . Daddy's heard it"—I interrupted myself with the sharp compact smack of the leather crop against her hot shuddering globes—"all before."

Her cries were those of a little whimpering girl and she sobbed as if distraught beyond imagining. But even as she flinched she was already maneuvering her crimson hemispheres back into position in case she missed anything.

Later on, after she'd squirted all over my face and I'd come all over her tits, she was enjoying a cigarette, which she insisted on exhaling out the window, as we chatted aimlessly about movies and TV shows and mock-lamented the time we wasted binge-watching them. I was still marveling at how flush-faced and refreshed she looked after being caned, paddled, whipped, licked, and facially fucked, when . . .

Drinnnggg Drinnnnnnnng

I was sure it was my downstairs neighbor again ready to complain about the noise now that it had stopped but when I opened the door there were two uniformed police officers looking very serious, if not a little nervous, standing in the hallway, and another one stationed strategically further down the stairs in a black bulletproof vest over a white T-shirt. They were all doing their best to look past me into the apartment.

"We got a call saying there was an argument," said the younger one.

I looked at them all, standing there, prepped for serious action. I had answered the door in only a T-shirt so I wasn't keen on opening it too wide.

"Erm, it was actually the opposite of an argument," I said.

The guy down the stairs understood immediately and began to look away as if already thinking about his next case, but the other two were still hosting thoughts no longer applicable. When Caitlin appeared behind me in knee socks and stilettos, holding a tote bag to her chest, her blushing face was almost as red as her ass had been earlier. I opened the door a little wider so they could see exactly how I'd spent my afternoon.

"Hahaha, it's okay, officers," she squealed delightedly, "there's no trouble here."

The two cops grimaced with embarrassment and perhaps even disappointment. They thought they were coming to rescue a damsel. I was grateful for her cigarette because if she had already left I might have been in handcuffs. On her way out she stopped in the doorway and raised her right hand to high-five me.

"I can't wait to tell my friend Stefan," she said.

Whack.

Barney barked as she descended the stairs.

• • • •

Having nudged my cart like a dung-beetle all the way over to Prince Street, I was stunned to look up from my padding feet to see a group of strangers in my spot. Too drenched in sweat, confusion, and self-hatred to make a scene, I continued on to the next block and set up there instead. I tried to make it look like I did this every day but secretly I was furious and terrified.

It looked like an entire family had descended on my precious spot. There was a Mongolian-looking woman, or at least I think it was a woman, and horizontal-eyed men of varying ages, none of whom acknowledged me as I passed.

It was the fallout from the Laurence Hotel's anti-vendor policy. It wasn't a permanent arrangement but its effects might be. What if these people preferred their new spots? I still had far too many books to get rid of. And yet as I looked around me I realized I had the entire street to myself. I had never seen anyone set up on Crosby Street and for the moment it seemed like I had stumbled on a new frontier.

If not greener grass then concrete less gray.

As I rumbled past Stone Cold Joe earlier he shrugged as if to say, "There was nothing I could do." He was incapable of refusing anybody anything. He probably helped them set up and handed them a "yellow." He didn't even seem perturbed by the fact that the jewelry and scarves displayed on their tables looked similar to his own. This had to be why he had lasted so long out there, he just didn't have an ego.

But my very livelihood was being threatened, my homestead was overtaken, my territory seized. Shouldn't I do something? Because they were eating when I passed by they actually looked like they were having a picnic on my spot. It added to the affront.

I wasn't thinking straight.

I was rebounding between Marian's news and the Laurence Hotel's strategy. Why was I out here at all? What was the point in continuing to humiliate myself if Marian was no longer an option? To sell books? The books weren't selling. At least not as well as they had using her ass.

I would have loved to hear Christine's opinion on both matters but I couldn't risk the humiliation. I had laughed openly when her Wall Street guy had walked out on her but now it was starting to look like I might be the source of similar if not superior entertainment. All those fellatio-induced confessions about how I was hurting Marian by not contacting her. How I had been such a terrible boyfriend by refusing to ask her to live with me. How she must miss me.

How embarrassing.

I couldn't bring myself to give her the satisfaction of knowing she was right. That Marian had in fact been systematically punishing me. For years. Three years to be exact. Even more unsayable was the fact that she had been getting on with her life while I was still frozen to the moment we broke up.

I consoled myself that at least now I knew she'd been dumped she would suffer like I had.

It was merciful to have found out. Otherwise my state of confused self-flagellation would have continued indefinitely. The longer I marinated in guilt (Marianated?) over the wrongs I'd done her, the longer she owned me.

In fact I had more in common with her ex now since we had both dumped her. He'd obviously had enough of her shit too. Actually he'd dumped her *twice*. We'd certainly have a lot to talk about. I imagined the two of us meeting for coffee like a scene from a French film where jealousy and rage went unrecognized in the service of highly unlikely scenarios. But I then was repulsed by the realization that any dialogue between us would have to take place in the shadow of his dick.

Not going to happen.

Pedestrians flowed around me like dirty water as I stood there frozen to the pavement. I was afraid to move in case I caused some new calamity. My literary aspirations and my ruined relationship were intermingled: find a girl you love, hurt her viciously, dump her unceremoniously, and then immolate yourself trying to win her back by street-selling your self-published books recounting the entire story.

"I like that you're out here doing this."

His name was Jared and he was saying something about how I represented the death of the bookstore. He turned out to be a writer for *Esquire* and *Vice* and *GQ*. He stroked his chin as he considered me and my situation.

"What exactly is required to be 'out here'?"

Madness, *self-hatred*, and *masochism* presented themselves as possible answers. But before I could answer he began to talk about his own self-published book and how he felt "this" might be a good way to get it seen and what did I think about it. I thought he should go fuck himself but out of sheer habit I feigned interest in case there was the chance of a post on his Instagram. As it turned out there wasn't. In New York you were only allowed to pitch to someone while they waited to pitch something to you.

I called Ursula and tried in vain to convince her that she wasn't a sex addict. If I could gaslight her into thinking she was just codependent there might still be a chance of having my balls siphoned. But she was adamant, she'd already been to three SLAA meetings and she was talking about going to a Buddhist group.

"No, I've reached rock bottom."

There was a pause after she said this and it took me a few moments to realize she was referring to me.

I was her rock bottom.

But I made some decent money that day.

I sold books.

I even began to get the hang of the card reader, swiping credit cards like I was running an actual business. Availing themselves of my bulk price they almost always added an extra book when they paid with the card. What's another $10 when you're already spending $20? If this continued I wouldn't need a publisher at all. This was more lucrative. And more importantly it was cooler. Better to be a self-published-street-vending-underground-anonymous writer than yet another corporate bitch. And as if that wasn't enough, on the way back from taking a piss in the Apple Store I'd see Stone Cold Joe, Arrest-Me, Forgive-Them, and even the Mongolians looking miserable and unvisited. I forced a sad expression into my face so that they couldn't glean from it that my new spot was so much better than where I'd been and they still were. I didn't want to have to fight them off when they tried to muscle in on my new territory.

Isabel waddled all the way up the hill to ask why I'd moved.

"I needed a change," I said.

She looked at me hard, like there was more to it. She wanted me to elaborate, to complain about the Mongolians. She wanted to start a war. But that was the last thing I wanted. I had to assume she already knew why I had moved up here but I didn't want her to know I was making more than before because then I'd be a target. The other vendors always knew how well or badly you were doing. I was happy for her to think I was sulking. I certainly didn't want to appear like I was doing too well or I'd have to deal with all of them migrating up the street and arranging themselves either side of me. Then because she seemed to be talking to herself while she looked at me I began to worry she was putting some Haitian voodoo curse on me. I unleashed some mumbling of my own in the form of the Lord's Prayer and hoped my lapsed Catholicism was still strong enough to combat her pagan equivalent. It was the nearest I was ever going to get to a street fight.

TITS SO BIG HER T-SHIRT READS EW YOR
#TheOxygenThiefDiaries

Burrrrrrrrr

"I've pissed on guys for money."

She was the latest respondent to my Craigslist ad. I had suggested a quick phone chat prior to meeting, but two wide-eyed and ear-cocked hours later I was still listening to a goth girl called Pearl casually confess to all sorts of outrageousness. For instance, Brendan Dooley, the Irish actor who seemed to have a cameo in every film ever made, had once paid her $2,000 to give herself an enema while he watched and masturbated. He was very specific about what she should eat. Indian curry, no rice. In lingerie and heels she teetered on a mirrored table while a transparent tube emptied the contents of her alimentary canal into Tupperware. Reclining in an armchair Dooley watched, wanked, and winked. He winked at everyone. It was his happy-go-lucky Irish affectation. On one occasion he turned up with a red-haired hooker who straddled him as Pearl siphoned herself. He found time to wink at both of them.

Another client liked to be supervised while eating the contents of a toilet bowl. Demonstrating an impressive talent for administration Pearl scheduled that session directly after Dooley's so that the contents of his Tupperware could be repurposed.

Yet another client, a septuagenarian financier, liked to be strapped into a gynecologist's chair, ankles in stirrups, vibrator in ass, while girls in lingerie pinched his nipples and jerked him off. Pearl was able to make herself sound almost lifeless as she talked about all of this. Or maybe she was experienced enough to know that presenting mind-scorching scenarios in such a matter-of-fact tone prevented the listener from deriving any pleasure he hadn't paid for. Was she waiting for me to suggest she write a book? Was she hoping I'd write one about her?

There was more.

A litigation lawyer from Miami who liked to be cuckolded. He loved to be reminded that he was a piece of shit and that his wife was looking forward to being fucked by his business partner whose cock was so much bigger than his. He longed to hear how they laughed at naked pictures of him while they fucked on his desk.

A friend introduced Pearl to *the scene* when she was eighteen. She interviewed at the various "dungeons," all of which were owned and run by Russians. They actually tried to discourage her at first by asking her to *breadboard* one of their regulars. Breadboarding, they explained, involved nailing the loose skin of the scrotum to a chopping board, or a floorboard, or a door. If she was in any way squeamish about this she'd refuse and save everyone a lot of time and money. But she delighted the client by turning up in a nun's habit (lingerie underneath) carrying a scaled-down wooden cross. After she crucified his balls he happily paid extra.

The dungeon itself was a converted dance studio with the windows painted black and partitioned off so that the moans and groans, shrieks or shouts of your fellow patrons added to or subtracted from your enjoyment depending on your preferences. Shelves groaned too, with a mind-boggling compendium of sexual paraphernalia. Everything from Anal to Ziplocs.

But I was three years too late.

When Pearl gave birth to their son her live-in boyfriend told her she'd gotten flabby. Her response was to change the locks to their Tribeca apartment. Mind you it didn't help that he'd been unfaithful. At the time of our phone chat she was selling the place to buy a bigger apartment in the same building. She'd bought it with money she'd earned working "freelance" as a dominatrix. The dungeon took 80 percent but on her own she made $900 an hour. She paid for the apartment in cash. The seller didn't ask where the money came from.

He didn't care.

She spoke without embarrassment or hesitation about how, on her own time, she'd fuck guys with strap-ons and make them suck on her "dick" just like they'd do to her, given the chance.

"What would you say to them?"

"I'd say 'Suck it bitch' and 'You're not doing it right.'"

She actually knew what she was talking about.

She'd ram the strap-on down their throats just like any self-respecting male would do.

"And pull them forward by the ears so they gagged on it."

Here she laughed wickedly, obviously enjoying the memory and perhaps savoring my discomfort. It was unnerving to hear a girl play the role of a guy who knew that the only reason we wanted to fuck women in the ass and shove cocks down their throats was because it gave us not just a sense of power but of revenge for all the indignities we'd had to suffer just to get them legally naked in the first place. Or was that just me?

Pearl was past caring.

She had her twins and her apartment and there was nothing to gain by being coquettish.

And anyway men paid good money to be humiliated and beaten with their own notions so why should she pretend she didn't know what to do? She charged $900 an hour for these extracurricular house visits. Plus she was thinking of writing a book and presumably needed to sound as knowledgeable as possible about her chosen subject within earshot of a potential publisher. Which I assumed was how she saw me.

As long as she didn't have actual sex with any of them she could advertise herself under the *services provided* listings. Plumber, Electrician, Dominatrix.

And because she had her phone on *record* right up to the moment she swiped their credit cards there could be no question of future misunderstandings—legal or otherwise. I wondered if she was recording our call. I also wondered if force-feeding men with a strap-on came under the heading of "actual sex"?

Seemingly not.

One of her more sought-after services involved the insertion of Sounds. These were thin smooth rods not unlike knitting needles that were inserted into the eye of the penis. She inched them down the sperm duct till the tip touched the base of the penis and excited the prostate gland. I'd seen this phenomenon in Japanese porn clips but because there was no English spoken I had no idea what I was looking at.

I heard myself speak. I sounded like a little boy.

"Will you do that to me please?"

"I will if you ask me to."

Which was a strange response because that was exactly what I had just done.

Maybe it was a legal thing.

Drinnnnggggg

Her face in real life was much prettier than her photos but her body just took on the shape of the clothing that contained it. At one point as I searched for a breast in her bra it felt like the cups were filled with liquid. She effortlessly summoned the mocking tone of voice and disappointed-in-you demeanor of an arch-bitch dominatrix but I couldn't help thinking it was merely an affectation left over from a time when she was younger, thinner, and firmer.

These suspicions were confirmed when my hand ventured into her jeans. I didn't dare unbutton them for fear that the room would fill with liquid Pearl. It was the first time I hoped I'd have my hand arrested before it reached anything resembling pussy. The lumpen geography leading up to it was uneven and loamy. Everything seemed to be shifting around. It was as if a bomb had gone off in the vicinity some years previously.

Meanwhile she stroked my cock through my jeans and I had no problem with this whatsoever. She traced a fingernail carefully over the denim with just enough pressure to ensure that the cock below was teary-eyed and magnificently maddened. But having dispatched my manual scout and finding nothing resembling terra firma there was nowhere to go, nothing to aspire to.

236

"What are you thinking?"

It was becoming an exercise in Olympic politeness. *What was I thinking?* This was at odds with what I expected a dominatrix should ask or demand. Meanwhile she was still stroking my poor confused cock under my tight bulging jeans. But far from being all dungeonesque and domineering she was coming across as seriously insecure. Should I make her feel more confident about her ability to dominate me?

"I'm thinking how cool it is that you know exactly what to do," I lied.

"And what are you thinking now?" she said, still stroking me.

"I'm thinking about how experienced you are."

"And now?"

"Well . . ." I'm thinking . . . is this part of her domination thing? Ask him what he's thinking from moment to moment . . .

Once the blood required to irrigate a man's mental acuity has raced south to inflate an erection, his ability to lie is considerably reduced. He might feel like he's brandishing a Claymore but to a woman it's a flesh-covered lie-detector. Trying to hide what I was really thinking under a believable lie, while yearning for the cock-stroking to continue, was beginning to feel like I was back in a relationship.

Torture indeed.

THREESOME? I CAN BARELY HANDLE A ONESOME

"Hey, boss, you mind if I sit down here? I'm pretty quiet really. I won't hurt your business."

"Sure," I said only because I had no idea what he meant.

He wanted to sit down? Who was I to deny him that? He looked like he might be homeless but not disgustingly so. New York's street people seemed to have a better sense of fashion than other cities I'd lived in. It was probably because the clothing donated here was of far higher quality. Comfortably attired in a black hoodie, sweat pants, and what appeared be a new pair of Nikes, he made straight for the trash can on the corner and began to rummage in it. I watched him rip the edges of a pizza box until he was left with a large white square. When I looked again he had transformed into a panhandler. Hunkered down on the corner he had settled in for what looked like a long haul. His technique was devastatingly simple.

Crouch behind a cardboard sign and cry.

He raised his wet face intermittently so that the full effect of his abject misery could be better appreciated. A girl swathed in black limped past in a complicated leg brace and crutches.

"Help meeeeeee," he wailed after her.

She stopped and read his sign:

HOMELESS, PLEASE HELP, VERY LONELY, MISS MY MOM, NO FAMILY.

She immediately began to rummage in her expensive purse. I couldn't see the numerical value of the note she inserted in his transparent plastic cup but from his reaction it had to be more than a dollar.

'Thankgewww," he wailed as she limped away.

There's a story they love to tell in copywriting courses where a bum, not unlike my new neighbor, sits on a street corner with a sign that reads, I'M BLIND. He may or may not be blind, we're not going to get into that. The integrity of the client is none of our business. We are merely charged with improving his communications. The point of the story is to demonstrate that emotion has a huge part to play in a purchasing decision. The bum does not receive any money, although being blind, you might wonder how he knows this for sure. He might be getting hundreds of dollar bills silently shoved into his cup before being stolen by clever thieves but again, let's not exceed our brief by delving into the client's security arrangements or corporate culture. A passing copywriter identifies the problem, whips out his pen, and adds three words to the blind man's sign.

It now reads: I'M BLIND AND IT'S SPRING.

This guy knew to raise his head at just the right moment so that the passersby received the full brunt of his emotion. There wasn't a great deal of difference between the two of us really.

I taxidermied my angst while he trawled similar depths. But that day, Nolita's well-to-do chose his brand over mine. Here was a real-life homeless person on the streets of New York.

Someone from whom they could purchase freshly secreted, debatably organic, artisanal servings of self-esteem. While-u-wait. Many had already walked past before their haughty self-assured expressions fell away. Stricken with guilt, they were already searching for wallets or unshouldering bags before turning to kneel before his majesty, his humanity. As cash was presented his anguished face contorted anew, this time in gratitude. Could it be that some barely hoped-for light had breached the impregnable vault of despair in which he found himself?

"Thanggggewwwwww."

Having bestowed blessings on the faithful, the transaction was complete. The honorarium was removed as soon as benefactors left so that prospective donors need not be burdened with unnecessary details. A modest dollar or two was visible in the cup. No doubt this was the reason it was transparent. I saw him energetically throw change at the backs of those who dared put coins in there.

"You're kidding, right?" he shouted after them and they were too ashamed to respond.

I watched him, transfixed.

What the residents of Nolita knew about hopelessness they'd gleaned from HBO. The real-life equivalent was more than likely too medicated to be able to come up with this sort of marketing strategy. After all, if someone had it together enough to select a corner located among the demographic most likely to sympathize with his cause and having arranged himself there, could cry on cue, he deserved more than a few dollars in a plastic cup—he was an entrepreneur. As one woman shoved what looked like a sizable denomination into his receptor, the Lamen-teer shot me a quick look that seemed to say, *This is how it's done, asshole,* before reverting back to hopelessness and despair.

I blinked.

Had I really seen that?

Had he really stepped out of character for a second to gloat? His sign changed slightly from day to day but the basics were always present:

**MY FAMILY WERE REMOVED BY
HURRICANE SANDY, MISS MY MOM.**

Efficiency itself.

In a headline every word needed to earn its place. You only had seconds to get your point across. It shouldn't take more than four seconds to read. Make your point and if pos-sible back it up with a strong visual. In this case the image of a grown man deep in the throes of despair. He wielded the same emotional stopping-power as a pet shop window . . . on fire. And if that wasn't enough, he was white. This guy could be your cousin, your brother, your dad. The vain wannabe-hipster selling his self-published, self-involved, self-serving memoir was invisible beside such a confession of humanity.

Stony-faced bitches who moments earlier looked ready to physically fight anyone impeding their progress went limp. In fact I was often the unintended recipient of the softened look that actually belonged to him. Their eyes would rest on me as the decision took hold in them to stop. They would then retrace their steps, summoned by the tug of his vulnerability, often dropping unironically to one knee in front of him. And having been wrung dry of their daily emotional allowance there was no fucking way they were stopping at my table. The sentiment on my sign seemed so self-satisfied and cynical in comparison.

THIS WOBBLY WHEELED–TROLLEY DASH
THROUGH THE COSMIC SUPERMARKET
#TheOxygenThiefDiaries

I was secretly thrilled when a tough-looking, heavily tattooed out-of-towner noticed him sitting there in the street crying. As he approached he began to shake his head in disbelief. Having spent the day in SoHo he had been big enough to forgive the indignities visited on him by fashionistas, photographers, and faggots, but here was something he could not let slide.

"You fucking pussy. Be a man . . . Jesus . . . embarrassing."

He had barely walked past when change and cardboard exploded from the pavement and the Lamenteer rose to his own defense.

"Fuck you, you fucking fat asshole in your fucking cowboy boots and bullshit tattoos, you think I'm afraid of you? Is that what you think? An asshole like you? Look at you. You think you're a big man, come back here and I'll kick your fat fucking ass, bitch, yeah you, you little bitch, look at you, come on, I'm waiting here for you, no? That's right, walk away you little bitch, you fucking better . . ."

The guy looked like he was about to shout something back but just then quarters, dimes, and pennies rained on him, and his shocked reaction unmanned him. It was already over. The Lamenteer beckoned to him in a seemingly friendly manner as if he was more than happy to continue their chat. The pleasantness advertised his willingness to fight and fight dirty. The tattooed guy harrumphed and mumbled.

It was over.

But crouching back into his spot the Lamenteer now seemed like just an ordinary beggar. Where were the tears? Could it be he was unable to get back into character? He stood up again. And this time he just walked away, leaving the cardboard sign and transparent cup there. It was his equivalent of storming off the set. Maybe now I'd sell some books.

It was still early and I might benefit from the rush-hour foot traffic at the Prince Street subway as Nolita's retail and corporate staff completed their daily commute to Brooklyn. A well-preserved older woman shoved her worried face into mine.

"Where's that man? I bought food for him."

The concern on the woman's face was laughable. I'd seen her pass earlier and she had obviously decided it was worth waiting in line in a high-end sandwicherie to buy this poor man some food. The crisp brown recycled paper bag confirmed that even the most basic sandwich would cost $20. There would have to be some french fries in there too because homeless people love french fries and a ridiculously priced bottle of water to wash it all down with. How did I know this? Well, because it was I who ended up devouring its contents. I had done my best to look as if I hated to be the one to set her straight but we members of the middle class had to look out for each other.

"He's a complete performer."

I looked furtively left and right as if giving out this kind of information put me at great risk.

"He actually asked me if it would hurt my business if he sat there and then after a few minutes he started his crying routine."

"You're kidding." Her eyes were wide with disbelief.

"No," I said, "I'm not."

She looked at me longer than was necessary.

Her disbelief was testament to his performance.

"Well, he had me fooled," she said and after another moment's hesitation held the bag up.

"You should take it. Turkey sandwich and french fries."

I feigned reluctance and mimicked gratitude.

The next day he was already in position as I rounded the corner with my cart. The first thing I saw was his miserable crying head soaking up all the attention for miles around. Taking it away from me before I even set up. And even more annoying was the fact that he was completely within his rights since he had gotten there before me. Cursing, I unfolded my table as far away from him as was legally allowable. Which wasn't nearly far enough. I'd get fined if I was too close to a hydrant or a store entrance. Caught between a mock-mourner and a financial fucking. And people looked at *me* accusingly. Why wasn't I doing something about that poor man? Did I not see him? What kind of uncaring prick was I? The last thing they were thinking about was buying a book. He was ridiculously effective.

Not selling books was bearable if people still took photos and posted them. But even that wasn't going to happen with him around. In the end I went over and asked him nicely to move up the street a little bit, if he didn't mind. Suddenly there was no indication of the uncontrollable sobbing and involuntary twitches he'd been subjected to only seconds before.

"Why would I do that?' he asked quite reasonably.

"Well, because, people are asking me if you're okay."

"No," he said calmly. "I can hear perfectly, you're cursing the customers out after they don't buy nothin' and that's just not my problem. You need to change your pitch."

I couldn't believe what I was hearing.

'I'm not doin' nothin'. I'm just sittin' here. They're not askin' if I'm okay. That's just a lie."

But as he spoke he started to get up, so I wasn't about to slow him down by defending myself. Plus I was stung into even greater depths of annoyance by the fact that he was right. I *was* indeed cursing the passersby and him too if his hearing allowed. As far as I was concerned, he was costing me sales and media exposure. People didn't feel comfortable pulling out wallets and handing over $20 for a book when there was a wailing man on the pavement expiring behind them. Change my pitch? Did he have any idea who he was talking to? I had sold multimillion-dollar ad campaigns to some of the most revered clients on the planet and won awards doing it. Change my pitch? Where should I begin to explain to this subhuman just how superior I was? Did he ever manage teams of creatives? Had he ever shepherded international ad campaigns from conception to execution? Had he any idea who the fuck he was talking to? I was failing at being on the street. So much so, I was now being berated by a more successful beggar. I had thought in light of Marian's latest revelations I had reached the rock bottom of my descent but it seemed like I had just found a trapdoor. I retreated behind my table while he made himself hoarse shouting at me. People physically ducked to avoid being caught in the crossfire.

"You're a fucking liar and you know it, I have done nothin' wrong here, I even asked you . . ."

It suddenly made sense that this stretch of pavement went uncontested by other vendors. Even after the Laurence Hotel's enforced reshuffle, no one wanted to deal with this.

". . . you won't even sell one fucking book today, I guarantee it."

It was the curse of the Lamenteer.

I began to freak out.

Would he suddenly reappear behind me with a homemade shiv? Would my paranoid prediction of appearing stabbed on the six o'clock news come true? He'd enlist the help of innumerable street felons summoned from hollow sidewalks. An unkempt man stopped and fixed me with what seemed to me to be an African American version of a Charles Manson stare. He looked like he had my eyes. I tried to hide the relief from my face when he resumed walking but then he turned suddenly as if remembering where he'd seen me before.

He held my frightened gaze in his.

I hoped he was another of Françoise's orphans, bent on payback for the cynical little shit who had invented her. At least that would be better than street-fighting over patches of New York pavement. I was terrorized by my own wrongdoing. Was this really what had become of me?

Waddling back toward my table I could now see that he wore his skinny jeans so low he looked like he'd shat himself. The hand protruding from his black felt poncho held a smart-phone that he now positioned over my book. Suddenly two very pretty, slightly stoned-looking white girls appeared either side of him and began to browse aimlessly as he took photos, first of the cover and then, opening it, the first page. Without lifting his eyes he kept saying the same thing over and over.

"I gotchoo bro . . . I gotchoo bro . . . I gotchoo . . ."

The thumbs on both hands hopped up and down on his screen as the girls linked arms and nodded approvingly.

"This'll be good for you," one of them said in a whisper as if she was afraid the caped one would hear. As if she was a prisoner smuggling a message out. She seemed almost jealous of me, as if *this* was what she hoped would happen for her.

They didn't buy a book.

"So you sell more books when I'm not here? Yeah right."

I jumped as the Lamenteer reappeared behind me. Drawing on all the mock-concern at his disposal—which judging from his daily matinee was bountiful—he looked so sad I almost mistook his expression for sincerity.

He'd been watching.

Stunned by his supernatural ability to appear and disappear I had nothing to offer but silence. He nodded slowly and smacked his lips as if this new development tasted very good indeed, but he was merely collecting himself for the string of well-aimed abuse that would follow.

"If you were a real writer there'd be no reason to be out here standing in the fucking cold . . . no reason at all. You're just a little bitch. A little lying bitch.

"You should write a book about a homeless guy who ruined your business."

His voice trailed away as he made his way slowly across the street and pedestrians changed pace and cars slowed down to accommodate him. As if they could intuitively tell who this section of street belonged to. He launched an afterthought over his shoulder.

"Lil Bitch."

I'M ALL SOUNDTRACK AND NO MOVIE
#TheOxygenThiefDiaries

We'd like to stock your book in our stores as a matter of some urgency. Please get back to me at your earliest convenience.

The letter, text, email, and voice mail from the Barnes & Noble head buyer were all identically worded. At first I was reluctant to respond. Where had they gotten my information? It felt too corporate. Like I suddenly had a job and this guy was my boss. Plus I needed to get my story straight. Was I the marketing director of G Publishing or the production assistant? Or the creative director? I certainly didn't want him knowing I was the writer. But all he seemed to want was a contact person with whom to place orders. Someone called Eileen Flayed was cc'ed on the email and a quick google revealed her to be one of the most powerful people in publishing since it was she who decided which new books were placed on Barnes & Noble's shelves.

Could I please contact him at my earliest convenience?

Replying, I tried to sound as much as possible like the female creative director of G Publishing. He responded almost immediately saying they were getting walk-in requests for my book all over the country. Did I have inventory on hand? Where should he send purchase orders? He would loop in his logistics guys. Whom should he contact to send around a UPS truck to expedite shipping? He would loop in his transport people. As the stack of names cc'd on his emails increased, the answer to all his questions was the same.

Me, me, and me.

Drinnnnggggg

"UPS to pick up your boxes?"

She was certainly stocky enough but would she be able to single-handedly carry seventy boxes down my stairs and load them herself? Barnes & Noble was paying to have them picked up from my apartment and I didn't want the moment ruined by anything that resembled manual labor. I'd done my fair share of lugging those fucking things up and down the stairs, and she didn't look like she could handle it.

Not on her own.

But at least I wouldn't have to hump them all the way to the post office where, over the previous weeks, I had made myself deeply unpopular. I basically had to beg the staff to take the boxes from me. I didn't tell them I'd ordered ten thousand more from Korea.

Burrrrrrr

"I like your numbers."

These were the first few words out of the mouth of a big-time literary agent called Quinn Whitaker. He didn't even try to pretend he'd read the book, he was interested only in how well it was selling. And according to Amazon, Barnes & Noble, and iBook sales, it was now among the top sellers in the country.

"My biggest problem will be to get you more money than you're already making but what I *can* promise is, I'll get twenty copies of your book into every store in the country."

The fact that pond-life like this was starting to show interest confirmed that I was doing something right. By now I was getting so many orders it no longer made sense to be on Prince Street. Pretty soon I wouldn't need to go out there at all. I could stack eight boxes, each containing sixty books, on my cart and ferry them to the tiny post office two blocks from my apartment. That was 480 books per run. I was doing two, sometimes three runs a day availing myself of their very reasonable media rate, which applied to books and CDs.

But I was visibly hated by the post office staff.

I felt like an unpopular visitor in a low-security prison, desperately looking for an inmate to converse with. Any inmate. The Latina lady with impossibly long fingernails simply pretended she couldn't see me. Or hear me. The one time I did approach her I had already overstepped my welcome just by speaking.

"Whoa . . . hold up. One word at a time."

My Herculean adventures bottlenecked here?

I learned quickly. You didn't speak until spoken to and even then you needed to be so deferential you almost knelt. I watched as cocky professionals clutching manila envelopes sighed and harrumphed in response to what they obviously regarded as shoddy service. I winced on their behalf. They would be left there to ponder their mistakes alone and ignored. Not just by the staff. There was no way they were going to solicit the support of the rest of us standing in line, lest we be tainted by their stink.

Meanwhile I was being contacted by the likes of *Publishers Weekly*, *New York* magazine, and even *The Guardian* in London, all of them wondering if I could put them in touch with Anonymous. They wanted interviews either in person or over the phone. Would this be possible? They would of course respect his/her anonymity. After creating yet another alias email address I responded as Cynthia Long, saying I would pass on their inquiries to the author, who was presently hard at work on a third book. There seemed to be doubt about Anonymous's gender so I was careful not to come down on one side or the other. Fuck them. The more intrigued they were, the better. But where had all this attention come from? Black Charles Manson had posted photos of my book under an inspired caption,

Ima check this out

He had three million followers.

• • • •

"Okay let me see . . ."

My first date with Emmeline was going suspiciously well.

I had just invited her to tell me *everything* and she paused now deciding where to begin.

She wasn't just a model, she was an art model. This meant she was comfortable baring not just her body but her soul. For a girl so beautiful and well read she was surprisingly down-to-earth. Would I soon hear how she had been abused or beaten or similarly mis-raised? I hoped so.

The normal ones were boring to me now.

I wasn't surprised to hear she'd just been hired as the concierge for a newly opened über-trendy boutique hotel on the Lower East Side called the Palindrome. It went without saying that she lived in Williamsburg. Two weeks earlier she had arrived at my table with both books already in hand and posed with them, waiting for me to take a picture. It got 212 likes.

"Okay I have it . . ."

Suddenly inspired, she straightened herself.

"One night when I was fourteen, my parents were at the opera and I invited a thirty-two-year-old man from a dating site over to my house. I blew him in the hallway and sent him away again. I needed someone to practice on . . . Is that the sort of thing you're looking for?"

It was.

"He thought I was eighteen. I texted him my real age later."

I winced on his behalf.

By the time she really was eighteen she'd already offered herself as a nude model to a forty-eight-year-old alcoholic painter who bathed her in paint, filled her with absinthe, and pressed her onto canvases.

"We lived together *under a bridge* in Austin."

She seemed to relish the phrase, presumably because it conjured an aura of bohemian homelessness, but when I asked her to clarify, it turned out they'd shared a large studio in the renovated arch of a railway bridge. And when, after eight drunken months, they broke up, he gave her the paintings in a self-pitying passive-aggressive attempt to be rid of her, she slashed them with a carpet knife, paying particular attention to the imprints of their copulation.

"He was Irish too."

The use of *too* inferred I was already being included in her résumé. While working with him she met another Irishman, a photographer, who had a reputation for being a *complete pervert*. Again she offered herself as a nude model. She was already a veteran at nineteen. I couldn't tell if she was just killing time with me on what was, after all, St. Patrick's Day (an Irishman would surely want to get drunk and maybe even pay for the drinks on such a day), or whether she really was enjoying herself as much as she seemed to be. We were sitting in the café attached to the McNally Jackson bookshop and the quiet respectable atmosphere, as Noho's well-to-do pored over books and phones, provided an inviting hush for our salacious conversation. Or at least it did until she described the sort of stories she liked to write.

"Nazi porn," she called it.

Her favorite featured an innocent but rather better-looking Anne Frank being discovered and sodomized by two SS officers. Lost in the telling of the story, she seemed unaware of her surroundings, but I saw that we were becoming a source of free entertainment and potential controversy as our neighbors held their breath for the next development. When she got to the part where blood from the girl's sodomized anus was being used to lubricate her virgin pussy I thought it prudent to intervene.

"Shall we walk?"

She was already standing.

I held the door for her and as she brushed past I caught the whiff of a deeply musky scent that emanated from her like heat. She said it was a relief to be out with an Irishman because we were more intelligent and educated and generally that much more witty than Americans. I was so flattered by this I felt it would be insulting not to at least *try* to kiss her and so, grabbing those slender shoulders, I turned her toward me right there on the sidewalk. Her head tilted back like a film star ready for her close-up.

I began placing well-intentioned fish-kisses on her pouting mouth but since such pecks were ridiculously innocent compared to the outrageousness she'd conjured inside, I felt the need to introduce my tongue, which she immediately met with her own. Pushing the envelope even further I sent a manual scout down the slope of her back to the firm round mounds of her magnificent ass.

"Holy fucking shit," I whispered.

She looked worried.

"That's an amazing *arse*," I said, using the Irish nomenclature to score more points.

"Thank you," she beamed.

"I might have to devote a sonnet to it." Again, it seemed like something an Irish writer might say.

"I might have to hold you to that."

"Yes, hold me to it," I said, pulling it closer.

Her smile lit up the entire street and a couple of adjoining alleys. I accompanied her to Eleventh Street, a walk of some twenty blocks, stroking that young firm ass along the way and even managing the occasional caress of her dancer-sized breasts as she bounced along beside me flushed and distracted. She was loving it. I pointed out every lustful look she received from every man we passed and yes, even some women, and she was astonished at their frequency. Wasting no time on false humility, she openly regretted that she could never seem to witness the phenomenon for herself. Admittedly I did overdo it a little by projecting lustful intentions onto complete innocents, among them a young boy who was not yet out of puberty, but I wanted to keep her physical beauty alive as a subject and so, it seemed, did she.

A woman won't interrupt when you're celebrating her looks.

And yet I still couldn't be sure if she was just tolerating me. Playing with the poor old bastard's libido while he escorted her to her real date for the evening with some young stiff-pricked stud on Eleventh Street. I wouldn't know for sure if I'd see her again until I received confirmation the next day.

We discussed sexual etiquette as we walked.

"It's just rude," I said, "for the guy to come before the girl."

I don't know if she believed me but she definitely liked hearing it. So did a guy who happened to be passing at that same moment. It brought him involuntarily to a standstill. When I let her know he'd heard what I said she immediately announced to the air around her, "I'VE PERFECTED THE BLOW JOB . . . AND I LOOOOVE TO SWALLOW."

She threw her head back, laughed at the good of it. I took a rest to enjoy the sight of her enjoying herself. New York approved of her and she could feel it.

"I'VE GOTTEN VERY GOOD WITH MY MOUTH," she continued far too loudly before kissing me with it.

"Okay, let's keep in touch," she said and strode off up Eleventh Street before I had a chance to realize we'd reached our destination. I nodded like I was confident about seeing her

again but I wasn't. Somehow I managed to wait until the following afternoon before texting her.

*So I've begun work on my ode to your ass but I'll need to
do some more research, can you bring it to my place on Sunday night?*

The three dots indicating she was typing appeared almost
immediately.

*haha I might be able to swing that but I'll be getting off
late so I might have to stay . . . may I update you during the
week?*

It might have been an evasive tactic but it might also be
the fucking jackpot. The next day I checked and rechecked my
texts, trying to get an idea of whether she was serious when
she said she'd visit. I wouldn't know for sure until I saw her
actually ascend the stairs to my door. And I couldn't imagine
that happening. She was a model for Christ's sake. Undressed,
I was going to look like a seal beside her. In fact she'd be doing
me a favor by *not* sleeping with me.

Ping.

I can be there in a half hour if that works?

Oh Jesus!!!!

I would have preferred at least three hours to shower and
shave and clean up and I had intentionally resisted the temptation to prepare for her visit because I was pretty sure I'd be
disappointed if I did. It was astonishing what I achieved in
the intervening half hour. Make tea, provide snacks, shave,
shower, iron a shirt, and sweep the apartment.

Drinnnnng

"You look nice."

She complimented me as if I was the one who needed to be seduced. Looking crisply perfect in the blazer, blouse, and skirt ensemble required by her job, she stepped out of her introductory pose in the doorway and strode past me to the couch where she picked up a copy of my book and began reading. Reciting random snippets she playfully tilted and turned her head, foiling my repeated attempts to kiss her lovely mouth.

"Romance has killed more people than cancer . . ."

My hand between her thighs got her attention.

Tossing the book aside she stood up and I marveled as she slipped out of her jacket with a private smile fully aware of the effect she was having on me. Clothes leapt from us in all directions on the way to the bedroom. The sublime slopes of her lovely young body had me giddy with lust until she rolled onto her stomach and I saw the purple bruises on her otherwise perfect ass.

"Someone's been getting spanked," I said, trying to hide my disgust. Not because she'd been spanked but spanked so recently the marks hadn't had time to heal. Was this a remnant of her rendezvous at Eleventh Street? The mauve marbling on what should have been a pristine pair of buttocks felt like vandalism. My gift had already been opened and rewrapped. My newspaper read. I was okay with the idea of her seeing other men but being confronted with such irrefutable evidence was disturbing. Not so much fingerprints as handprints. And it had been so seriously beaten up she obviously liked it. Until that moment her general demeanor had bordered on aristocratic but now it seemed that under all the affectation and intellectual polish she was just trash.

Or yes, I was jealous.

I dove down on her.

I would need to at least match my rival if not surpass him.

I brought all my experience to bear on the situation; a steady uninterrupted application of dual finger-fucking augmented by a combination of thumb-in-the-butt and rhythmic tonguing-of-clit usually produced spasms and shrieks followed by a howl of orgasm. I looked up from my ministrations to see her head thrown back in abandon while her long elegant hands pushed against the headboard for leverage. Her face, neck, and shoulders were already flushed but I wasn't taking any chances.

"Fuck my face," I hissed and she began to undulate accordingly. When the shuddering began I curled my fingers against the fleshy coin of her G-spot.

"Ooooooooohhhhhh . . . argggggghhhhh fuck yesssssssssss- sssssss."

As her orgasm subsided I teased and caressed her lovely body, drawing spontaneous eruptions of gooseflesh along the way. Follow that, you bastard, whoever you are.

Back in the living room, over what was left of supper, she enthused about a photographer she'd met earlier that day.

She'd been a fan of his for many years and had dreamed of collaborating with him. Her former boyfriend back in Austin (I would later learn he was her husband) forbade her from contacting this guy because he knew from personal experience that "collaborating" with him meant having sex with him. He knew this because that was exactly how he'd met her.

I made a conscious decision to be flattered that she trusted me enough to confide that she did indeed intend to fuck him. This was what it would be like to be with her. You'd be expected to show interest in the constant airing of her artistic and erotic ambitions. Could I do that? For the moment I could, because I wasn't in love with her. But what about when I was? Or when I was willing to admit I was. I decided to like her less. To protect myself. I forced myself to notice that there was something unwashed about her. Smelly even. And she was still so inexperienced. Yes she was filthy-minded and debauched but she hadn't yet developed the skill set to match her intentions. She had yet to progress beyond the obligatory blow jobs and feigned wifely concern that had served her so well in Austin.

"More tea?"

"Awww you're so sweet."

I winced.

She had already made it very clear she loved darkness in men. Men like @drkroom. A casual glance at his work and you knew you were dealing with one seriously sick fuck. Naked women draped over scaffolding like butchered meat, rapey Polaroids, security camera voyeurism, broken doll bondage.

He was art house elite and even I could see they were made for each other.

At this point I'd seen her splayed on couches, backlit in forests, spotlit on roofs, submerged in baths, glistening in oil, wrapped in plastic, bathed in sunsets, dipped in milk, and suspended from ropes, but the more naked she was the less visible she was. In the same way a truth is more elusive when there are thirty different versions of it, the countless conspiracy theories thrown up around the Kennedy assassination had the same collective effect as the endless supply of images purporting to represent this girl.

Rather than reveal they enveiled her.

Scrolling though her pictures, it was interesting that the most erotic among them were the self-portraits. I decided she was an artist trying to be taken seriously. A bookish girl trapped inside the body of a lingerie model, fascinated by the antics of the latest contender. Like the Korean man halfway up a ladder washing the windows of the Palindrome who persisted until she gave him a false phone number. I was amazed she considered this even worth reporting. Surely she was hit on constantly.

Apparently not.

"It's impossible for me to find friends."

I felt the heat of panic rise up in me, she had just said the one word I did not want to hear.

Friend: (noun) the enemy of sex.

And yet it had to be difficult to find people she could be honest with. Would I be able to withstand her honest appraisal of the world? I'd only be valuable to her for as long as I could. The moment my jealousy showed she'd spot it and be gone. It was safe to assume she was fucking half of New York. For the moment I was just happy to be included in the fucked half.

• • • •

You get off at 3PM right?

I do.

Would you also like to get off at 3:01PM, 3:06PM and 3:09PM?

She had two responses to indicate laughter. The first and most sought-after was a long train of *ha's* usually extending to two lines. The second was what I received now.

Haha

I tried again.

Your pussy whispers obscenities in my ear "pleath leth me thuck your cock"—she has an adorable lisp

A further rummage in her Tumblr revealed rather tantalizingly that she was still married. To a distinguished looking gent who looked, in their artsy wedding photo, like he might burst into tears any moment. She had probably fucked him up quite a bit. After all I was in a bad way after only knowing her a week, what would it be like to be married to her? I had not yet received a reply to my carefully crafted text explaining the meaning behind band names like Spandau Ballet and Steely Dan. (*Spandau Ballet* came from the grotesque dance performed by hanged war criminals, and *Steely Dan* was a metal vibrator.)

Ping

Exhale.

You're full of entertaining tidbits.

This was like being called *sweet* again but at least it was a response. It was followed by an unexpected bonus.

When I return to full health I'll come and darken you doorstep again

I liked that. Yes I did. It was so unsolicited it verged on considerate.

Darken my doorstep, darken my duvet, darken my wood.

Hahahahahahahahahahahahahahahahahahhhahahaha

At last.

Drinnnnnngg

Turning sideways now, she offered me a classic profile framed by my doorway. She was joking but she looked fucking amazing.

She had an unusual habit of holding her head fixed while her eyes swiveled sideways to look at me. I wondered about it until it struck me rather logically that taking unassisted self-portraits required this sort of discipline. You'd need to hold a pose while leaving your eyes free to dart around checking camera settings and angles.

I jumped on her a little too enthusiastically, kissing her,

groping her, inhaling her heady scent. And though she didn't resist she obviously wasn't ready to get straight into it.

"So you missed me," she said, translating my breathless pawing into words.

I had snacks laid out for her. Nuts and biscuits presided over by a teapot of freshly brewed strong Irish tea.

"You certainly know how to treat a lady," she said.

This was *you're so sweet* in eight words.

"Just the thin veneer of civilization," I said, trying to appear world-weary.

She beamed at this and there might even have been a hint of relief. The last thing she wanted was another older man (in truth much older) mooning over her. And then as if to confirm the impossibility of us ever becoming anything even resembling a couple, not that I wanted that, well, not really, she began to tell me about her latest suitor.

The Korean window-washer had metamorphosed into a revered war photographer. Any trace of levity left her face when I asked about this. She turned and looked at me full on, no side-glances now.

"Oh yes, he's very good."

The fact that this guy had supposedly been in combat zones immediately gave him a very good chance of getting into her pants. Any mention of death or decay and she was almost sexually aroused. A section on her website featured beautifully composed black-and-white photos of executed collaborators from World War II. Slumped in armchairs, propped on park benches, or lifeless on linoneum, they were all female and oh so glamor-ous. As if Rita Hayworth, Katharine Hepburn, and Grace Kelly had been carefully killed so as not to ruin their outfits. The Korean guy took her to a bar where he knew all the staff.

"He kept saying *we're not going to have sex,* he didn't mean it, but he kept saying it."

She paused to select a treat.

Oh the luxury of indecision.

He groped her in the bar and felt her up in the cab. He said they should go back to his place to *say good night*, which was illogical since she lived in Williamsburg and his place was in Carroll Gardens but obviously they were way beyond reason's reach at this point. And I was far too relieved to hear he hadn't managed to fuck her. And flattered. Secretly I thought myself better than him. More intellectual. More civilized. And yet he'd taken her out and spent money on her, which was more than I would have done. But I was shocked to hear she'd met him at all since she told me the last time she'd given him a fake number. This meant I wasn't significant enough to keep track of the lies she told me. But any mention of @drkroom was conspicuous by its absence.

"So you're still prepping for the Nazi shoot?"

I feigned nonchalance, a fellow artist interested in an un-usual project.

"Oh that's not happening"—there was a pause as she swal-lowed before finishing her sentence—"till next week."

My nerves were shot.

The day before I had paced my floorboards hoping to hear from her during a long silence necessitated by a supposed cold that I assumed was merely a delay tactic to enable her to see @drkroom instead of me.

But then, I thirstily received two texts in a row.

What are you up to this week? and *I'm on the mend and feeling horny*

She obviously hadn't fucked him yet if she was feeling horny. But now that I had brought the subject up I would learn far too much about her plan to lure him to her apartment that Saturday.

He'd texted her about a dream he'd had where he was a serial killer about to go on a spree but had deliberated before setting off because he couldn't decide what color towels to take. Red or white. He couldn't decide whether to celebrate the blood or conceal it. She told me this like it was the cutest thing in the world. There was a pause now while she shot me a sideways glance before nibbling delicately on a cupcake. Aware of my adoring eyes she fingertipped the excess crumbs from the sides of her mouth and shamelessly sucked them off before continuing. Her apartment had been suggested as a possible location for their upcoming shoot. Who suggested it was left unsaid. And if they were going to work without interference from her roommate, they would need to use . . . wait for it . . . her bedroom. She had either forgotten or didn't care that she had already told me she couldn't have visitors because of her "uptight roommate." But she was okay with @drkcunt coming over to photograph her naked? In her fucking bedroom? Holding her phone up to my face, she invited me to look at the photo of it she'd sent for his professional appraisal.

It was completely empty.

Nothing in it but floorboards and a window. No bed, no chair. Nothing. One deft tap of her finger and I was eavesdropping on their text exchange.

It's empty!! he squawked.

It now has a bed in it, she demurred.

Ahh so you don't sleep in a coffin?

No, she replied, *I sleep naked.*

I want to see that.

She put the phone down and cupped some nuts.

"Up to then I thought I was losing my touch," she says.

Losing her touch? Who did she think she was talking to? How good a job I must have done convincing her I could care less who she fucked. Or maybe she knew exactly the effect she was having. That exquisite torture caused by the shift of two diametrically opposed tectonic plates in my mind. One representing affection, love, and cuddles, the other, punishment, cruelty, and despair. Was it masochism to want to fuck her even as she shared her intention of fucking someone else? *You better fuck her fast before she changes her mind.* It was not an elegant thought but it was the real reason I nodded when I offered to refresh her teacup. Still munching on my humble supper she began to remove items of clothing.

Nothing too revealing. Just making herself comfortable. The big incongruous eighties-style sneakers and a vintage wristwatch. She was the hardworking New York executive visiting her bit of fluff. There was no need for pretense, she could be herself around me. I wanted to take this as a huge compliment and decided that if sex ensued then this indeed was what it was. It was the first time in my life I'd felt like the mistress while the girl behaved like a visiting adulterer.

Meanwhile I had to hear more about this fucking guy.

As I had suspected, he was the real reason I had received no texts for the preceding days and now it was being confirmed that the Nazi shoot was indeed set to happen that weekend. At her place. In her bedroom. She removed more clothes; the tight little cardigan, the starchy blouse, and reaching to her side for the zipper on her pencil skirt, she lamented her chances of getting fucked by a taller, younger, better-looking guy than me and I didn't care. The removal of clothes was strangely clinical until I realized that for her, it was business as usual. Turn up at a studio, make some small talk, perhaps over a cup of tea or coffee, and then down to business. But the more she talked about @drkroom the more I wanted to fuck her. To compete? No. I wasn't so optimistic as to think I could ever seriously rival him. I was merely trying to grab as much fruit as possible from this slowed-down truck before it gathered speed and left the area forever.

SKINNY-DIPPING IN NEW YORK'S GENE POOL
#TheOxygenThiefDiaries

I didn't realize it was her until she had already walked past. I mightn't have recognized her at all if it hadn't been for her most striking feature. We had a running joke that the security guard at her studio spent so much time looking at it she should replace her ID photo with a picture of her ass. I felt the familiar warmth spread across my midriff that only it could produce in me. Still with her back turned she slowed almost to a stop and tilted her head as if straining to hear something. Was she waiting for me to call her over? She couldn't have known I had moved to this new spot. She was probably as surprised to see me as I was to see her.

If it *was* her.

She had presumably decided against coming over to talk to me because the last time she'd done that I asked her to go away. *Told* her to go away. She wouldn't want a repeat of that.

When she resumed walking and began to mingle with the other pedestrians, I rose onto my toes, memorizing every nuance for later analysis. But just as she got into her stride she disappeared.

Had she entered that café?

A quick google revealed that Vito Veritas on Prince Street was a high-end sandwich shop specializing in gluten-free fare.

So that was it.

Her stomach would act up if she ate anything other than gluten-free sandwiches or cakes.

I had often made the mistake of insisting we eat at diners (mainly because they were cheaper) and it turned out to be an expensive decision in that it cost me more sex than I was willing to admit. At first I thought she was putting it on, pretending to have stomachaches just to make me work harder for her affection. I still wasn't convinced the whole gluten-free thing wasn't a scam created by cafés so they could charge an extra $4 for bread.

I wondered how many times she had eaten here when I was encamped two blocks away. What a relief I hadn't had to watch her strolling along arm-in-arm with her boyfriend. That would have been even more torturous than the mental JPEGs I already received of her impaled on his . . . I blinked the image away.

I was suddenly elated I hadn't called her over.

When I first spotted her there I was convinced she was stalking me but now I could see that on the way to treating herself to a posh sandwich I had popped unexpectedly out of the pavement. She lingered for those few moments like she half-expected me to beckon her over and I probably would have if I hadn't been so leery of further revelations, most feared among them being the possibility that she had been fucking the Californian while we were still together. Naturally I obsessed on the café door for the next thirty minutes and only wrenched my eyes away to answer the occasional question.

"You'll be here tomorrow?"

Yeah yeah, I nodded impatiently. Why did they have to lie? Why couldn't they just fuck off if they weren't going to buy a book? Why try to convince me they were coming back?

I didn't know it would be my last day out there.

I had only come back out because a journalist wanted to take some photos of the table to accompany an interview celebrating my marketing genius.

While Marian hesitated, waiting for her name to be called, I couldn't help thinking her hair looked far too dark. Was she now dyeing it? Had I caused her lovely dark heavy hair to go gray?

I felt the familiar tightening in my throat. I didn't dare cry. I had too much hoarded away in there. She was like an effigy of how I remembered her. There was a time when I would have blamed myself for her appearance. Surely I had reduced her to this. But now I had an accomplice. Or more accurately a scapegoat. A big-dicked Californian scapegoat. He could take his share of the responsibility. Or as far as I was concerned, all of it. I was off the hook.

It was striking how little I felt for her now. I was free. No guilt, no pleasure, no warmth. No fear. No pity. No interest. She might have been a stranger. Just another sad, annoyed-looking girl taking a lunch break from a mind-crushing job. She wore a pair of well-tooled leather shoes, the kind hipster girls like to wear sockless, and she had rolled up her navy blue trouser legs the better to expose them. There was definitely something tragic about being able to regard the girl I'd recently keened over and feel nothing but relief that I hadn't had to talk to her. And anyway what would I have said? I would have embarrassed myself by inferring she was stalking me. At least I was spared that.

And for all I knew she might have been on her way to a date. Why not? She might have stipulated in her datemedotcom profile that she preferred gluten-free food and a well-meaning, gainfully employed young man might have invited her to lunch.

So crazy to think I was outside selling books containing intimate details of her life, including her sexual preferences, while she might be interviewing for a new relationship only yards away. Objectively she was a professional woman, independent in appearance, on her way to enjoy a specialized meal from an upmarket eatery in a stylish part of downtown Manhattan. The woman in question passed a street vendor selling books.

Would I have felt better if she looked incredible? I wanted to feel something but no emotion presented itself. No sign of the fluttering in the stomach that was at one point synonymous with even the thought of her. Now all that remained was a factual recognition of someone I used to know. It should have been insulting that she might have seen me and walked past. But I had to concede that if she had stopped she would not have been welcome. What impenetrable knots we tie.

Fuck. There she was again.

Striding purposefully now in the other direction without even a glance back for me. She had taken no more than five paces when a young man ran past me in the direction of Vito Veritas. He looked like he was about to run past her too until he sort of jumped and twisted himself in midair so that when he landed he was facing her. She stopped abruptly and I held my breath as I waited for her to burst into tears as she had once done when some students carrying a sign saying FREE HUGS had embraced her in the street. But the young man, whom I now recognized as the Streetmeet coach, simply smiled. As his lips began to move he made deliberately slow, unthreatening gestures as if addressing an excitable deer. Nodding reassuringly he blushed as if aware of his own ridiculous predicament while slowly, theatrically, moving his right hand toward his breast pocket. It was as if she had a gun on him.

His eyebrows, raised higher than was reasonable, were comically interrogative.

But she didn't cry. Instead she began to sway in the same way she'd done at my table two months earlier. The same way she'd done so many times when she needed to effect an override of logic. Passing men now began taking notice of her, and she did not need to turn around for me to know she had deployed her dizzying smile because it was obvious from the delighted expression on the guy's face. He handed her his phone. She took it and began to type. Now at last I did feel something.

Sick.

Even as it was happening I knew the entire exchange would be available to watch on Streetmeet.com. Everything he said, her responses, his tactics discussed, her looks graded. It'd be worse than watching her getting fucked. But I knew I'd never watch it, it was torturous enough to know it existed. *I hate that this exists!* She'd be a Streetmeet case study, the subject of helpful commentary and slo-mo replays. She wouldn't like that. Or would she? She was single now after all. Or at least she was for the moment. And there I'd be, like a fucking meerkat, forever in the background.

． ． ． ．

Prnnnnngggg

That night I was just drifting off to sleep when my phone vibrated on the bed stand. A text from Emmeline, it was 2:30 AM.

Okay, it's official, this girl does NOT understand the workings of the male mind

Then another.

But I seem to understand you so that's something!!

Does this mean your shoot was less than you hoped for?

We didn't meet at my place, we met at his, the entire thing was ridiculously erotic, suggestive hints, it went on for hours, he touched me countless times, and then nothing, I just left

And then another.

I don't even know if he's straight or . . . I am just so confused

She was asking me to console her because she hadn't managed to get him to fuck her.

I'm shocked, I replied truthfully. *He didn't take any photos?*

He did.

Pause.

Of me crawling around naked on all fours while he whipped me in his Nazi uniform

I'm crying. Again I was being truthful.

Yeah

274

He spent 90% of the time staring at me while smiling. I have no clue.

No bulge in his trousers?

I mean I'm not imagining it, could he be messed up when it comes to women? . . . yes it was there.

And he made no attempt to take it out? Maybe he just sees women as porn that he can jerk off to later . . . some guys can't handle the real thing in 3-D . . . you can't be feeling very flattered right now.

No

Was it just you and him?

There was a pause now while I waited till 3:20 AM to hear how cheated she felt at not getting impaled on a competitor's cock after spreading her ass cheeks in front of him all evening.

He just wrote me to say he "had so much fun" and "you're fascinating and smart"

And then she sent another, presumably answering my question twenty minutes earlier about them being alone together.

Yes

That's so weak, I ventured. *"you're fascinating and smart" you're scorching hot*

Thanks, that makes me feel a little better. Oh well.

I'm sorry to hear all of this but maybe you'll get a couple of cool shits out of it

She ignored the typo.

He basically implied he wanted to see me again . . . but i dunno . . .

Implied? I'm sorry but shouldn't he be a little more enthused?

It was enthused but i'm not sure why.

You mean he got off on being aloof or something?

I can't tell

Hmm strange indeed

There followed another long pause of about twenty minutes until I received a screen-grab of their text exchange. Their dialogue immortalized.

@drkroom: *That was very productive thank you*

Emmeline: *You're welcome, I hope I wasn't too awkward?*

@drkroom: *Not at all you were perfect*

Emmeline: *Unless of course you find that sort of thing charming*

@drkroom: *Very charming*

Emmeline: *I wasn't too inexperienced or naive?*

@drkroom: *Not at all . . . you were great?*

Emmeline: *Sorry I'm just so bad at reading situations . . . new in town and all that*

@drkroom: *Naive about . . . ?*

Emmeline: *Imagining there was something going on between us beyond just a photo shoot?*

Emmeline: *Talk about awkward!! Please don't even answer that . . . I'm soo sorry.*

@drkroom: *Hahah yes, I felt it too*

Emmeline: *Hah ok that is SUCH a relief . . . I'm not going crazy after all*

And then a text to her eavesdropping eunuch.

Are you cringing? Was that the most awkward series of text messages you ever read?

So you haven't lost your touch after all . . . calm and quietude return to the realm . . . exhale

Not exhaling . . . just breathing

She had been literally on her hands and knees begging him to fuck her. The next day she communicated with me in a way that immediately made me suspicious.

She initiated an actual phone call.

But the reason for dusting off what was, for anyone under twenty-five, an anachronism was to ask the old Irishman if she could use his apartment for "a Mr. Darkroom fetish shoot." She managed to make it sound like I should be honored. Like it was something I'd tell my grandchildren about.

When I recovered from her insult I had a pathetic thought.

"Only if I can be present."

She remained calm.

"Hmmm not sure how that would work, I don't think he'd want someone watching."

Watching? I was superfluous in her mind. The cheeky cunt thought I was going to allow her and this sick-fuck loose in my lovely apartment? For a second I thought it might be cool to have such filth being shot in my place (I could product-place my books) but what would I do while they fucked in my bed, or worse, on my coffee table? I'd be livid with jealously. I already was. She continued to plummet in my estimation. Or maybe I was just jealous. My last remaining hope was that he was only into humiliating her. That he'd stop there. That she'd still avail herself of my services after he was done with her.

"So it sounds like you've got him in the bag," I said, trying not to sound too crestfallen.

"Yeah but I'm not going to get laid because I made the mistake of saying I love being tortured for ages before being rewarded . . . so now I'm going to have to clean his floor and lick his boots."

• • • •

Burrrrrrr

Emmeline called to tell me that @drkroom took photos of her in her Williamsburg apartment and after meticulously covering her naked body in baby oil finger-fucked her. I couldn't tell if she actually got off on telling me all this or whether she saw me as her male girlfriend. The only reason they hadn't actually fucked was because a text arrived from her meddling roommate just as she heard the sound of what she imagined to be the unbuckling of his belt.

"Imagined?"

"Oh, I forgot to mention I was blindfolded."

She related the story breathlessly as she walked to work at the Palindrome. Was she looking for my opinion? My opinion was, I didn't like it. *I* wanted to be the one fingering her all oiled up and blindfolded. Even so, I was happy I hadn't agreed to let them use my apartment, not just because I'd spared myself the anguish of jealousy but because baby oil would be a bastard to get off my leather club chair. He had apparently confessed he was in a sexless relationship with his live-in girlfriend. Could it be that actually fucking Emmeline would count as infidelity but all the other stuff was okay?

I don't know why I was encouraged by the fact that he hadn't actually penetrated her yet. It wasn't as if I was doing such a great job in that department. But at least it bought me some time.

After hanging up I saw she had forwarded me a list of demands she'd set out for her newly acquired slave. Yes, that's right, her slave. Some guy had emailed her on deathlete.com, her commercial website, begging to be her slave. She thought it was a joke. But when he listed the tasks he hoped to perform for her—*pick up her laundry, walk her dog, clean her apartment, pay her rent* (pay her rent?)—she realized it was a serious proposition from a real person. Attached were confirmation orders for a pair of Jimmy Choo shoes and an entire season of gothic lingerie. She promised she'd wear them for me the next time we met. So I was still in the running.

She didn't know the city well enough to suggest locations so she now wanted my opinion about where she should meet him. I was aware of being sucked in but I couldn't resist the titanic pull of her sexual machinations. In fact I surprised myself by how easily the ideas came to me. He should book a room at the Tribeca Grand and a table in the restaurant downstairs.

She should have him freeze one of his own turds and use it as a butt plug.

*hahahahhahahahahahahahahahahahahahahahahaha
hahahahahahahahahahahahaha*

But the more she involved me in her antics the more insatiable those appetites seemed to be. I tried to convince myself that there would naturally be a period of adjustment as she sampled all these new flavors but an intuitive voice cautioned me.

Within the hour she texted me his emailed receipts showing the room he'd booked and the restaurant reservations made in her name. Also attached were confirmation orders for an array of whips, paddles, and restraints.

She picked up the language effortlessly.

Maybe in reality she was already an experienced dominatrix who knew exactly what she was doing. Slowly coaxing me into obsession. She sent a JPEG of the finished Nazi shoot and it was suitably depraved. Completely naked except for an officer's cap she crawled on all fours, aiming that stupendous ass at a semi-silhouetted SS officer in full uniform of jodhpurs and jackboots. The riding crop he held at an angle explained the dark stripes across her white buttocks.

Her plan was to have the slave book hotel rooms two or three times a month and then "kick him out so I can invite someone more interesting over."

i.e. you or @drkroom

Oh and she was leaving her job so she'd have much more time off soon.

Drinnnnggg and *Burrrrr*

When the name of an AA newcomer came up on my screen at exactly the same moment the doorbell sounded, I did something that surprised even me. I deliberated. Where did my loyalties lie? On the one hand I owed my life to AA, everything good that had happened to me in the preceding seventeen years had been directly attributed to the teachings of its program. All that was asked of me in return was that I help a newcomer find the same freedom I had. On the other hand there was the smoldering hot pussy perched on long shapely legs standing in the hallway. I answered the door.

I knew she'd met @drkroom earlier so I had to assume it hadn't gone well or she wouldn't be calling on me. He can't have impressed her or at least I hoped not.

Between munches and sips she had just begun to tell me about her slave (his name was Marc) when she received a text from who I would later find out was her estranged husband saying he was filing for divorce. She said they'd met for a drink earlier in the week but she was "definitely done with him now." So accustomed to shoring up the egos of the men she was with, she obviously thought I needed to hear this. Didn't she realize she'd already told me about her attempts to fuck @drkroom? Telling me she was done with her husband was hardly a consolation.

"So he's your ex-what, exactly?" I said, inviting her to tell me what I already knew.

"Husband," she said, sadder about having to give up the truth than the marriage. It turned out she'd left him only two months earlier and he had now followed her to New York to try to get her back. She'd seen me four times in those two months and fucked god knows how many other men while holding

down a job, picking up a slave, and cultivating a collaborator/
lover. It was so flattering to even get a text from her let alone
have her tonguing the tip of my cock like she'd do ten minutes
later.

"I guess I should reciprocate," she said, meaning she should
give me a blow job. And just as she was about to put it in her
mouth she stopped and smiled.

"This is my first uncircumcised penis."

The three Irish guys she'd been with were obviously not
native-born then. And the sight of her perfect model's body
leaning over to suckle on the tip of my being was difficult to
endure only because I felt so strongly that I didn't deserve it.

She tongued it.

Her beautiful face was frowning and determined as her
stiffened tongue strafed the helmet. She was willing to make
herself ugly in the service of my orgasm. But I wasn't able to
pay her the compliment of coming because I wasn't confident
enough to believe it *was* a compliment. I could tell by the increased frequency of her flicking tongue that she was expecting
me to come but somehow I was still unable to release myself.
I grabbed the cock away like a schoolmaster admonishing a
schoolboy and beat him until he was in tears. When I handed
him back, suitably chastened, he was much more forthcoming.

Gushing in fact.

I came and came and came and laughed and she laughed
too and I came even more and still tonguing me she laughed
again as I continued to writhe, yelp, spasm, and gasp. She was
flushed and visibly turned on by what she had caused and I

could feel her perfect pussy getting even wetter around my still embedded fingers. Her body was maddeningly erotic, even more so now after orgasming.

"He's falling for me. I can see it in how he looks at me."

She said it like she was disappointed. Like even he was fallible. She had initially approached him because of his dark brooding persona but now this millennial Marquis de Sade was reduced to: *I've been thinking about you all day.* Closing his text she rolled her eyes.

"What I've just been on, was definitely a date."

She looked so well bred and conservative. Well mannered. Like an upper-class English heiress with an edge. So when she said something potentially cruel it sounded like she was merely reporting the facts. She wanted very much for me *not* to fall for her. But I knew I was already past that point. Secretly I was thrilled to hear that the dark and dangerous @drkroom was just a pussy like the rest of us. After another thumb-pummeling during which she was polite enough to obtain all manner of multiple orgasms, she reviewed me favorably.

"You really know how to get me wet, you'll have to tell me your secret."

She might have been complimenting my chicken salad. Her screen lit up on the bed stand. It was another text from @drkroom.

She read it aloud.

"How are you?"

"Yes, how are you?" I asked, inviting her to juxtapose her present situation with her new understanding of @drkroom.

"I'm very good indeed," she purred, smirking down on me like a wet dream come to life or, more accurately, a wet nightmare, a dark and thrilling ride to nowhere.

• • • •

After a dinner she ordered but didn't eat, she whipped, kicked, and ordered her slave around the hotel room. Striking poses in her new lingerie, she tipped champagne onto the carpet and demanded he lick it up. He wasn't allowed to sleep in the bed. Or the bath. He slept on the floor like a dog. Then, having whipped him mercilessly for spilling all that expensive bubbly, she dispatched him uptown to a specialized wine merchant to fetch a ridiculously expensive bottle of Beaujolais. Attached to the bottle was a message she'd dictated to an embarrassed sales assistant with instructions to drive his *Owner* to an address in Brooklyn where he should *wait outside while I get my brains fucked out by a real man.*

It was a nice touch to enlist the sales clerk. Was she really new at this? From the back seat of his own car he was shown @darkroom's photo and invited to understand just how worthless he was in comparison. All this as he drove her over the Williamsburg Bridge in the dawning light of a sunny Saturday morning after a night of frustration spent in a hotel room with his cock in a cage. Under Mistress Emmeline's supervision he had willingly locked his cock and balls inside a clear Perspex cage (available from all good BDSM stores) before handing her the only key that she wore on a precariously thin thread around her ankle. Hardly the most secure location for such a valued item but it ceased to matter when she flushed it down the same toilet he was busy, at her command, licking clean. Presumably there was a spare but this was unconfirmed.

"I hadn't expected it to be so funny," she confessed over the phone. This was endearing. She was like the incestuous younger sister I never had. The night before, during what must have been the first few hours of her new adventure she texted, *I'm a natural at this.*

Selfies of her being fucked by her brooding bull-like Brooklynite photographer appeared on her slave's phone while he looked in vain for a parking space. GIFs of $900 wine being splashed on and then licked off her bullet-hard nipples.

And yes there were stabs of jealousy when I heard she'd headed all the way over the Williamsburg Bridge to Brooklyn instead of the East Village but then what would I have done with a bottle of rare wine? And did I really want her coming over to my place early on a Saturday morning in gothic lingerie and heels? Of course I fucking did.

And yet it was her I envied, not him.

Imagine being that beautiful and that young and that clever in a city like New York. Oh the damage you could do.

"I could get used to this," she said.

The success she was enjoying with one slave began to inspire notions of more. After all, the mechanics of humiliation would work just as well on one guy as the next. They might even be made to feel jealous of each other. And her presence, her physical presence, wasn't even required to maintain dominance over them. In fact her absence, selectively applied, could in itself be harnessed as a form of punishment. With two or three of these guys on the go she'd get her rent paid, her fridge stocked, and her wardrobe lined.

Her reports were so gloriously detailed and so deliciously unedited I was at first flattered that she should take me so deeply into her confidence. But then I began to see I was merely a repository for her exploits. A sort of unofficial biographer. Exhibiting her perfect body no longer provided the exhilaration it once had. Having developed a tolerance for it she was searching for ways to get even more naked. The photographers had been mere stepping-stones toward an ever-increasing adulation. If that audience could expand to include the readers of the book she knew I was writing then so be it. She knew I could be relied upon to chronicle her antics as she strutted and posed on the newly mounted New York stage. But then as if to prove my theory wrong everything went quiet.

Weeks passed without even an Instagram post . . . except for one. A beautiful black-and-white shot of her ass with my sonnet projected on it. My poem clung like literary lingerie to its subject.

> *At first I touched it with my mind*
> *A rear so rare I roared inside,*
> *A rump so worthy of a sonnet,*
> *I vowed aloud to write one on it,*
> *Like starv'd dogs on meat releas'd*
> *My thoughts upon thy cheeks do feast*

Oh luminous moon now cleft in twain,
Hark the serenading wolf-pack baying,
Pour qu'un écrivain se rince l'oeil
Montes-moi ton joli cul.
Behind thy back we doth conspire
Till whipp'd and spank'd tis set afire

I added one more *like* to the 2,056 already there.

And no, I wasn't credited.

But apart from that nothing. No texts, no calls. It was disconcerting. She was no doubt embroiled in new intrigues and I'd soon receive a full report. I was sure that managing a job, a growing Rolodex of slaves, and a darkroom full of sexual depravity was probably enough to keep anyone occupied, but even so it was unlike her not to narrate. Maybe it was just too awkward to continue seeing me now that @drkroom was getting so cozy. Then one day while negotiating a particularly treacherous patch of tarmac behind my hand truck I felt a welcome tug in my pants pocket.

Ping.

He dumped me.

My mind whirred.

I was sure that @drkroom, having the pick of New York's filthy-minded art models, had simply inhaled Emmeline and moved on. Now she'd turn to me for consolation.

"I'm sorry to hear that," I lied.

Be still my trembling thumbs.

But I was wrong, it was the slave who dumped her.

Fired her in fact.

This was the closest Emmeline would ever get to having her heart broken. She was in shock. Smarting from being rejected by a masochist for not being sufficiently sadistic. It totally unsettled her. The language used was the same as always: *It's not you it's me . . . I'm not getting what I want from the relationship . . . I need to take a break.* By inviting her to be his dominatrix he had paradoxically remained in control from day one.

"Can I come over for tea and sympathy?"

She was confiding in me and not @drkroom. Should I be encouraged by this or had I already been demoted to *friend*? Was I on the brink of three more years of half-truths and ill-definition? It'd be Marian all over again.

Not if I could help it.

When she did finally arrive she looked somewhat depleted. The euphoria of her first few months in New York had worn off and something close to reality had settled onto her like dust.

Her husband was serving divorce papers, she'd resigned from her job, hoping to be supported by a cluster of slaves that never materialized, and most troublesome of all she was trying to decide what to do with the fact that @drkroom had invited her to move in with him. This last item was accompanied by an eye-roll but the flush in her cheeks betrayed her.

"He's so into me it's embarr—"

I lunged at her in midsentence.

If I was going to be rejected I'd get it over with.

But she not only melted into my embrace, she flicked her tongue against mine encouraging me to continue. If she had pulled away and explained that we could no longer be physical because she and @drkroom were getting serious I would have known how to behave but I had no map for this. Maybe they had an open arrangement. Or was I being given the chance to match the bid made by a competitor? Shedding clothes as she led me to my own bedroom, she was naked and on all fours before I even had my shirt off.

With her head and upper body buried in the pillows all I could see was a two-limbed alien, vertically split at its intersection. A lisping creature unaware of culture's mores, uninterested in anything but a sucking, salivating need. It might have been trying to speak, or more likely it was hungry. A gentle swaying enhanced its hypnotic effect.

It should have been a fantasy made flesh, the very coordinates of a wet dream arrived at. I imagined all the men in New York . . . in the world, who would gleefully throw me aside and force-feed this seething slit with what it craved. The image I'd once had of New York's female elite amassed outside my apartment was now replaced by its male equivalent.

The moment hung in the air.

Reaching back, her long elegant fingers tickled under my balls. Her optimism was still intact. Her young mind had yet to encounter the far-off phenomenon of a cock gone soft. No, I wasn't teasing. There would be no victorious docking and no exaltation as I proceeded to the next challenge of desperately trying not to come. Amazingly, she did not stop, turn around, sit up, and stare at me in disbelief. Instead she behaved like she was languishing in orgasms already achieved. Maybe it was easier to do that than confront a subject that was going to be very tricky to discuss. One that required an intimacy we didn't have. I was under no illusions we'd become any sort of couple. I didn't even want that. And neither did she. Or at least not with me.

But even in his most depraved moments @drkroom still demonstrated a willingness to commit. His moral compass, battered as it was, tended toward monogamy—a spanked, bruised, tied-up, and choke-fucked monogamy but monogamy nonetheless. Meanwhile I was hard pushed to produce a sufficiently stiff cock.

This was when I had the idea.

It occurred to me rather gently that the concept for my much fretted-over next book had already existed before I'd even begun writing the first one. It had just been waiting for me to notice it. I felt no regret or self-admonishment for not having seen it sooner, it was simply ready now to be seen and so here it was, emerging in this most unexpected of moments.

Aisling's book of romantic photo-essays.

With my newfound publishing clout I could easily produce such a book and drop it into the slipstream of my recent success. So many people had asked if she ever published her version of events. But Aisling wouldn't be the one producing this book. Emmeline would.

Or more accurately, Emmeline and I.

I might not be able to physically fuck her but intellectually and artistically I could penetrate her harder and more deeply than anyone alive. Even more than @drkroom.

I'd invite him to collaborate.

It wouldn't be any more difficult to pull off than some of the ad campaigns I'd worked on over the years. And Emmeline was born to do it. Not only could she effortlessly play the part of Aisling but her various slaves could stand in as captains of industry as they endured the heat of her displeasure. They wouldn't even need to pretend since many of them were already one-percenters who needed to be taken down a peg. Or pegged? In her capacity as dominatrix she could insist they sign waivers allowing the use of their imagery (face optional) as part of their sado-humiliation. It was the perfect project to demonstrate her skills not just as a photographer/model/artist but as a cultural activist fighting the corroding forces of capitalism and the power of the patriarchy.

It was so much better than just being written about; it would give her a chance to create a showcase of her talents for which I could provide a combination of bohemian credibility and mainstream exposure normally unheard of in her circles.

And I'd be granted the sort of closure I had no right to expect. By publishing the book of cynical romance photography that *Diary of an Oxygen Thief* had been written to prevent, I'd intentionally produce the very book I had been so afraid of.

As Emmeline's cum-summoner held me in its sway I imagined working out the details.

I would take Aisling's initial idea and expand on it. Step-by-step photo-stories following romantic liaisons initiated by Aisling (played by Emmeline) as she systematically reduced the world's most privileged pricks to tears. It'd be easy to create biographies for the various participants: an Oil Executive, a Merchant Banker, a Litigation Lawyer, a Plastic Surgeon, and of course an Irish Advertising Creative Executive.

I'd be able to art direct my own life.

For the shoot we'd book the same room in the same hotel. Room 901. Emmeline wearing Prada just like Aisling had done. We might even get a fee for product placement. Candid black-and-white photos of an actor playing the part of Anonymous, taken in and around downtown bars and cafés would mimic the impromptu shots Aisling took of me. More of the same in the back of the cab on the way to the hotel. Then maybe a quick visit to Ireland for more shots in Dublin. The Temple Bar and Hotel Constance and finally back to New York for a detailed reenactment of that notorious roll of film shot in the Cat and Mouse bar: the raised finger, the embarrassed poses, the salutary pint of Coca-Cola.

It'd be fun casting the guy who played me.

I thought about approaching Aisling to offer her the chance to collaborate. But why would I do that? If I produced this book I'd reclaim that part of my life and maybe even acknowledge that yes she might have had a point. That maybe it *was* arrogant, stupid, immature, and entitled of me to expect her to drop everything when I arrived in New York just because I had some preconceived ill-informed notion of how girls are supposed to submit to a guy. Why shouldn't she just fuck me once, or twice? After all, she hadn't lied. She had been very open with me saying she was not looking for a relationship. By producing the very book I was so afraid to see realized I'd show how much I'd grown.

The public would be encouraged to wonder if the book contained the actual photos taken that night in the Cat and Mouse. No one knew what Aisling looked like so it would be impossible to decide if Emmeline was or wasn't her. No one knew if Aisling was even real. No one except me. And I might have imagined everything that had happened between us.

Or I might not.

Someone claiming to be Aisling might come forward but it would be difficult to make a case. Such a person would be easy to dismiss as an attention-seeker. After all, how could I be accused of stealing an idea that had only ever been mentioned in a work of fiction? A work of fiction I had written. If the book was fictional then so was she, and then so was her claim.

In fact if anyone owned the idea, I did.

In the meantime I'd prepare a backstory for Emmeline as Aisling. Most people weren't going to look any further than LinkedIn, Facebook, Instagram, Tumblr. A few back-dated posts just to give her a sense of history. A website based around Emmeline's own work would purport to be that of Aisling McCarthy with studios in Dublin and New York. Imitation ads for tastemakers like Gucci and Prada would lend credence to the success of her website. She had to be doing well if brands like that advertised with her, right? We could even sell limited edition prints of Emmeline's work masquerading as Aisling's. The book would of course also be available for purchase.

I might even "come out" and take a well-earned bow.

On the other hand, probably not.